THROUGH THICK BLACK LASHES,

Sheffield regarded the enchanting face of the girl who shared his bed. The sight of her lips curving with pleasure made him wonder what she could be dreaming about. Like silken honey, Courtney's hair curled back over the edge of the pillow, inviting the touch of his fingers and revealing the slim, sweet column of her neck.

Aching with regret and longing, Sheffield let his golden gaze examine Courtney's sleeping body: face, arms and tantalizing outline of breasts, waist, hips and thighs beneath the shirt and sheet that covered her. Could he leave her without making love to her? Perhaps more to the point, could he leave her after *making love to her?*

---

Crimson Intrigue

DEVON LINDSAY

A CHERISH BOOK
New York, N.Y.

This novel is a work of fiction. Names, characters, places and incidents are either the product of the author's imagination or are used fictitiously, and any resemblance to actual persons, living or dead, events or locales is entirely coincidental.

A CHERISH BOOK
Published By Cherish Books, Ltd.
New York, N.Y. 10018

First Cherish Printing—1984

Printed in the United States of America

For
André Raveneau
and
Charles

Crimson Intrigue

Chapter One

"What am I going to *do?*" wailed Courtney Ashton, sinking into a Sheraton side chair.

Lisabeth glanced over from her station at the window. "What's wrong this time? Honestly, Courtney, you look spectacular. Timothy will be rendered speechless." She turned back to scan Georgetown's dusty Duck Lane. Although Beth was, at seventeen, a year younger than Courtney, her gentle face and indulgent tone were indicative of her unfailing, serene maturity. "At what time were you expecting him to arrive?" she asked her sister.

Midnight-blue eyes deepened to smoldering violet. "Oh, Beth! You're no help at all. Haven't you gotten it through your head that I wish he'd find some other girl to drool over? The way Father has been pressuring me to become Mrs. Timothy Lamb, I've begun to feel like Marie Antoinette on her way to the guillotine."

"That's the silliest thing I've ever heard!" Lisabeth crossed the room to perch on the bed, next to her

1

sister's chair. In spite of Courtney's gloomy expression, she made an enchanting picture in a day dress of thin white muslin. A ribbon of spring-green silk encircled the Empire waist and set off the snug bodice, while a second ribbon wound through Courtney's luxuriant honey-colored curls. "There probably isn't an unmarried female in either Georgetown or the capital who would not change places with you!" Lisabeth pursued. "It's a sin that you find fault instead of counting your blessings. You're beautiful, well bred, and Timothy Lamb is all that any girl could ask for in a husband."

Courtney rolled her eyes. "A matter of opinion, dear Beth. I find Timothy tiresome and unappealing."

A deep voice resounded from the hallway. "Have you forgotten that there's a war on?"

Gerald Ashton appeared in the doorway, his size and blazing blue eyes intimidating. Lisabeth paled but recovered in time to nod triumphantly at her sister, while Courtney herself cringed almost imperceptibly. The older she became, the more openly she displayed a resistance to her father's efforts to manage her life. Yet the habits of childhood were hard to break, and Ashton was a man of tremendous will, accustomed to controlling his family of females.

"No, Father, I have not forgotten about the war." Daringly, Courtney edged her tone with acid irony.

His penetrating gaze narrowed, and he advanced. "I thank you for reassuring me, daughter, and I hope that perhaps you'll consider this matter realistically for a change. When the British come here, as we know they will, I shall be leading my unit proudly into battle and may not live to take care of you. Lamb rests on his elective office and a cushion of family wealth. He will never be called on to risk his neck in the fray. Whether or not you find him *unappealing*"—Gerald's voice mocked her icily—"the reality of the situation is clear. You are the older daughter. Once you are safe and secure in your marriage, Lisabeth will be free to accept a marriage proposal of her own, and I'll be able to do battle against the enemy without worrying about the future of my children should I be killed."

Courtney was barely able to refrain from tilting her head to one side, closing her eyes and making a loud, rude snoring noise. It seemed that she'd heard a version of this guilt-provoking speech a thousand times. Right now she longed only to avoid even one more tyrannical sentence. "I understand, Father. I have understood all along . . . but I would like to feel that whatever choice I make concerning my future will be of my own free will."

Ashton recognized the determination in his daughter's eyes by their amethyst hue. It was a shock to realize that the challenging upward curve of her brow duplicated one of his own most habitual expressions: silent, defiant resolve. Raking a hand through his sandy hair, Gerald glanced toward his younger daughter. At this moment, with her brown eyes reflecting her distress and her soft brown hair framing her sweet face, Beth was a replica of her mother. It would take more than a common-sense argument to bring about Lisabeth's defection; she was as certain of her father's infallibility as she was rigidly optimistic about the future.

"Well, Courtney, you have every right to your point of view." He smiled with flinty cunning. "It's obvious that you don't wish to discuss this matter further with your father, and I certainly don't want to be accused of delaying your decision." Extending a hand toward Lisabeth, whose eyes were round with admiration, he added, "We shall inform your mother that you will be down directly and the tea will be kept hot. Since Timothy hasn't arrived as yet, I suggest you steal a few minutes to . . . collect your thoughts."

As the clock on the parlor mantelpiece chimed for the fourth and last time, Courtney sipped her cold tea and tried to appear interested in what Timothy Lamb was saying. Something about weakness in America's military.

Her father was nodding adamantly. A moment later he interrupted with several minutes' worth of his own assessment of the war situation. From time to time he paused to allow someone a murmur of admiration. Usually Beth or Mrs. Ashton provided these, but now Gerald was looking toward his future son-in-law.

Gamely, Timothy pushed back a stray lock of blond hair and ventured, "That's a very clear picture you present, sir! I'll wager that President Madison himself isn't better informed!"

Lisabeth, who had been working industriously on a piece of embroidery, looked up to declare, "I believe that if the President were half as intelligent as Daddy, he wouldn't have gotten us into this horrible war at all!"

"Well, well." Gerald chuckled. "I appreciate those sentiments, but I'm afraid you're both biased. Why, Lamb, it seems as though you're part of our family already!"

Courtney, seated near Timothy on the green and white Hepplewhite sofa, squirmed. Her feeling of dread grew when she saw her father nudge her mother. It was a familiar cue that Amity Ashton had learned to recognize.

Smiling brightly, Amity exclaimed, "I cannot resist mentioning what an attractive couple the two of you make!" Still beaming, she looked at Gerald and added, "As usual, dear, I have to agree with you. Mr. Lamb *does* look just right sitting there next to our Courtney."

At that moment Mrs. Belcher, the housekeeper, arrived with a fresh pot of tea. Beth held out her cup.

"It's as if fate has brought him to us," Amity concluded with satisfaction.

Congressman Lamb shifted in embarrassment and watched Mrs. Belcher refill his china cup, glad for the diversion. "I . . . uh . . . certainly appreciate your hospitality. You have . . . all become important to me . . ." He cast a nervous glance at Courtney.

Courtney had frozen, feeling helpless and outraged. Expectant eyes, including the chocolate-brown pair belonging to Timothy, waited for her to say the appropriate words. Unwilling to lie and unable to tell the truth, she finally murmured, "I'm also happy that Mr. Lamb has such a congenial relationship with all of us." Managing a tense smile, she stood up. "Knowing that, I feel better about slipping back to my room. I've a nasty headache, but I'll wager you'll all be so busy chatting that you won't miss me for one minute!"

Then, like a rabbit bolting from a trap an instant before it snaps shut, Courtney hurried toward the hallway, barely mustering a parting smile.

Wistfully, Courtney gazed down from the window seat in her bedchamber, watching the cool flush of twilight spread over Duck Lane as she reviewed the tangled situation of her life, searching for some bit of logic that would set her free. Instead, Courtney saw the faces of her parents, of Lisabeth and of Timothy Lamb as they had been late that afternoon. She felt suffocated all over again by their expectations—each person's prompted by a different reason.

It seemed to Courtney that her family's lives were ruled by such silly rules and worries. Amity Ashton was a virtuous, gracious, still-beautiful woman whom Courtney and Lisabeth had idolized since infancy. Never had she been known to say a bad word about anyone, except, possibly in an apologetic whisper, to explain to her daughters the reason why someone wasn't invited to a party or why she couldn't allow them to visit a certain family. Never had she spoken sharply to Gerald, or to them either, for that matter. Her manner was invariably ladylike; she deferred to her husband in all matters, and the primary criterion for her entire behavior was propriety.

At some vague moment during Courtney's journey through adolescence, she had struggled with the notion that her mother's ways were not necessarily the best and that she, Courtney, might wish for something else in her life besides the absence of criticism. Slowly, she had begun to resent the rules and plans her father set down . . . and had wrestled with a stabbing guilt that twisted more in light of Lisabeth's serene acceptance. It was painful and confusing to face the reality of her parents' weaknesses and flaws. Amity Ashton had been residing on a high pedestal for years, but as Courtney approached womanhood, she found herself outraged by the way her mother acceded to her father's tyranny. Suddenly Courtney saw that there was no equality in their relationship, no passion, no effort at understanding. A spark of anger flared within her sadness when she realized that Gerald Ashton might be less a bully and more a human being today if Amity had stood up to him the first time he'd given an order to his bride.

Amity wanted Courtney to marry Timothy Lamb because it was the socially proper thing to do and because her husband wished it. When Courtney tried to talk about her own feelings, the expression in her mother's soft eyes was baffled. Timothy was a fine, kind, ambitious young man with a respectable career. What more on earth could Courtney want than a husband who would care for her, a home of her own and children to raise?

A reasonable question. But Courtney knew just how passionate a person she had grown into, for thus far she had yet to meet someone who would accept her true self. She burned with curiosity about dozens of things. The first few facts of any new subject were like the beginning of a thread that she felt a compulsion to pull, on and on, happily absorbing fresh knowledge until she was sated. She read and wrote energetically, and in between she dreamed of all she wanted to learn and see and do. On one side of her dreams was a shadowy male figure whose very presence would set her life sparkling, like icicles do on a sunny morning. He'd be irresistible. A true man . . . and he'd love her just as she really was.

Courtney rose from the window seat. The fragrances of supper wafted up the stairs; roast beef, caramelized carrots, saffron rice. As she lit oil lamps with a taper from the fireplace, Courtney thought about the dreams she'd nurtured, and for the first time compared them with the reality of her life and the world in which she lived.

The war cast its shadow over all of Courtney's days, but the darkness had intensified during these past months of 1814. When the fighting had begun two years ago, partially because of poor, delayed communications between America and England, skirmishes had taken place in the distant north: Michigan, New York, Canada and eventually Lake Erie and Pennsylvania. However, the tide had turned in light of Napoleon's recent abdication following his defeat by the British. English ships had been freed from blockading French ports, and veteran English troops had been sent from the victorious Wellington. It had taken forever for Georgetown and Washington to become aware of the British buildup of ships and troops during the early months of 1814, and recently Gerald Ashton and Timothy Lamb told tales of the two-pronged attack being launched by England. The first blade struck southward from Niagara, sweeping Americans from the Great Lakes, while the second thrust out from Montreal to push American troops down the Hudson Valley to New York. Wherever one went these days, citizens of the capital whispered and wondered about the British who had won their war with France. Now that Wellington was free to concentrate on America, what would his strategy be? Was the American army as ineffectual as rumor suggested?

Women weren't supposed to listen to such conversations, according to Amity Ashton, but Courtney was ever curious, and it seemed foolish not to understand all that she could about the war, especially since she lived a stone's throw from Washington. She knew that, after twenty years of disarmament, her country had not been prepared for battle. America's navy and equipment supplies were tiny compared with Britain's, but equally as frightening was its lack of commanders. The need for vigorous leaders, as well as for the troop training and discipline, continued to be disturbing problems, while the average citizens worried about their safety and hard-won freedom. Where Courtney lived, the fear of attack was real . . . and all the more paralyzing because the city was newborn, like a barely begun drawing.

During Courtney's thirteenth and fourteenth years, she had been dazzled by Washington society. It was a far cry from London or Paris, but she certainly didn't know that. To her impressionable eyes, the city was intoxicatingly cosmopolitan and blessed with a variety of inhabitants who were familiar with the grandest modes of Europe. Diplomats might yell about sidewalks that ended in sloughs of mud, but Washington as a whole enjoyed itself. Georgetown, older and more confident, took on an even warmer glow.

Before the war, Washington had relished its reputation as the home of America's most beautiful women; privately, people called it a marriage mart when eligible daughters were seen flirting with ambassadors, senators and captains. The receptions had continued since the war's commencement, but the threat of invasion had recently cast its cloud over the capital. Furthermore, it seemed that most of the handsome local bachelors had, one by one, enlisted in the army or navy.

Courtney thought about the likelihood that her father would join his regiment. It was true that Timothy Lamb, as a congressman, would remain in Washington.

When she attempted to imagine life without her father —or even warmhearted Timothy—her stomach felt cold and empty. One voice inside her called out, "No, it will never happen to anyone close to you!" and was answered by another that cried, "Oh, yes, it could! As easily as a trip in the dark . . . and then what will the future hold? How will you feel?"

Slowly, Courtney surveyed her bedchamber, which reflected the quiet, warm elegance of the rest of the house. The mahogany field bed and bureau were Hepplewhite designs, set against cream walls and a thick Aubusson rug of primrose yellow and Delft blue. There was a wonderful puffed, quilted counterpane over the bed: pale gold striped with blue. The two Sheraton side chairs flanking the small fireplace had seats upholstered in the same silk stripe, while the bed hangings were fashioned from a muted ivory muslin. Courtney loved the room in spite of the restless hours she'd spent within its confines.

In fact, her life wasn't such a tragedy after all. Her parents were both alive, she had everything she wanted as far as clothing, food and other material things were concerned, and nearly every girl her age from miles around would have given her eye teeth to receive a proposal from Timothy Lamb. After all, the truth was that for all Courtney's dreams about a dashing true love, she had yet to meet a man who moved her an inch. The brave, reckless ones had gone off to war, leaving behind an assortment of foppish dandies, middle-aged widowers, dull government officials and tongue-tied boys who broke out in new blemishes if she gave them a dance or five minutes' conversation.

"Courtney?" Lisabeth tapped lightly at the door. "Are you awake? Supper is ready."

Courtney was staring out the window again, dimly aware of the purpling dusk that descended over Georgetown, Rock Creek and the sparse outlines of Washington.

"Oh . . . yes, of course I'm awake. I'll be right down, Beth." She blinked slightly, readjusting her thoughts to the present, to the supper waiting downstairs and the conversation she would have with her family. Everyone would be overjoyed to learn that the wayward child was mending her ways; that the family member who had been chronically out of step was ready to resume her place in line.

Courtney felt a kind of peacefulness, not unlike that of a condemned prisoner, settle over her. It stemmed from the realization that there would be no more arguments, confrontations or embarrassing war. Her selfish days were over! From now on she'd try to tame her restless curiosity and appetite for physical and emotional adventures. Her byword would be cooperation.

Courtney opened the door and walked toward the stairway, whispering the word "cooperation" in a firm tone. Unfortunately, it tasted like plaster.

Chapter Two

May 24, 1814

Moving through the sea of people, Timothy Lamb searched eagerly for Courtney. He had looked forward to this evening, the occasion of their engagement announcement, for a full fortnight, reassuring himself that she would no longer keep him at arm's length once the betrothal was official. How odd and thrilling, after ten years' immersion in studies and an election to Congress, to find himself caught up in the addictive spell Courtney cast so effortlessly.

Once more Timothy made a methodical tour of the Ashton home. The entry hall was divided by an arch, its curve filled with a fanlight, and although Dr. William Thornton stood beneath it, sipping rum punch, there was no sign of Courtney. Even filled with crowds of chattering people, the house was beautiful. Timothy appreciated fine things, and he cast an admiring eye at the wide-planked floors of Georgia pine and the thick rugs from China, Persia, England and France. In the dining room, where the table groaned with an assortment of fragrant, colorful temptations, there were corner cabinets filled with Chinese export porcelain that took Timothy's breath away. He went through to the library, his gaze scanning the paneled walls of warm pecan, the gaming table that was ringed by men with cigars and brandy glasses in their hands, and the Sheraton reading chair, in which President Madison sat perusing a volume from Gerald Ashton's extensive collection. Only servants were in the kitchen, at the back of the house, so Timothy returned to the parlor with an impatient sigh. Where in heaven's name had the girl disappeared to? Could she be ill?

The long parlor ran the length of the east side of the house and was classically and fashionably Federal. The walls were Adam green, the furniture Phyfe, Sheraton and Hepplewhite; the hardware was small-scale, with brass locks and doorknobs. The focal point of the parlor was the wide, curving bay window at the far end. This area was known as the "music room" and boasted a pianoforte, a harp and a plush velvet window seat that held ten people. Candles magically illuminated the little nook, and Timothy saw Lisabeth sitting at the harp, talking to a foppish young attorney. She looked fragile and trusting, but her companion had a predatory air that irritated Lamb. A fitting time to enlist Beth's aid in his search for Courtney!

From the hallway, Courtney leaned forward in the shadows to watch her fiancé make his way through the crowd to speak to Lisabeth. When he sat down on the piano stool and struck up what looked to be an involved conversation, Courtney felt her chest relax. The tight feeling eased, and she could breathe again. Now seemed the proper time to investigate the refreshments, and she slowly traversed the hallway, smiling and greeting the guests as she went. Even these few minutes of reprieve from Timothy and the impending engagement announcement filled her with a sense of euphoric freedom.

"Darling girl, what have you done with my future son-in-law?" Amity's question was drenched with honey, but Courtney could see the reprimand in her mother's gold-brown eyes. The consummate Washington hostess, Mrs. Ashton was stationed at the dining room table, supervising the rotation of dishes.

Feigning nonchalance, Courtney plucked a plate from the translucent stack and proceeded to fill it with tiny, edible masterpieces. "Timothy was deep in conversation with Beth when I spied them just moments ago, so you needn't worry that he has deserted me, Mother."

Amity's properly arched brows flicked upward. "That was not precisely what concerned me, dear," she replied softly. "However, since you're here, you may help me for a few minutes by watching the table while I go to the kitchen. If any dish is emptied, come and inform us, won't you, darling? I shouldn't be gone for more than ten minutes, and then you'll be free to return to your fiancé."

Courtney tried for a smile to match her careless shrug. "Fine. I'm always eager to help, as you know, Mother."

Alone at last amid the guests, Courtney began to eat the savory appetizers and sweet cakes that dotted her plate, her midnight-blue eyes skimming the people who milled about. Apparently all the best citizens of Georgetown and Washington were here tonight: the Madisons; Elizabeth Kortwright Monroe, who was internationally known for her beauty; Mrs. John Van Ness, the heiress; Dr. William Thornton, architect, inventor, painter, horse racer and husband to Anna Maria, who had studied with Gilbert Stuart and acted as William's draftsman. Joe Gales was eating oysters and regaling Martha Parke Custis with tales of the latest goings-on at his newspaper, the *National Intelligencer.* Courtney knew that this group was just the tip of the iceberg; the parlor was crammed with dozens more people of power and influence.

She took a sip of wine and yawned. In spite of her indecently thin, high-waisted gown of white muslin, she was warm. The room was stuffy. To pass the time, she compared her gown with those worn by the other girls and couldn't repress a tiny, pleased smile. Nearly everyone wore white muslin, but hers was stunningly embroidered at the neck, sleeves and hem with swirling stems and leaves of silver gilt dotted with minute blue and rose flowers. The rich border seemed to accentuate the low neckline and the creamy curves of her breasts that swelled above it, while the puffed, gilt-trimmed sleeves added a touch of innocent contrast.

Courtney could feel the warmth in her cheeks. The smudge of color set off her large blue eyes and the cascade of caramel-gold curls that fell from the Grecian knot fastened high on her head. More than one middle-aged respectable husband had cast a lustful glance in her direction this evening, but Courtney wasn't capable of coyness or even polite flirtation. Not one of those men, most of whom clung to the old fashions of breeches, stockings and powdered hair, stirred even an ember of desire in her. Nor could she muster any enthusiasm for the numerous posturing dandies who thought themselves dudish and irresistible in their long pantaloons, tail coats with high, rolling collars and tall, light-colored hats.

Taking another sip of wine, Courtney fought the wave of sadness that threatened to engulf her. What is wrong with men these days? she cried silently. Everyone is so preoccupied with marriage potential that there's no time for passion or romance. If just one of you silly fops could have behaved like a real man and swept me off my feet, I wouldn't be caught in this trap of Father's and Timothy Lamb's!

Scanning the room once more, Courtney turned her

eyes toward the doorway. It was almost as if she had
sensed he would be there . . . arriving to rescue her
heart in the nick of time. Incredible eyes of molten
amber captured her own and penetrated to her soul.
Courtney was shaken, and it took a full minute before
she could think to look at the rest of him, for at first it
seemed that this man was a product of her desperate
imagination.

He was gorgeously masculine, chiseled and lean.
Jet-black hair was cut in ruffled layers that looked as if
they had been brushed backward by an amorous wind.
A few negligent locks fell over a starched, white shirt
collar around which was tied an intricate cravat. Fault-
lessly cut clothes skimmed the man's tall, hard phy-
sique, emphasizing the width of his shoulders and the
narrowness of his hips. His frock coat was dark blue,
his long, close-fitting trousers a champagne shade that
led one back to those amazing amber eyes. Courtney
could scarcely credit that a man could have such
eyes . . . and such a face. Where was the flaw?
Bronzed skin, slashing brows—one went up now as her
staring became unmistakable—a thin nose that bent a
bit arrogantly just below the bridge. Appraising his
mouth, she blushed. It was firm—sensuous and intelligent all at once—and finally came a square-cut jaw that
emphasized what she was certain must be the core of
him: unyielding, confident and secure enough to show a
little of himself, to share something of what made him
special with a woman.

Courtney shivered as she watched him approach,
feeling like a spectator in a tantalizing dream. Tanned,
elegant fingers caught her hand and lifted it to the
mouth she already knew so well. When the lips touched
her skin, she was startled by a strange sensation that
blossomed under her thin muslin skirt.

"Sir . . ." Courtney heard the quaver in her voice
and blushed, which only intensified her embarrass-

ment. The man must think her a stammering schoolgirl! "I . . . I am Courtney Ashton. Have we met?" As if she wouldn't have remembered!

He grinned. It was like the sudden flash of a knife on a moonlit night. "No, Miss Ashton, I don't believe we have. I'm Damon Sheffield. The Monroes asked me to join them tonight."

It seemed as though her nerves, bones, wits—all of her—were melting away on the Chinese rug. Never had she craved anything as passionately as she craved Damon Sheffield.

"I understand you are engaged to be married," he was saying, his voice wry and soft. "Is there no hope?"

"Oh. Well . . . I, uh . . ." Damn Timothy and her father and anyone who could keep this man from touching her, kissing her!

"You don't sound very definite." He smiled, one side of his mouth bending upward to mock her gently.

"I . . . well, there hasn't been any announcement yet." It sounded silly and childish even to Courtney, and when he grinned again, she knew he was aware that the announcement was to be made tonight.

"In that case, I'd be a fool to give up so easily. Could I possibly persuade you to continue this conversation in the garden? I find crowds smothering and irritating . . . and certainly not conducive to changing the mind of a maiden on the brink of betrothal."

Courtney smiled a bit, thinking that he could have asked her to go home with him and share his bed and she would have been powerless to refuse. "I agree, Mr. Sheffield, that this house is oppressively warm and crowded. I would be delighted to walk in the garden with you."

It was unthinkable to go off alone with any man, let alone a stranger. Courtney had used this very rule to keep Timothy from being alone with her. She shrank from the idea that he might try to kiss her. Damon Sheffield, on the other hand, brought out a predatory instinct she hadn't known she possessed. At this moment it seemed entirely possible that *he* might have to fight off *her* kisses!

A few pairs of curious eyes followed them down the hallway to the entrance to the garden, but Courtney didn't care. She still felt as though she were watching someone else's dream. When Damon's long fingers grazed the small of her back to guide her out the French doors, a crazy shiver ran up her spine and along her scalp. What on earth was happening to her?

It was a balmy evening—starlit and fragrant with honeysuckle and white moonflowers. The Ashton garden was charmingly sylvan, bordered by ivy-colored walls that ran back to a small cottage where their gardener, now fighting in Michigan, used to reside. The centerpiece of the area was a gray stone fountain from which radiated a dozen flagstone walkways edged with boxwood hedges and encompassing tangled bushes of azaleas and magnolias.

"So . . ." Courtney ventured as they strolled toward the bubbling fountain, "are you new to Washington, Mr. Sheffield? A fresh addition to our government, perhaps?"

The stranger smiled most enigmatically, his amber eyes flickering off toward the western wall. "Yes, Miss Ashton, I am recently arrived here, though I live in your own Georgetown rather than in Washington proper. I like the cozy charm of this town more than the capital's rough edges."

"Have you a house?" They had paused beside the fountain, and Courtney observed the expression on his face and the movement of his hands and body with a longing that made her ache inside.

"No, not yet. I am staying at the Union Tavern until I decide whether I wish to bring my business here on a permanent basis."

"Oh!" Something in his voice kept her from prying further. "Well, I certainly hope you do decide to remain, Mr. Sheffield. Georgetown—and Washington —is greatly in need of good men . . . and businesses, of course."

"I'm relieved to learn that," he replied in a low voice, eyes agleam in a way that made her blush furiously. "And the female citizens of your fair town . . . are they in need of good men?"

Briefly, Courtney thought of the reaction such a question would elicit from her mother and sister. If she were as ladylike as they, she would redden and display shocked indignation at his audacity; but, of course, she was different. Incurably, it seemed. "As a matter of fact, Mr. Sheffield, I'm afraid we female citizens *are* in need of good men—desperately so."

Behind them the water splashed moonlight, and a sudden breeze sent goose bumps over Courtney's bare skin. Strong hands slid up her arms, and a voice whispered, "Miss Ashton, I insist that you call me Damon." He smiled, gently amused. "Are you cold? Here . . ." Hard, lean arms enfolded her. Courtney's cheek brushed his pleated, starched shirt front and well-cut waistcoat.

"I—my name is Courtney." She looked up, but could scarcely hear her own voice.

"And I am Damon." His eyes literally warmed her; they were like cognac over a fire. When he caressed her nearly bare shoulder with deft fingers, she trembled then swayed when his hand grazed her collarbone and the slim column of her neck.

Yearning washed over Courtney in a powerful wave, striking with such force that she didn't bother to struggle. She smiled a little, glorying in the feeling of this steely, masculine body pressed against the length of hers, and saw him smile in return. He was going to kiss her, she knew it, and was filled with blissful anticipation. His mouth was going to cover hers . . . demandingly? Did he want her? Find her desirable? Dark fingers traced her cheekbones, brow and jaw line, and then his lips hovered above hers just long enough to send another shock of sensation to the unknown place between her legs. She could almost taste the brandy and cigar smoke on his warm breath.

"Courtney! Is that you?" As Gerald Ashton shouted into the darkness, Damon released her. Stunned, she took a few steps in her father's direction. "Courtney, I've been looking everywhere for you—we all have! Do you expect me to announce your engagement at breakfast?"

Panic and desperation choked her, and she looked back, praying Damon Sheffield would rescue her. However, like a hand extended to a drowning person, then cruelly pulled away, he had disappeared. Numb and confused, Courtney followed Gerald into the parlor, where Timothy was waiting. The expression on his face reminded her of the helpless love of a stray puppy she had found years ago. Touching though it was, she realized more sharply than ever that worshipful adoration was not what she wanted from a man.

The guests listened politely to the Ashtons' announcement, then crowded around Courtney and Timothy, pressing congratulations and best wishes on the lovely young couple.

Courtney's heart sank as she felt her fiancé's damp fingers press her hand. Beth was blinking back a tear while she kissed her sister's cheek and whispered, "You're so lucky. . . . Thank heaven you finally saw the light."

Although Courtney struggled to display the appropriate joyful pose, she was frightened. She felt like a bird caught in its cage, moments away from having its wings clipped forever. Instinctively, she scanned the guests again, searching hopefully for Damon Sheffield. Had he been a mirage? A product of her romantic, eager imagination?

At the first opportunity, Courtney slipped away from Timothy and the others and returned to the garden.

Heart pounding, she scanned the darkness for Damon but was surprised to recognize, instead, the outline of her father's back and head.

"Father?" Courtney queried hesitantly. "Are you all right?"

"Why, of course! Never better. I just wanted a moment to think." Gerald surprised her again by putting a gentle arm around her shoulders. "I'm happy tonight, my dear. I know you have reservations about this engagement, so I thank you for trusting my judgment. Lamb will make a find husband. Maybe he's not a dashing hero, but believe me, daughter, those types only exist in romantic novels. You know that I only want what's best for you and Beth . . . the kind of contentment your mother and I have known." Quickly, he bent to kiss her gold curls. "Now I can go to war if need be, with my mind at rest. Lamb is a responsible, trustworthy sort, and he'll see that all three of you are safe."

"Ashton! Is that you out there?" the voice of Dr. Thornton boomed. "The President has a question about one of your ships. Come to the library!"

Gerald, snapping back to his usual bluff distance, gave Courtney a pat on the head and strode into the house. For a long while she remained in the garden, strolling near the fountain, staring at the moon and thinking. Gerald's words had filled her with despair because his convictions would not be altered by any argument she could offer. He was certain he was right. On the other hand, it was heartening to realize that his tyranny was rooted in love after all.

Chapter Three

May 29, 1814

Pennsylvania Avenue was not quite as dusty as usual this afternoon, but Courtney decided this was a mixed blessing, since the fine weather brought out more men than ever to loaf under the poplars. Washington seemed to attract adventurers of every class, and the less savory congregated on the avenue. There were literally crowds of dandies, while, for balance, fancy girls mingled among them in their provocative, off-the-shoulder bodices. Like Courtney and Lisabeth, they wore lots of jewelry: long gold chains twining about their necks, bracelets, armlets and rings.

"They look better in their clothes than the great ladies at the President's Mansion," Courtney whispered. She was strolling between her sister and Timothy, who overheard her and made a strangled noise.

"Courtney, darling, how can you—"

Beth interrupted him with affectionate indulgence. "Please, Mr. Lamb, if you're going to marry my sister, you must get used to her shocking outbursts."

"Oh, stop it, both of you!" Courtney tossed sun-dappled honey ringlets which fell from an emerald clip atop her head. "I simply meant that the fashions suit them better. They feel more at home in those scandalous gowns. Somehow the turbans that are all the rage look chic on them, and even the cashmere shawls seem to hang more gracefully."

"Well, since you put it that way . . ." Timothy muttered doubtfully. "However, I, for one, think that you—and Lisabeth, of course—are more beautiful than all the fancy girls and great ladies combined."

Courtney wanted to roll her eyes, but instead, she smiled dutifully and kissed his cheek. "That is kind of you." She paused, choking on the next word. "Dear."

They were passing the Bathe House, which seemed to do a thriving business. A large sign over the door proclaimed: WARM, TEMPERATE AND COLD BATHS FOR THE USE OF THE CITIZENRY. TERMS, THREE WARM AND FOUR COLD BATHS FOR 100 CENTS. A handsome young man was emerging, still tying his cravat, and winked at Courtney. Aghast, Timothy rushed to distract her with conversation.

"Did your luncheon with my mother go well? She's been looking forward to getting to know you for weeks. It was a terrible disappointment to us both when she took ill before the engagement party."

Courtney averted her eyes and strove for a neutral tone. "Well . . . it went smoothly enough." She was positive that Mrs. Lamb, a widow with smothering maternal instincts, wished Courtney had never been born. Further, she would swear that the party-day illness had been no accident.

Lisabeth spoke up, "Frankly, it was a relief to see you approaching the house to fetch us. If your session in Congress had gone late, even ten more minutes, I fear, Mr. Lamb, that Courtney would have had us walking unescorted all the way home to Georgetown."

Timothy could only groan and easily assume an

expression of sick apprehension, his crescentic eyebrows disappearing into the careful swirls of blond hair topping his earnest face like whipped cream on vanilla pudding. Courtney had come to the conclusion that his brown eyes, alternately alert and dreamy, must be the hazel nuts, added as an accidental surprise.

"Your mother and I disagreed on a few points," she told him, not the least bit penitent.

"A few points!" Lisabeth stopped under a poplar to stare at her sister. "You two were arguing like—"

"Well, she kept saying the most ludicrous things, such as the war was all England's fault! When I mentioned that the quarreling had started because we wanted them to revoke the orders-in-council, she acted as if I were speaking Latin! I had to tell her that the orders prohibited American ships from trading in European and West Indian ports, and that England revoked the darned things but we didn't find out in time to keep from declaring war, and then our damned pride wouldn't let us back out! Honestly, Timothy, your mother behaved as if I were making it all up just to start an argument!"

"Courtney, darling, what you don't seem to understand is that most women don't take the time, as you do, to grasp politics and world events so—"

Timothy broke off at the sight of a tall, dark figure coming toward them from the doorway of the *National Intelligencer*. The man was the picture of rakish, sardonic good looks, and he was smiling at Courtney as though he knew what she looked like beneath her gown. There was something familiar about him . . .

"My dear Miss Ashton," the stranger was saying, obviously amused by some private joke, "I think it would be wise for you to keep your voice down. Your charming tirade was audible inside the newspaper office, and Joe Gales wondered aloud if you had joined the British!"

Astonished, Timothy glanced at his fiancée and was

further stunned to see that she was blushing hotly. How did she know this scoundrel?

"I don't believe I've had the pleasure," the man went on easily, extending a strong hand in Timothy's direction. "I was privileged to attend your engagement party, sir, but unfortunately, I was called away before I was able to meet you formally . . . or the lovely, younger Miss Ashton." The word *younger* seemed intended as a tiny jab in Courtney's direction, but Timothy couldn't be sure. Was it merely his imagination? "My name is Damon Sheffield."

They shook hands, Lamb managed a few wooden pleasantries, then Sheffield turned to Lisabeth, gracefully raising her pale hand to his lips while smiling at her with his eyes uplifted in a roguish way that reddened her cheeks.

What was it about this impertinent devil that turned these girls' knees to water? an outraged Timothy wondered. Was this what Courtney wanted from a man? Suggestive winks, sexual innuendo and insolent conversation riddled with double entendres? Sheffield had somehow fallen into step with them, and before he knew it, Timothy found himself engaged in a discussion about the war and the news Sheffield had heard of Congress. His manner was completely charming; he seemed to admire Timothy and his role in the government. Names of prominent citizens, from President Madison to Dr. William Thornton, were casually strewn among Sheffield's sentences, leaving no doubt that he had visited and been made welcome at the homes of at least a dozen prominent families over the past month. It appeared that they all were coaxing him to remain in the area permanently.

Suddenly the group was in Duck Lane. Timothy was shocked to realize he had become so engrossed in conversation with Damon Sheffield that he hadn't noticed how much progress they had made toward Georgetown and the Ashton house.

"This was much more enjoyable for me than return-ing to the Union Tavern alone," Damon said. "I hope my presence hasn't been a bother to you."

"On the contrary, Mr. Sheffield, it has been lovely talking with you," Lisabeth assured him.

"How kind of you to say so." Amber eyes smiled at her, then turned their gleam in Courtney's direction.

She mustered a pretty grin. "Are you fishing for compliments?"

"I . . . I do hate to interrupt," Timothy said, point-edly clicking his pocket watch open and shut, "but I must be getting back to Washington. Courtney, I'll see you tomorrow night at dinner and . . ." Uneasily, he drew her aside. "And please don't worry about your troubles with Mother."

She nearly laughed aloud. "No, I'll try not to, Timothy."

After he bade a general farewell all around, the two sisters and Damon watched him turn the corner. Just then a head popped out an upstairs window. It was Mrs. Belcher, the housekeeper, and she called sternly, "Lisabeth Ashton, get ye up here! Yer mother's been waitin' all this past hour to fit this dress on ye!"

Moments later Courtney found herself alone, except for Duck Lane's passersby, with the mysterious stran-ger. They stood together on the steps outside her house, and for all Courtney knew, both her parents were watching them from the window. Still, excitement was choking her. Ever since the moment he had stepped out of the *National Intelligencer*'s offices, Damon Sheffield had filled each of her senses. She knew every detail of his polished knee boots, of the double-breasted green riding jacket that was cut high to his waist in front to display a flat, hard belly. When he'd walked briskly beside her down Pennsylvania Avenue, she had observed the flex and stretch of the long muscles of his thighs, snugly encased in cream-colored trousers. Now the late-afternoon sun was deepening the tan of his face and splashing gold over his raven hair. Courtney was entranced. For days she had dreamed of him and wondered if a dream was really all he was, in spite of the gossip being spread about the mysterious Mr. Sheffield. Now she knew he was neither myth nor dream, and wanted only to be touched, kissed . . .

"So, Miss Ashton, you will soon be Mrs. Lamb?" The amber eyes mocked her knowingly.

Hearing the name change, Courtney felt an inner wrench. "Well, that is the essence of it, but the wedding won't take place until the end of August."

"I see." The smile had left his eyes, replaced by something that gave her pleasurable chills. "Congressman Lamb's gain shall be the local bachelors' loss."

"Well . . . I don't think any of those bachelors will expire of a broken heart." Courtney met his smile, thinking, Go ahead! Touch me! I want you to. I'm dying for it . . .

"I wouldn't be too sure about that."

"Is that why you left the party the other night, Mr. Sheffield? Couldn't your heart stand the strain of hearing my betrothal announced?"

He blinked, then let out a burst of laugher. "Touché, sweet Courtney." Recognizing her reaction to his use of her first name, Damon leaned closer, eyes agleam. "It wasn't nice of me to leave you so . . . unsatisfied."

Her pretty mouth formed a little *O*. "I don't have the faintest notion what you're talking about, sir!"

"If you say so." Wickedly, he lifted her soft hand and surprised her by turning it over and kissing her palm. His mouth scorched the creamy surface of her skin; a long shiver ran up her arm and along one shoulder. "It must be torture for Timothy Lamb," he murmured.

"Whatever do you mean?" Belatedly, Courtney pulled her hand free.

"I mean that you are cruel to allow him to come this

close, then tell him he must wait three months to take you to bed."

Before Courtney could gather her wits and reply, Mrs. Belcher pushed open the window and leaned out again. "Yer mother says to come in!"

Sheffield was smiling as the window slammed shut. "She couldn't have been more definite than that! You had better go inside, Courtney, where you'll be safe."

"But—"

"Perhaps we'll meet again. At your wedding?" He made a mock bow and had turned to retrace his steps up Duck Lane when a slim hand caught at his coat sleeve.

"Please . . . wait. There is something I want to ask you."

Mrs. Belcher, Amity and Lisabeth were congregated in the sitting room, which was off the master bedchamber. Courtney found her sister standing on a stool while Mrs. Belcher pinned alterations to a new, daringly cut gown of pale green muslin. Amity sat behind them on her favorite chaise, holding an extra pincushion and supervising the operation. The French Toile de Juoy wallpaper behind her provided a becoming backdrop.

All three heads turned as one when Courtney entered.

"Darling," Amity admonished in a soft, hurt tone, "please do me the favor of joining us. We're anxious to her *all* about Mr. Sheffield." When Courtney was seated on the chaise beside her, she added, "Really, dear, it was quite improper for you to remain on the street alone with a man of such reputation. Especially since you're about to become another man's wife."

"In three months, Mother. I am not quite on the brink yet." She wanted to add, "I hope."

"Why, I must disagree!" Amity replied, her voice carefully, sweetly, polite. "You stepped to the brink when you became engaged."

Courtney wondered how much her father had been going on about this, since it wasn't like Amity to stir up conflict. "I see your point, Mother, and I'll keep it in mind for future situations like today's." She waited until Mrs. Belcher, garbed and coiffed as always in the servants' fashions of the Revolutionary War, swiveled her powdered gray head back to Lisabeth's waistline.

With studied nonchalance, Courtney inquired, "I haven't heard anything untoward about Mr. Sheffield. He seems a perfect gentleman to me. What is this reputation he has acquired?"

Mrs. Belcher clucked her tongue three times but did not speak. Amity sighed and shook her head sadly. It was Lisabeth who finally found words.

"Everyone is talking about him, Courtney, though in truth I must admit it seems to be only a crazy quilt of rumors—some laughably dissimilar. The general consensus, however, is that he's a rake who shows little evidence of scruples and has yet to give definite answers concerning his birthplace or family background." She had been looking at the far wall as Mrs. Belcher pinned, but now she stole a glance over one shoulder at her sister. "There is also vocal agreement among the females I've talked to that he is irresistibly good-looking and his wicked charm is as tempting as the devil's."

Courtney had to smile at Beth's uncharacteristic bluntness. "Don't tell me you were affected?"

"I cannot tell a lie . . ."

The two sisters laughed together while their mother widened golden-brown eyes at this unseemly conversation.

"Well," Amity said with an air of finality. She'd feel much better when the subject shifted to the menu for tomorrow night or the fact that the dogwood trees had blossomed. "As long as both of you have been fair warned, we can put Mr. Sheffield out of our minds and let the wittier, more sophisticated women deal with him."

Courtney brushed stray ringlets from her brow to hide a wince. "I must tell you all—it's the silliest thing, but, you see, I had no idea that poor Mr. Sheffield was so disreputable. I was feeling sorry for him because he's new in town. I thought he might enjoy some proper conversation instead of trying to talk to diplomats who can do nothing but complain about the District of Columbia . . . so . . ." Her mouth had gone dry.

"Yes?" Amity seemed adverse to saying even that much.

"So . . . I invited him to join us tomorrow night for supper."

In the silence that followed this announcement, Lisabeth came down from her stool and stared at her sister. "Oh, Courtney, really! How could you?"

Chapter Four

May 30, 1814

An uninformed observer would probably have taken them for a cozy, intelligent group of friends, and it was precisely this brave facade of friendliness that amused Damon Sheffield to such a degree that he enjoyed his role as unwanted guest. If the Ashtons smiled any more sincerely, their faces would crack, and even Timothy Lamb, the poor fool, was making a valiant effort to appear warm and gentlemanly.

Courtney and the food were the only things Damon trusted. In the center of the candlelit table reposed a platter laden with a magnificent striped bass encircled by dozens of succulent stuffed clams and topped with a perfect almondine sauce. Two nights ago he had dined with Dolley Madison and Jemmy, who was both her husband and the President. They had at least three chefs, but none was as skilled as the Ashtons', in Sheffield's opinion. Even the wine was impeccable—as delicate, clean and spicy as the intriguing young lady who was seated across the table from him. Candlelight put diamonds in her honey curls and a glow in her cheeks, and accentuated the creamy beauty of her bare shoulders and partially uncovered breasts. If Timothy Lamb had any sense, he wouldn't have let Damon in the door tonight.

Gerald was studying the engaged couple from his vantage point at the head of the table. As if he didn't have enough trouble selling Lamb to his daughter, now there was this lawless-looking scoundrel—eating with them, no less!—against whom she could compare her prospective husband. Since Amity was twittering about someone's new baby, Gerald had no qualms about interrupting.

"Timothy, my good fellow, I've been meaning to ask you something. As a member of Congress, what do you think about the situation in Chesapeake Bay?"

Engrossed in a dreamy perusal of Courtney's arm, hand and as much of her bosom as he could stare at with decorum, Timothy had to be queried twice before his obligation to respond sank in. He blinked at Ashton, flushed guiltily and shifted as he sensed Damon Sheffield's maddeningly cool gaze.

Lisabeth came to his rescue. "Honestly, Father, poor Mr. Lamb has to wrestle with those problems all day long. I imagine he's exhausted! The worst part is that I must admit to some of the blame, for I had him explain the entire situation in Chesapeake Bay this very evening while we waited for Courtney to come down. It certainly is complex and confusing!"

Timothy had gathered his wits by then. Actually, political discussions were exactly his cup of tea, and he squared his shoulders confidently.

Mr. Ashton did a perfect job of cueing him by apologizing for his thoughtlessness, then adding, "But now Beth has me more curious than ever, *son*. Won't you enlighten me?"

"Oh, for heaven's sake!" Courtney burst out just as her fiancé opened his mouth. "What is so complex and confusing? The British are strutting like peacocks in Chesapeake Bay, but now that we have our gunboat flotilla and Commodore Barney, it won't be long before they go back where they belong." Her eyes were deep violet. "Commodore Barney will show them that we aren't a bit weak and ineffectual, that spirit and passion are stronger than sheer numbers and arms, just as they were thirty-five years ago!"

"Well said, daughter!" Gerald shouted, and when he raised his glass to toast her speech and the American ideal of liberty, the others joined in with impetuous enthusiasm. Courtney, flushed with pleasure and patriotism, glanced at Damon. She expected to see his amber eyes alight with dawning love and admiration, but instead, he seemed pensively detached, despite his raised glass and polite smile.

"Is something troubling you, Mr. Sheffield?" she asked.

"I should say no, but I find my curiosity overcoming the embarrassment I feel in betraying my ignorance. You seem to be quite expert on the subject of Commodore Barney, so perhaps you can help me."

Courtney felt as if she were alone and skating on ice for the first time. His eyes holding hers, and the sound of his voice speaking to her, preventing any rational thought. A tiny part of her mind didn't believe Sheffield. Moreover, she suggested his casual attitude masked a sharp interest in the subject that he didn't want to advertise or explain.

"Well, certainly, Mr. Sheffield, you may call on me for assistance at any time." The indifference in her smile vanished when he grinned suddenly in return, white teeth flashing with devilish amusement. The mutinous part of her mind was cast aside and forgotten.

"Your kindness overwhelms me, Miss Ashton." Damon managed to squelch the grin, but laughter flickered in his golden eyes. "The truth is, incredibly enough, that I grew up in a remote area of . . . ah

. . . Maine, and I fear that my education has been sadly neglected regarding Commodore Barney. I know a few things and am aware of his importance to our side, but I would be grateful for more details of his past exploits."

Gerald made a blustery sound, as if clearing his throat, but it was obviously his less-than-tactful way of letting his family and Timothy Lamb know exactly what he thought of a man who didn't know the details of Commodore Joshua Barney's life.

Damon, in the process of lighting a thin cigar, slanted a wry smile in the direction of his host, then shrugged, mockingly apologetic.

"Mr. Sheffield, I'd be pleased to enlighten you," Courtney said. A maid was clearing the table, followed by Mrs. Belcher, who poured fragrant, steaming coffee into the fragile cups and curled her lip at Damon. "I can certainly understand, since you are new to Washington, that you might not have heard—"

She was interrupted by another snort from her father. "Courtney, you had better let Timothy tell this tale. After all, he is—"

"No!" Violet eyes scorched first Gerald, then Timothy, for good measure. "You may be shocked to know that I am as knowledgeable as any man on most subjects, Father. Now, Mr. Sheffield"—she turned slightly to shut Gerald off—"Joshua Barney began his career in the navy during the Revolution, when he went to sea at the age of twelve. He was a prisoner of war several times, but upon his last capture, he was sent to prison in London. He escaped, lived there unrecognized for several weeks and finally found his way back to Philadelphia by the spring of 1782." She paused to sip her coffee, conscious of Damon's admiring gaze and the surprised attention of her family. "Back in America, Commodore Barney was given command of a convoy of trading vessels on its way down the Delaware River. When they were attacked by a British sloop-of-war, he managed to turn the tables on it, so that he brought not only the convoy safely into Philadelphia but also the eighteen-gun *General Monk* as a trophy of the war's last important naval action."

"Courtney . . ." Timothy breathed. "How have you remembered all this?"

"When we had him here for supper last month, I asked him questions, he reminisced and I remember because I am interested." The caramel-hued eyebrows arched.

"I believe I can supply the next event in Barney's life," Damon offered. "He sailed the *General Monk* to France and was kissed in public by Marie Antoinette!"

Everyone laughed at this while separate portions of strawberries and cream were served. Courtney eagerly ate one of the perfect, plump berries before speaking again.

"I'm not surprised, Mr. Sheffield, that you remembered the part about the beautiful French queen," she teased. "Unfortunately, after the war was over, it took eleven years for the first six United States frigates to be laid down. Poor Commodore Barney was angry and hurt when he was chosen as only the number four captain, and so he declined to serve."

Damon exhaled a stream of smoke. "Now I understand why he went to France to fight. He was both captain and commodore for them during their war with Britain, wasn't he?"

Courtney nodded. "He's a brilliant man, but terribly proud. To make matters worse, he offered his services to America in 1807 *and* 1809, but neither President Madison nor Secretary Monroe could find a place for him."

Sheffield's dark brows went up. "Ouch."

"Oh, Commodore Barney has certainly had the last word!" she laughed, and heard her father chuckle wickedly in agreement. "When the war began, he didn't bother with the navy. He just sailed a privateer. On a single four-month voyage, he captured eighteen British vessels!"

"It sounds as if Barney was after more than British blood," Damon muttered ironically.

"No doubt. His eyes light up when he speaks of being begged to take command of this gunboat flotilla. He said his orders had to come exclusively from the naval department, and he got his way!"

"I must say I'm reassured now that I have the full story. I was feeling rather pessimistic about our chances, but it sounds as if Barney has a talent for miracles!" Unable to resist another opportunity to make Courtney blush, Damon smiled at her again. "Thank you for the lesson, Miss Ashton. If I'm ever able to return the favor . . .?" He felt a shock of white-hot desire at the sight of her delicious, shy expression and the rosy curves of her breasts.

Sitting next to Courtney, Timothy felt nauseated. He saw the way Sheffield looked at her and was humiliated to realize that Courtney was most definitely moved . . . and the man was several feet away! What increased Timothy's agony was the presence of the other Ashtons. Without even glancing at Lisabeth, he could sense her pity and uneasiness, while Amity, seated next to Damon Sheffield, appeared stricken. Only Gerald Ashton betrayed no hint of embarrassment. His blue eyes blazed until Timothy felt compelled to turn and meet them; somehow he received Ashton's exact, urgent message and took strength from it. Do something! Courtney was talking to Sheffield again—flirting —while she ate her strawberries so slowly and sensuously that it seemed the meal would never end. Timothy's brow and palms grew wet as he tried to think of something to say that would regain her attention and put Sheffield in his place.

Suddenly he heard himself burst out, "While we're on the subject of Commodore Barney, you might be interested to know that he's already begun to drive back the British navy!"

Conversation ceased. Everyone was clearly startled, waiting for him to continue.

"Why, Timothy!" Courtney exclaimed. She swiveled to stare at him with interest. "You cannot tell us that much and nothing more! Besides, whatever news Congress has heard will be all over town tomorrow." Anxiously, she took his hand. "Please! You know you can trust us."

Lisabeth spoke up. "Perhaps Mr. Lamb would rather keep his own counsel after all."

Ordinarily, reason would have prevailed and Timothy would have shut his mouth. But the essence of the report Congress had received today from Barney seemed valuable enough to win a large measure of Courtney's regard. The satiny, cool touch of her hand over his made Timothy oblivious of Beth's tactful warning or the alert sharpness in Damon Sheffield's demeanor. "No, no . . . I think you should know." He searched Courtney's beautiful eyes. "It would be selfish of me to keep such good news to myself. You see, a day or two ago our good commodore took sixteen vessels and attacked Tangier Island—the location of Cockburn's encampment."

"Bravo!" Gerald boomed. "I knew he'd send them squealing, those red swine!"

Courtney wrinkled her nose and glanced quickly at Damon, who responded with an ironic quirk of an eyebrow. "But, Timothy," she said slowly, "what was the outcome?"

"Well . . . well, as far as we know, it was decisive, but—" Damn! Was she already withdrawing? "But you can bet that the British are properly shaken up. *And,* Commodore Barney has no plans to let up. In fact, on June first, he will—"

"Mr. Lamb!" Lisabeth cried. "Please, we wouldn't want you to reveal any plans for future conflicts!"

Timothy's mouth closed as if frozen. Oh, my God, he wailed inwardly, how could I have come so close? "Of course not! I only meant—that is, knowing Commodore Barney, I'll wager he gives those pompous British no rest from now on."

Lisabeth was the first to break the uncomfortable silence, smiling as she pronounced, "Well said, Mr. Lamb. I know we all share your confidence in the commodore, and in all the men under his command."

During this long discussion about the war, Amity had remained properly silent, but now she startled the others by firmly taking control. Standing up, she declared in her pleasant, ladylike voice, "Now, I *know* you men are anxious to move on to the parlor for some brandy!"

With that, Amity left the table. As she passed into the hallway, the other occupants of the room realized they had no choice but to follow the hostess. A relieved Timothy Lamb took out his handkerchief and blotted the moisture from his brow.

In the parlor, Lisabeth watched her sister's pale fiancé take large swallows of brandy. She decided he needed a respite from the pressures of dealing with Courtney, their father and Damon Sheffield. It made Beth sad to see Timothy acting this way, for she had spent a good deal of time chatting with him when Courtney was unavailable, and she knew him to be a young man of engaging earnestness who could converse intelligently about art, history and birds. Beth sensed he worried that his real personality and interests were too dull for Courtney's taste, but unfortunately, his attempts at playing the dashing rogue only made him look worse. How could Lisabeth persuade him that it was better to appear a bore than a fool? If only Courtney could be more serious and sensible about her life . . . and about men!

"Mr. Lamb?" Beth was seated on a green-and-gold-striped loveseat; she mustered a warm smile and patted the empty place to her right. "Could you spare me a few minutes of your time?"

He was glad to escape the casual cat-and-mouse game he believed Damon Sheffield was playing. Never had he felt so frustrated or doltish. Every time Sheffield's eyebrow arched even a fraction, Timothy's insecurity plummeted lower. Lisabeth, on the other hand, had a soothing effect and even appeared genuinely interested in being his friend. Sitting beside her, Timothy felt his tensions ease. He thought that her soft brown eyes were as serene as a fawn's. Minutes later, Lisabeth was apologizing to an unconcerned Courtney for "stealing Mr. Lamb away for a bit, but he has kindly agreed to help me in my efforts to learn to play chess."

Damon watched them retreat to the cherry gaming table to one side of the curved music room, thinking it would be a criminal injustice if Courtney Ashton had to spend the rest of her life with that man. He was agreeable and reliable enough, but totally ill-suited to the spicy Miss Ashton. If nothing else, Damon could at least try to extricate Courtney from such a tedious fate.

"Father," she was saying, "I've been meaning to ask you if you've acquired a copy of *Thanatopsis* yet."

The three of them were standing in front of the carved mantel. Amity was doing needlework in her chair, and had brought out the square of embroidery Courtney had been working on since Thanksgiving, but her daughter would have no part of it. To Gerald's consternation and Damon's delight, Courtney had joined the men's discussion with her usual high spirits.

"Do you mean that piece by William Cullen Bryant?" Gerald was irritated by her presence and by her insistence on changing the subjects he broached. "You must know I have more important matters on my mind, daughter! Besides, you ought to be reading the works of more established, respected writers."

"Honestly, Father! I have read Shakespeare and Voltaire and Donne—in fact, every revered writer from

England or Europe." She could sense Damon's smile, but went on emphatically. "The point is, I'm annoyed by this attitude among Americans that our culture must copy Britain's. Supposedly, American manners and literature are somehow deficient. Either our own authors are not read, or, if they are, negative opinions are pre-formed because the writer is not English!"

"Courtney, you talk too much," her father said bluntly. "Can't you vent these cockeyed ideas of yours upon your female friends? I am certain that Mr. Sheffield and I can find more significant topics—"

"On the contrary, Mr. Ashton," Damon protested, a slight edge in his voice. "I find your daughter's views refreshing and thought-provoking. Please, Miss Ashton, do finish what you wanted to say."

Courtney's cheeks grew warm and her throat tightened. How was it possible that one man's voice, eyes, smile, could affect her this strongly? "Oh, um, well, I was only going to say . . . Oh, yes! I simply felt that, as a society, we contradict ourselves incessantly. First we shout that we don't want to be associated with England or led by the nose by her, and we are forever celebrating the independent nature of our country. On the other hand, there is the hypocrisy of America's attitude toward our own artistic endeavors. If we regard British manners, history and literature as the pinnacle of distinction, then why did we wage war to free ourselves of them?"

Gerald rolled his eyes heavenward. "All this because I failed to show the proper enthusiasm for *Thanatopsis!*"

Damon lounged against the mantel and took a sip of brandy. When Courtney looked up at him, almost shyly, his eyes were warm with genuine admiration. "I think you're a fortunate man, Mr. Ashton, to have raised a daughter who not only looks beautiful but also is not afraid to exercise her mind and voice her views with confidence." To Courtney, he made a brief toasting movement with his glass. "Your argument was interesting and valid, in my undistinguished opinion. I look forward to the time when we may discuss your ideas at length."

Courtney thought he must be making a fuss to irritate her father, because Sheffield's mouth was bent ever so slightly and ironically, as though mocking the formality of his words. Still, she basked in the flattery. Whenever she behaved in an "unladylike" fashion, she was corrected by her mother or blustered at by her father. Timothy reacted in an uneasy way. Somehow, in spite of Damon Sheffield's air of detached amusement, she sensed that he enjoyed her unconventional conduct and regarded her almost as if they were equals.

The exchange of words and expressions between his daughter and the rakish Mr. Sheffield caused Gerald to draw his sandy brows together worriedly. If Timothy couldn't come up to scratch and take Courtney in hand, there was no telling what sort of trouble she might fall into. Gerald wished he knew what Sheffield was up to, and that he and Amity had spanked Courtney— frequently!—when she'd begun doing and saying as she pleased during infancy.

"Ahem! Mr. Ashton, sir?"

There was Mrs. Belcher, hovering at his shoulder like a nervous gray bird. "What is it?" he demanded, one eye on Courtney and Sheffield, who were chatting in low tones about something that was apparently quite amusing.

"Sorry, sir, but Drummond, the new coachman, is at the garden door, askin' fer a word wi' the master. Seems one of the horses is hurt."

An exasperated growl came from Gerald's throat. He didn't trust Sheffield with Courtney even in the same room with her family and fiancé, but there was no help for it. Excusing himself, he followed Mrs. Belcher out of the parlor.

"Now," Damon whispered conspiratorially, "tell me what books by Americans you have been reading!"

When he leaned over, his intoxicating, masculine scent drifted into Courtney's nostrils and sent a shiver of longing down her spine. She could see the intricate details of his expertly tied white cravat and admired the chiseled line of his deeply tanned jaw. Then her eyes wandered up to his mouth, firm and sensuous, and Courtney blushed dizzily.

"Are you feeling unwell?" Damon inquired dryly.

"Yes! I—it must have been that rich meal. I'm a bit drowsy." She took a step backward and two deep breaths of the air she was used to.

"The books?" he prodded.

"Well, you see, that is part of the problem. Because of the prejudice against non-British authors, there haven't been many American books published. I have to struggle to persuade Father to buy the ones that do turn up at the bookshop. Sometimes it occurs to me that he's merely being stubborn in order to thwart my independence."

Courtney suddenly colored again, and Damon thought she might be the loveliest girl he'd known— because of the extra serving of enchantment provided by her headstrong, innocent, inquisitive personality. Keeping up with her quicksilver mind and moods required all his concentration, especially in light of Courtney's distracting beauty. Clad in an Empire-waisted gown of topaz velvet, she was irresistible, her hair a mixture of honey and caramel, her eyes starry-lashed and royal blue. A voice of reason in the back of his mind told him that if he used his wits, he'd take his attraction for Courtney as fair warning and stay clear of her. Right now, as her cheeks warmed duskily and a shy dimple winked beside her mouth, Damon was deaf to all voices of reason or prudence.

"Why on earth are you blushing?" he asked, barely stopping his hand from caressing her cheek.

"I was trying to decide whether to mention the last book I *did* read by an American author."

"Ah! Are you inferring that it was somehow *improper* reading material for respectable young women?"

"I knew you'd laugh at me if I told you!" She tried, unsuccessfully, to suppress a grin. "Well, it wasn't *indecent*, if that's what you mean, but it has become the sort of book parents hide from their daughters."

Damon let out a crack of laughter but bit his lip when he saw Timothy, Lisabeth and Amity staring puzzledly. "Please don't keep me in suspense any longer. What is this evil book?"

"*Charlotte Temple*," Courtney whispered. In spite of her embarrassment, she was having fun.

"Hmm. After my admission of ignorance concerning Commodore Barney, I hate to say this, but I have never heard of *Charlotte Temple*."

This struck Courtney as being almost unbelievable. How could such a man of the world be ignorant of Commodore Barney *and Charlotte Temple?* It was incredible. "Mr. Sheffield, *everyone* has heard of *Charlotte Temple*. It was written over twenty years ago, and it's still one of the most widely read books in America!"

Damon pretended to cringe with shame. "All I can say is that it's lucky I came to Washington and met you before I passed another year in such nescient darkness."

Still dismayed, Courtney took hold of his coat sleeve. "Come on, I'll show you the book." Without a thought for her mother or her fiancé, who was happily instructing a rapt Beth in the finer points of chess, Courtney led Damon down the hallway to the library. Amused, he watched as she took a book, bound in red leather, from the shelf and opened it to display the title page.

"You see," she explained, "Susanna Rowson, the author, ran a finishing school in Boston. She wrote *Charlotte Temple* to warn impressionable young girls about the 'gay seducer' type of man, who loves and runs away."

"Ah." Damon nodded soberly, biting his lip to keep from laughing. "An *important* work, of international significance. How could it have possibly escaped my attention?" He paused. "Tell me, Courtney, has *Charlotte Temple* achieved its purpose? Do you intend to heed Miss Rowson's sage warning?"

She gave him a tiny, mischievous smile. "The problem with the book is that she describes the gay seducer so effectively, he captivates all the innocent girls who read about him. Until *Charlotte Temple,* we weren't certain what we were missing!"

Damon laughed. "You're enchanting, Courtney." Tanned fingertips grazed her cheek.

She hurried to return the book to the shelf, anxious to put as much space between them as possible. "I must confess that I've read more serious and revealing books than *Charlotte Temple.* Mary Wallstonecraft's *Vindication of the Rights of Women with Strictures on Political and Moral Subjects* opened my eyes to ideas that had never occurred to me before. I imagine that if Father read it, he would ban it in this house before *Charlotte Temple*.

Respect glinted in Sheffield's eyes. "I have browsed through Miss Wallstonecraft's book myself, and I agree that its philosophies would be considered quite revolutionary in this house . . . and in most others, for that matter."

Courtney smiled a trifle sadly, then shook off the mood. Why was she discussing such things with this man? "At any rate," she declared, returning to lighthearted banter, "in spite of the temptations of *Charlotte Temple,* I must tell you that I don't wish to join the crowd of women *you* have been gaily seducing since your arrival in Georgetown!"

"Is it really a *crowd?* Already?" Damon feigned curious innocence. "Has someone been counting?"

Courtney furiously began to rearrange books as he crossed the room to stand behind her. "No doubt you find all this a huge joke, but I can assure you the women you've loved and left do not."

"What makes you so certain I've been rushing about breaking hearts since I arrived here?"

She couldn't resist the playful, honest tone of Damon's voice and pivoted around to face him, intensely aware of his hard body only inches away. "I had almost convinced myself that your true occupation was sweeping girls off their feet!" Courtney's voice was light. "Tell me, Mr. Sheffield, if you aren't spending all your time seducing the female population of the District of Columbia, what *are* you doing to occupy the daylight hours?"

He had to smile at her transparent nonchalance. "I keep busy. I meet with business associates and attend functions in private homes to which I've been invited. It's necessary for me to spend at least two hours keeping my correspondence up-to-date. And . . ." Damon's eyes moved to scan the shelves of books. ". . . I go riding every day north of Georgetown, in those lush little hills."

"Oh, really? I suppose you like to ride early?"

Damon's amber eyes slanted down into Courtney's, gently letting her know that he was not fooled. "No, as a matter of fact, I prefer the late afternoon, just on the edge of dusk. I do try, however, to be off High Street and into the hills before the start of the evening exodus of men on their way home from work."

"Oh! I see." Never had she craved anything as much as a long, deliciously ardent kiss from Damon Sheffield. "It happens that I also ride in that area quite often. Perhaps we will meet one afternoon."

He cocked a dark eyebrow. "One never knows, does one?"

Chapter Five

May 31–June 5, 1814

Courtney scarcely slept that night, which she found frustrating because the time until she would be alone with Damon was only lengthened. Through the night she repeatedly imagined the scenario: his face when he saw her approaching on horseback, the two of them cantering side by side in the dusky twilight, their long conversations in which she would captivate him with her wit and intelligence. Finally, hours later, Courtney fell asleep and dreamed that they had left the horses and come to a secluded clearing. Damon listened tenderly to her secrets, hopes, fears, problems . . . then he opened his heart to her and revealed the man no other woman had known. After declaring his love and begging her to marry him, Damon gently drew her into his arms and kissed her slowly, caressing her with long, tanned fingers. As the dream progressed, Courtney's body gradually became so aroused that she awoke with a start. Lying in the darkness, she realized that every sensation and nerve were heightened with sharp desire . . . for someone who was present only in her mind! What did that mean? With a sigh, Courtney burrowed back into her pillow and pressed her eyes closed, trying to retrieve the deliciously real dream.

The next morning she was too nervous to eat breakfast. Long hours were spent bathing, washing her hair and finally dressing. All the while Courtney daydreamed of the time she'd spend with Damon, plotting more variations of their dialogue, wondering if she should be candid or a bit indifferent or shy, and if she would have any control over her actions at all. Whenever Damon Sheffield was in the same room with her, Courtney's usually clear head somehow filled with euphoric clouds.

At lunch, Lisabeth watched her sister push Virginia ham and glazed baby carrots, usually favorites of Courtney's, back and forth and around her plate. First no breakfast, and now this. Concerned, Beth asked, "You aren't feeling ill, I hope?"

Courtney blinked as if to focus. "Hmm? Oh, no. I didn't sleep very well, that's all. You know, I've been a little restless lately, and I was thinking that some fresh air and exercise might do the trick. It's such a glorious day, I believe I'll go riding later . . . when the sun is less intense."

This made perfect sense to Lisabeth, yet she felt uneasy watching Courtney's painstaking, dreamy-eyed preparations for what was supposed to be casual ride. When Courtney donned her best habit, an entrancing light blue Glengarry, Beth stared. It was flattering and feminine for a riding habit; short-waisted, with lacy ruching running vertically on the bodice, standing out from the shoulder seams and bordering the long, snug sleeves that ended just above Courtney's delicate fingers. Lisabeth watched her sister fasten tiny buttons from the base of her neck up to her chin and tie a cravat into a bow with small, puffed loops.

"Beth, would you help me pin up my hair?"

The two of them executed a perfectly smooth Grecian knot from which escaped a profusion of honeyed curls that framed Courtney's fine-boned face.

"You must be planning more than a simple ride!" Lisabeth exclaimed at last. "Why are you fussing so over your appearance?"

"What do you mean?" Courtney's sapphire eyes were alert. "What could I be planning?"

"You needn't raise your voice. I'm not accusing you of going to meet a British spy to sell secrets! I merely thought you might be planning to meet . . . perhaps Timothy, so the two of you could spend some time away from the Ashton family. I wouldn't blame you, Courtney. In fact, I think it might be the very best medicine for your relationship."

"Frankly, I'm not anxious to be alone with Timothy any sooner than necessary! Don't look so shocked, Beth. You know I was pulled, struggling, into this engagement by Father . . . and you certainly helped! I realize you want me to fold my future into a tidy package, but you're deluding yourself if you believe that the word *betrothal* has transformed me into a smitten maiden. No one, not even I, can force my emotions to conform to Father's, Timothy's, Mother's and your own expectations. I'm a human being!" Amethyst sparks shot from Courtney's eyes; Beth's wilting expression could not soften her anger. "Since you seem to be so concerned for Timothy's welfare and so filled with admiration for him, I don't see why *you* don't marry him instead!" She grabbed her riding crop and blue plumed hat, adding as she exited, "I wasn't aware that it's a crime to take pride in one's appearance or to go riding on a beautiful June day! Why don't you worry about *your* love life for a change?"

For minutes after Courtney had left the house, Lisabeth remained rooted to the spot, her face flaming with humiliation. She tried to erase all thoughts from her mind, particularly those of Courtney's angry eyes and voice, and started slowly toward the door. She saw something red peeking from under the bed, and, being fond of order, she instinctively bent to retrieve the book. Courtney had never been good about putting books back in the library after she'd read them. With a sigh, Lisabeth continued into the hallway, straightening the binding, but when her eyes fell on the gold-embossed title, she stopped.

"Charlotte Temple . . ." Her voice was a thoughtful whisper. Suddenly she remembered the mental picture of the "gay seducer" which she had carried through her reading of the book, and realized with a shock that the rake of her imagination was identical to Damon Sheffield.

Drawing a deep breath, Lisabeth set *Charlotte Temple* on a hall table and went to put on her riding habit.

It was five o'clock. Courtney, frustrated nearly to the point of tears, reined in her mare, Yvette, at the edge of Parrott's Woods. High Street was cluttered with vehicles and horses traveling north to take country residents home to their suppers and port. For an hour she had trotted about with studied nonchalance, watching for Damon's dark hair and broad shoulders, all the while bubbling with nervous anticipation. Now, as Courtney faced the fact that he wouldn't be coming, disappointment squeezed her heart with icy fingers. Her need to see Damon Sheffield eclipsed her normal appetite for food, sleep and all the usual sources of pleasure in her life. On the verge of crying, Courtney pressed weary fingers to her brow and wished there were physicians for illnesses of the heart. If one appeared, surely she would be the first patient.

"Why, Courtney, hello!"

Beth! Courtney's head flew up to meet her sister's sweet smile. "What are you doing here?"

"You needn't sound so upset!" Lisabeth teased. "I'm not trespassing, am I?"

"Well, no, obviously not, but I just didn't expect to see you here."

"Your idea was catching, I guess. I've been riding for a while and was on my way home when I spied you and Yvette. I thought we might return together."

"Oh. Well . . ." Courtney glanced up and down Montgomery Road one more time. "That would be very nice."

Winding through the northbound traffic on their way home, the sisters had little opportunity to converse. Courtney wondered why she felt if she'd been caught by a parent with her hand in the cookie jar. After all, there was nothing for Beth to know, since Damon hadn't even appeared. Lisabeth, meanwhile, wished she could read her sister's mind. Nothing had been gained by following Courtney, but Beth continued to sense that something was amiss. Why would Courtney spend so much time in one place?

As they turned into the alleyway that led to the Ashton stables, Courtney glanced at her sister and felt a pang of conscience. Beth looked so worried!

"I don't want you to be concerned about me," she said, putting out a hand toward her. "After all, I *am* older. Please trust me to do what's best."

Lisabeth managed a wan smile. "I'm trying, but I have a suspicion that you and I hold different opinions as to what is best!"

When Courtney laughed in response, Lisabeth felt better. Perhaps it was all in her mind.

The next afternoon found Lisabeth picking flowers in the garden, a wicker basket over one arm. Timothy had joined the family for luncheon, and although Courtney had been absent, having the first measurement taken for her wedding gown, the rest of them had had a wonderful time. Now Beth hummed as she cut roses, remembering the warmth of their conversations.

"Oh . . . hello!"

49

Lisabeth turned to find Courtney, clad in a lavender riding habit, frozen on the path only a few steps away.

"Hello! Are you going riding? I'd love to join you! We had a marvelous time with Mr. Lamb today, and I'm sure you'd like to hear about it."

Courtney took a few steps forward. "Well, I'd like to, but not right now. I'm in the mood for a bit of reflection, if you don't mind."

"Reflection! I wonder!" Beth was shocked to hear her own voice. "Are you sure you aren't up to more than that?"

"Such as?"

"Such as . . . meeting some other man!"

Realizing the odds were against her even seeing Damon Sheffield today, Courtney was able to answer in good conscience. "That is the most outrageous thing you have said yet!"

The scornful tone of her voice reassured Beth, yet her doubts persisted like a nagging toothache. Had she seen a flash of telltale amethyst in Courtney's eyes before she'd turned away?

Later, Lisabeth changed into her riding habit and rode north on Market Street. She wouldn't reveal herself this time, and made a solemn, silent vow that if Damon Sheffield wasn't there today for a secret rendezvous with Courtney, she would never be distrustful enough to spy on her own sister again.

Three times between three-thirty and four-forty-five, Beth spotted Courtney's lavender-clad figure trotting between the trees of Parrott's Woods on the cinnamon-colored Yvette. And each time, she was alone.

When Damon Sheffield exercised his horse in the wooded bluffs above Georgetown, he usually followed Montgomery Street through town because of its parallel proximity to Rock Creek and the view of Washington beyond. On this fifth day of June he was tired, and glad for the peaceful feeling of this quieter pace. His thighs were sore after days of hard galloping over unfamiliar roads, yet he welcomed the prospect of stretching his tense muscles and riding for pleasure.

The weather was astonishing, the sky a vivid blue in contrast with cottony clouds. The meadow above Evermay was filled with flowers: lilac bushes in full bloom; red, yellow and pink hollyhocks decorating the stone fence; wild roses; clover; and sprightly daisies. The different scents mingled in the warm air to create a heady perfume, and Damon paused to fill his senses with the meadow's gifts. On an impulse, he dropped to the ground, thinking to pick a few daisies for his room.

At that moment a horse and rider emerged from Parrott's Woods, not far from Evermay. The rider came into the eastern edge of the pasture, nearly a quarter mile away, but Damon's alert eye saw that it was a female. From his position behind the hollyhocks, he watched her meandering progress across the meadow. The habit was a lovely powder-blue color, and he could see from afar that it covered a charmingly curved figure. The horse was a fine red roan, graceful and well-bred. Just as Damon's curiosity peaked, he discerned the true color of the girl's hair. Her fashionable plumed hat was tied to the saddle, so that the breeze and the sun were free to tease the curls which had been left out of a Grecian knot. At first the sun had fooled Damon into thinking the girl was a blonde, but now he saw that her glossy hair was the color of pure clover honey.

Courtney Ashton. After an instant's surprise, he remembered their conversation in the library and her flirtatious intimation that he might encounter her while riding one day. Was she here in search of him? And, if so, was this her first such attempt, or had she come each of the five afternoons he had been away? The implications of the latter dazed him.

Damon could see her face now, but it was obvious that she didn't recognize him behind stripes of hollyhock stems and circles of blossoms. Proceeding cautiously, Courtney eyed the gray stallion, which had crossed the road to graze on sweet meadow grass, and her eyes flicked in Damon's direction. He couldn't help smiling. No doubt she feared he was a disreputable type who might misuse her . . . and there were women who would say he fit that description.

"Miss Ashton, I'm speechless with surprise!" Damon's greeting was heavily underlaid with irony. For a moment he straddled the low stone wall with hard-muscled legs, smiling at Courtney, then dropped into the lush grass and went to meet her.

Courtney was paralyzed. After waiting, dreaming, watching and despairing for what had seemed an eternity, she could scarcely realize that the man coming toward her was not a mirage. One of the key factors in her swelling depression was the fear that Damon Sheffield's lengthening absence from Georgetown meant that he had left permanently. Could he really be here now, alone with her in a meadow of wildflowers?

He looked like a pirate. One rarely saw a man in public without both coat and cravat, but Damon wore only a finely made linen shirt, unbuttoned to reveal a few inches of bronzed chest covered by crisp dark hair that curled over the hollow at the base of his neck. Narrow hips and long, steely thighs were accentuated by fawn breeches which disappeared into the tops of dark brown knee boots. His hair gleamed in the sunlight, ruffled casually by the breeze, and Courtney was struck by some change in his appearance. When Damon flashed a white grin, the more vivid contrast with his deep tan made her think he must have spent every hour of the past several days outdoors, taking the full brunt of wind and sun. Even his muscles seemed more clearly chiseled.

Yvette skittered backward as this strange man drew near, but when he stroked her neck and spoke soft, comforting words, the mare relaxed. Courtney's heart thudded as Damon turned his attention to her, looking up with amber eyes that held the usual ironic amusement, and also a tender light that took her breath away.

"Have you forgotten me in these few days since our last meeting?" he couldn't resist teasing her. When she blushed, he tested further by taking one kid-sheathed hand in his and removing the glove. "Your silence is alarming and most uncharacteristic, Miss Ashton." Damon followed this remark with a slow kiss on the back of Courtney's hand and was startled to feel abrupt perspiration on her palm. If she were infatuated with him, that was fine, but it wouldn't do for Courtney to tie herself up in knots of longing that he could not, in good conscience, more than loosen.

"I . . . I suppose I'm just surprised to see you, Mr. Sheffield," she managed to whisper. "I thought that . . . perhaps you had returned to Maine."

His brow gathered in momentary confusion, then he remembered and laughed. "No, I'm in no hurry to travel to Maine." Dark hands encircled her slim waist before Damon slid Courtney from the sidesaddle and lowered her to the ground. Was she trembling? He traced the exquisite line of her brow, cheek and chin, smiling at the badly knotted cravat. "Dare I hope that I was missed?"

Tears stung dark violet eyes; it didn't help that she tried to hide them by pressing her face against his wide, muscular chest. Damon's own heart caught as he felt warm moisture soak through his shirt. In fact, the imprint of her delicate features on his flesh rekindled emotional embers that he had diligently banked for as long as he could remember. Burying his face in shining honey curls, Damon curved his arms around her back and tightened his embrace. The fragrance of meadow grass and clover filled his senses.

"Courtney . . ." He was determined to dissuade her, at least to the extent of regaining control of herself. Whatever was in her mind, heart and imagination had obviously erupted into a whirlpool during the time he'd been away. If he couldn't help her out of it, to a place where she could view him, and her own needs, with perspective and a bit of distance, everyone involved would suffer.

Damon spoke her name again, and finally Courtney mustered the courage to lift her head. All the carefully chosen words of reason turned to dust as he looked down at her. Tears clung to thick lashes above amethyst eyes, made a wet sheen over flushed cheeks and perched, twin drops of dew, on the rose petal of Courtney's lower lip. When Damon bent to kiss them away, her mouth trembled at the gentle touch, then grew fervent at his lips searched more intensely. It was as if a dam had broken inside Courtney. She gloried in the hard warmth of his shoulders and neck against her embracing arms, and though it seemed that Damon's kiss would leave her bruised and burned, she knew only that she wanted more and more.

Chapter Six

June 5, 1814

"I wish you'd tell me where you've been," Courtney coaxed. "If it's a secret, then that means you've been having a mysterious, exciting adventure, and I can't bear not hearing about it. I'm famous for keeping secrets. Once I give my word, even the British couldn't make me tell. They could torture me, starve me, ravish me—"

"The ravishing part would probably be a great treat for you," Damon interjected with a lazily sardonic smile. He was still marveling to himself that an audacious young virgin could have such success in persuading him to act against his better judgment. It had taken the last shreds of his willpower to refrain from educating Courtney in the finer points of ravishment, in broad daylight in a meadow next to Montgomery Road. She hadn't helped him in the least while he'd striven to preserve her maidenhood and reputation. When finally Damon had managed to put a few feet between his lust and her innocent fire, he should have bidden her good afternoon and ridden away. The fact that he hadn't, and worse, had allowed himself to be wheedled into "walking the horses in the woods, where the grass is ideal for grazing," convinced Damon that he was in danger of losing his reliably cool, sharp wits.

Courtney pretended outrage at his observation and took a step across the narrow path, one hand drawn back to cuff at Damon's arm. Amber eyes narrowed; tanned fingers flicked out to catch her wrist; brows went up in pseudo surprise.

"Tsk, tsk! You have a disturbingly short memory, Miss Ashton. You agreed to maintain a distance of three feet."

His hand gripping the translucent underside of her wrist sent goose bumps up Courtney's arm. She could feel traitorous hot blood rushing into her cheeks, and when she violently attempted to pull free, Damon released her so quickly that she almost toppled backward.

"You needn't act so conceited!" she cried. "I won't be transformed into a passion-crazed . . . *hussy* if you come within touching distance! *Somehow* I'll manage to contain myself!"

"Well, that's a relief," Damon said, choking back laughter. "I've never encountered an authentic *hussy*, but I have heard stories that would make your hair stand on end!"

Feeling his gaze riveted on her, Courtney managed to stave off an urge to break her riding crop in two. She wished Yvette had wandered away so that she could search the mare out and compose herself in the process, but both horses were only a few yards ahead, nibbling side by side.

"Meeting you alone today has been a very educational experience," Courtney remarked at last, slyly nonchalant. "It's plain you are on your best behavior in company, because I can see that the *real you* isn't to be trusted!"

"Indeed? On what do you base this wild accusation?"

"Well, first of all, you have taken advantage of my inexperience. Even my fiancé respects me enough not to compromise my honor before our wedding, but clearly *you* are ignorant of the ways of true gentlemen!"

Damon bit back another smile. "Egad! You have cut me to the quick!" Rubbing his jaw in mock distress, he fretted, "Do you suppose I might be labeled a male *hussy?*"

"There! You see? That illustrates my other point perfectly! Not only have you assaulted me physically, but your entire attitude is insolent!" Courtney was elated to feel herself getting a grip on the situation. As long as he didn't touch her . . .

Stopping in his tracks, Damon put his head back and laughed with rich enjoyment. When Courtney turned red and suddenly stalked away, he caught her easily and went down on one knee. Ardently contrite, he kissed her hands and begged her pardon. Courtney was still stung with humiliation, but the dancing light in his gold eyes melted her resistance. Something flip-flopped maddeningly inside her.

"You're adept at embarrassing me," she scolded. Hoping to avert her face before Damon saw her smile, Courtney tried in vain to pull free of his grasp. "For heaven's sake, get up! Why can't you behave, even for a few minutes, like a well-intentioned gentleman?"

"Please!" He kissed her hands again, the irrepressible curve of his mouth against her flesh like a flame. "I cannot rise from the dusty ground without your pardon."

"I never knew that any man could be so impertinent!" His nearness was unnerving her; it was as if the temperature in the woods had suddenly risen to a hundred degrees. "I am not dimwitted! I know when I'm being mocked!"

A gust of laughter escaped Damon's lips. At this, Courtney stepped backward, tugging one hand free, but when Damon shifted his left knee in her direction, his amusement suddenly turned to painful anger.

"Owwooch!" he howled, dropping back onto his hard buttocks and holding the injured leg stiffly out in the air. "Goddamn bloody sharp rock!"

Horrified, Courtney knelt beside Damon, oblivious to the smudges of dirt that appeared on the Glengarry riding habit. She was almost afraid he might hit her if she touched him, but put a hand on his arm anyway. "What happened? Where are you hurt?"

The initial explosion had passed, but Damon managed a stormy glare. "My *knee!* I cracked it right in the center on that cursed stone! If you would ever stand still—" For emphasis, he reached for the offending rock, which did indeed have a bladelike tip, and hurled it into the woods.

"Oh!" Courtney laughed derisively. "So it's my fault!"

Damon cradled his leg and soberly inspected the injury. "Clearly *I* could not be in error, so the blame must rest with you." His matter-of-fact tone was belied by golden sparkles in his eyes.

"I won't waste my time challenging such convoluted reasoning," Courtney murmured wryly. "Here, let's move over to where the deeper grass is. You can lean against the tree and recuperate for a few minutes."

Deftly, Damon stood on his right leg, keeping the other from touching the ground as he rose. When he gave her a look of dramatic agony, Courtney had to laugh. Shaking her head, she held his hand for balance as he hopped over to the lush carpet of grass and leaves that surrounded magnificent old oak trees.

After they had settled down comfortably, Courtney found her slim fingers still entwined in his. "You know," she said impulsively, "I noticed your hands earlier, while you were groveling at my feet and begging for forgiveness."

One of Damon's raven brows was arched high in disbelief, and Courtney had to stifle a giggle. She'd certainly gotten his attention! Realizing that he was waiting for her to finish, she said, "It's just that your skin is much rougher and even more suntanned. Look here." She turned his palm upward and pointed. "A blister! And those calluses weren't there a few days ago. I wish that you'd tell me where you've been!"

"I'm surprised to learn that you have spent so much time examining my hands and committing the details to memory." Although Damon's tone was laced with cynical amusement, he was not relaxed. "As for your curiosity about my whereabouts lately, I would appreciate it if you'd stop badgering me. I do not owe an accounting to you or anyone else in Georgetown . . . and that's the way I like it."

Stung, Courtney didn't speak for several minutes. Damon's hand became disengaged from hers. She watched as he negotiated a more comfortable position against the tree, then extended a welcoming arm to his horse. The stallion and the mare were returning from a short exploration farther into the woods, and after pausing to greet Damon and Courtney, they continued onto a new path.

"Can you tell me," she whispered, "if your absence had anything to do with the war?"

"Why do you ask?" His voice was tensely patient.

"Well . . . I realize it's none of my affair, but I have begun to feel that our . . . acquaintance has become—"

"Yes, yes, I get the point. And?"

"Some people have questioned your absence from the army in light of your strong physical health and . . . your state of unattachment." Courtney stared at Damon's profile. He had leaned his dark head against the tree trunk, and since his eyes were closed, only the tiny movement of a jaw muscle told her he was not only awake but listening. "Don't misunderstand! *I* have no doubts about your character or courage, but it frustrates me to hear these slurs, made behind your back, and be unable to defend you factually."

Damon's eyes were cognac-colored as he regarded her earnest, beautiful face. A smile flickered across his mouth. "I appreciate your loyalty, Courtney, undeserved as it is. You're a lovely creature, and, God willing, you won't have to suffer disillusionment for . . . a long time. However, I can't have you defending me. After all, you're betrothed to another man—" white teeth flashed "—and taking *my* scandal-tinged cause would only taint your reputation."

"Please, though, can't you give me some word? I know there must be a perfectly brilliant reason why you haven't at least joined a reserve militia, like Father—"

"Father, hmm? I thought as much. Well, I don't give a damn what Gerald Ashton or Timothy Lamb or anyone else has to say about me, but for your peace of mind, I will say this: I *have* fought in this war. I've killed more men than I can bear to count. I've sustained two serious wounds myself. And I consider myself as patriotic as your father or any other person who cares to compare his or her love of country with mine."

Courtney's eyes were wide with awed adoration. She soaked up each word, loving the proud, angry fire that Damon radiated. Even if he hadn't been away these past days on a secret, war-related assignment, he had obviously paid more than his share of patriotic dues.

"I wish you wouldn't look at me like that," Damon protested. "I feel as though you've canonized me and propped a halo above my head. Believe me, Courtney, I'm not a saint."

She gave him a crooked smile. "At least *you* realize it. I wish my father would say that about himself to

Beth or my mother from time to time. I think he actually encourages his own deification!"

"I've noticed that he seems to affect a rather regal air," Damon agreed wryly. "Why don't you share your mother and sister's belief in his infallibility? I find your comments and expressions all the more interesting in view of my early impression that your father arranged the marriage between you and Lamb."

Courtney shifted uneasily, examining a nick in her riding crop. The conflicting, confusing emotions she had regarding her father had never left the confidentiality of her own mind. "If I tried to explain, you would be so bored you'd fall asleep."

"Well, I doubt that." Damon kept his tone lightly reassuring. Casually, he traced the ruching that edged her wrist and let his tanned fingertip brush Courtney's satiny skin. "You know, I'm a good person to talk things over with because I've been so wicked myself that I've learned to be tolerant of other people's mistakes . . . and troubles. I don't pass judgment unless I encounter someone who is pretentious or otherwise false in dealing with others or himself. I can find no fault in people who are true to their own convictions and emotions."

Lulled by his voice and the feather-light caress of his finger on her wrist, Courtney sighed and leaned against Damon slightly, afraid he'd draw away, but his arm was warm and as unyielding as the tree that sheltered them.

"I've . . . never discussed this with anyone before. I don't know a soul, except you, who wouldn't lecture me and tell me how disloyal, misguided, and ungrateful I am."

"You don't have to confide in me, Courtney. I only brought it up because I like you, and I'm on your side. We all grow up believing that our parents are perfect, so if we turn out differently, it's natural to feel guilty." Damon brushed his lips over the caramel-gold tendrils that crowded her brow. "Guilt is a rotten emotion, and when it enters into crucial life decisions, it's downright wicked. One's thinking becomes so warped, an uncluttered perspective is impossible."

"Listening to you . . . saying those things . . . it seems totally unreal, as if I'm dreaming." When he didn't respond, Courtney let herself relax a little more against him. "If I were to pick one trait of Father's that upsets me most, it would be his inflated confidence in his own ideas, plans, opinions. He thrives on guiding other people along the route he has devised, and at home this is accepted as normal. When I was a child, Beth and Mama idolized him and lived to please him, and I acted the same way. We all, including Father, silently agreed he was so special and dynamic that it was unthinkable he could ever be wrong." Courtney shook her head in ironic wonder. "The hardest concept for me was the notion that Father might have flaws. When doubts about him first crept into my mind, they were so painful that it was easier to push them away and go on being 'a good girl,' never questioning. Father always reinforced our good behavior with enthusiastic approval. He really *is* dynamic, so his smiles and compliments—the extra attention—made Beth and me soar."

"And when he doesn't approve?" Damon queried softly.

"Oh, well, a person could freeze from Father's cold stares. Even now I feel sick when I see his mouth tighten because of something I've done or said, but gradually, over the years, I learned that frost is just a weapon he uses to try to regain control. I don't think even he is truly aware of what he's doing—the real implications of the way he manipulates lives. Father is convinced he's doing what's best, and he's trying to get me to do what's best. The problem is, he has it all figured out and wrapped up in a neat little present without any regard, or respect, for *my* views, *my* possible intelligence, the value of *my* opinions, *my* dreams!" Courtney jumped up and strode to the other side of the path. Making a fist, she hit the nearest tree, then watched dots of blood materialize on her knuckles. When she turned back to Damon, he saw stormy violet eyes and cheeks stained with emotion. "It's *my life!*" she cried. "It belongs to *me!*"

"Certainly," Damon agreed calmly. "Parents don't own their children."

It was almost impossible for Courtney to realize someone was listening to these ravings and saying they made sense. In an instant she returned to Damon's side, almost perching on his thigh as she leaned forward excitedly. "Do you really mean that? You aren't just trying to placate me?"

Damon laughed. "Do you suspect me of conspiring with your father and Lamb? Really, Courtney, you ought to have enough confidence in your own good sense and in my perceptive wisdom to believe we share a viewpoint that happens to be both correct and just."

"If I'm so smart, why does everyone else I know tell me I'm *wrong* about everything . . . and immature, selfish, irresponsible—"

"Well, you complicate their neat little lives by having a mind of your own and not swallowing the ideas they feed you. It took a lot of courage for you to listen to *your* voice rather than to your father's. The trouble with all the women I know is, they're so busy following all the rules laid down by their parents, society, a husband, friends and the church that whatever is unique and individual within them has become lost in a tangle of artificial manners."

"Most men are the same way, only in reverse," Courtney observed. "Don't you think so? A boy grows up with his own set of social pressures."

Damon slid a strong hand up Courtney's arm, feeling its supple outline under the sleeve of her habit. An ironic smile bent his mouth. "What do you suppose went wrong with us? Perhaps we didn't get enough milk or liver as babies."

Bubbles of euphoric delight swelled within Courtney. The warmth of Damon's amber eyes made her blush, but when she looked down, the sight of his hand curved around her sleeve only heightened her discomfiture.

"I . . . I wish you would share a little with me— about your life. How did you become such an independent thinker?"

"Oh, there's nothing very unusual about my past," Damon replied, shrugging. He looked beyond her, into the distant clearing where the horses had wandered. "My father was killed at Yorktown when I was three years old, so, you see, my problems were different from yours. Then my older brother died a few years later. I could sense that my future was being planned by my mother, but those trusty emotions, guilt and responsibility, tied my hands and silenced my protests."

"Do you mean that your mother is like my father?"

Damon studied her lovely face, so tense with concentration, and smiled. "No. She has more on her mind than her own ego or a desire to control me. I grew up in the country. We didn't have a great deal of contact with other people, and Mother had time to fuss about my being the last living male in our family. She wanted me to make my mark in the world, a mark big enough to share with the spirits of my dead father and brother. Once she saw that I was reasonably intelligent and physically efficient, no goal was beyond my reach as far as *she* was concerned. And no girl was good enough for me. She loved me well enough, but no matter what I did, she'd follow her praise by strategically detailing the ways I could have done better or her plan for my next, bigger achievement." Absently, Damon's dark fingers untied, then deftly knotted, Courtney's cravat in a series of quick, intricate folds. "Finally, a dozen years or so ago, I had a brush with death that made me take stock of my convictions. I realized I would have only one chance at life—perhaps only another day!—and that it was utter folly to let anyone else set my priorities, or even to humor Mother by letting her think I could be controlled."

"What did you do?" Courtney couldn't believe he was actually confiding in her, or that he had ever been an unsure child with a domineering mother. Her eyes flicked over her freshly tied cravat—identical to his own, marked by a perfection Timothy struggled for hours, in vain, to achieve. The long muscles of Damon's thigh braced the side of her hip, and bronzed hands held hers lightly from time to time. Courtney dreaded the pink encroachment of twilight. How could she bear to go home?

"I went to Mother and told her how I felt," Damon replied. "I thought about trying not to let her down. It was conceivable that I could have pursued my own goals, far from home, in a way that would have kept her hopes up. I could have stalled, made excuses, generally led her on without causing any difficulties for myself, but somehow I gathered strength to decide that my life must be my own. No half measures, no room for misunderstanding. So I talked to her, face to face, and basically said that I had my own plans and didn't want to hear any more of hers from then on—"

"Oh, it must have been devastating! I'd be shaking, but only because I've been conditioned to fear Father's wrath. But for you, to say that to your mother—a widow—when men are taught all their lives to protect women at any cost . . . Didn't you feel guilty?"

Damon looked at Courtney for a long minute. An unexpected little flame kindled inside him as he realized that she understood. There was no accusation in her voice, only the anxious hope that he *hadn't* felt guilty.

"I made up my mind that I wouldn't be. And I think I did the right thing for both of us, because she ought to be living for herself, not for me. I told her I'd have to do what I felt was best and that I hoped she'd begin to search for some pleasure and satisfaction for herself."

"Oh, it's so sensible! Why don't parents understand?"

Flashing a grin, Damon lifted her hand and kissed it. "You are sounding a bit superior, Miss Ashton."

"Well, maybe I am! It makes me so angry to think that Beth is always scolding me and telling me to behave myself, as though I were a child, simply because I don't believe Father is some omnipotent king. She's the one who needs the scolding!"

"Don't say that to her, Courtney. If you don't want her to meddle in your life, you have to set an example. Besides, words don't help very much in these situations. I'll wager the day will come when Lisabeth's eyes are opened regarding your father, but you can't force her to see. The truth is too difficult for her to deal with yet."

"How did your mother accept the rude awakening?"

His smile was grim. "I didn't have much luck forcing her to see the light, either. She prefers to believe that I'll turn up after the war and settle down to business . . . which makes it nearly impossible for me to visit her in the meantime. Intolerable, really."

"But it's not your fault!" Courtney cried.

Damon nodded. "Now, my dear, I have a hard question for you. If you're filled with fiery determination to lead your own life, why did you allow your father to maneuver you into a marriage with the irresistible Timothy Lamb?"

"I'm not going to apologize for that! You don't know how he'd been badgering me—Father, that is—and Timothy, too. And Mother and Beth. I was surrounded! But if it weren't for the war, I'd never have given in. Father made me feel it was my duty to make a good match so he could go into battle and face death with one less daughter to worry about. And I felt responsible for Beth's lack of suitors. As long as I, the older sister, was unattached, men called on me first."

"It's not because you're older!" laughed Damon.

The woods were hazy with beams of lilac and gold dusk. Courtney could see her bodice rising and falling with the throb of her heart. How could one man look so incredibly touchable? In the dusky shadows, his eyes were molten, the chiseled lines of his face appeared even more masculine and his mouth, open a fraction to reveal the whiteness of his teeth . . .

"Courtney, are you all right? I didn't mean to upset you," Damon said with soft concern. "I know families can exert an enormous amount of pressure, especially on a female, who is reminded that she is dependent—"

"If I'd only known," she interrupted, her voice barely audible, "no amount of pressure could have swayed me."

His brow gathering, Damon leaned forward to enfold her in his arms and let his hand run soothingly over her back. "Known what, sweetheart?" Was she going to cry?

Courtney whispered into his hard shoulder, "I used to dream about men like you . . . but I never really saw one. Only a lot of affected dandies trying to be rakes. After a while Timothy looked like a logical choice. I began to think I had been childish—living in a dream world—and with the war, it seemed time to wake up and face reality."

Damon was speechless and more than a little alarmed. "Courtney . . ."

Her face was turned up now, amethyst eyes brimming with tears that clung to her starry lashes. "Why couldn't I have met you even one day earlier? Why did it have to happen at the engagement party?"

"Look, Courtney, I—" Feeling her shivering, he tightened his embrace. Courtney pressed herself closer, slim arms creeping around his shoulders, and then her mouth was under his. Salty and sweet and fresh. The heat and depth of the kiss stunned Damon. It was as if they were drowning, eagerly, in each other's arms. He couldn't get enough of Courtney, and obviously a torrent of desire had been unleashed in her. Soft fingers touched the planes of his face, felt the texture of his hair and slipped under his shirt to test the strength and warmth of Damon's shoulders, back and chest.

Courtney was in a state of feverish bliss. The perfect cravat was untied once more, while his lips brushed her temples and found her bare neck, sending shock waves of yearning throughout her body. Fleetingly, she thought, I'm lost, out of control . . . but the thought slipped away before the faces of her family could appear to frown their disapproval. All she knew was that nothing had ever felt more right. Damon was intoxicatingly adept at heightening her arousal; each touch and kiss were torturously exquisite. Sitting across his thighs, she felt something rigid pressing through her riding habit. When Damon unfastened her ruffled bodice, Courtney thought her heart would stop beating. Gently, his fingertips grazed the silky covering of her chemise, and one breast swelled beneath his touch. Courtney closed her eyes as Damon bent, slowly freed her breast, then kissed the aching nipple with deliberate leisureliness.

Feeling her hands in his hair, the movement of her body against the hardness that begged to be satisfied, Damon was ready to take her. It was almost dark now, and there hadn't been a sign of another person for over three hours. Deftly, he shifted Courtney sideways to lie in the grass and moved halfway above her. When was the last time he had been so hungry for one girl? Ever?

"You are enchantingly . . . sweet," he murmured huskily. "Irresistible."

As his hand returned to the fastenings on Courtney's bodice, Damon gently kissed the column of her throat until he reached the delicate contours of her face and tasted warm tears. The appearance of Gerald Ashton himself couldn't have jolted Damon more abruptly. He pulled his hand from her clothing as if it were on fire and sat up straight.

"Jesus Christ, Courtney, what's wrong with me?"

Shocked, hurt eyes looked up at him. "Why? What is it? Are you worried about this?" She rubbed at the tears. "I'm not upset, I'm happy! That's why I'm crying! Please—"

"Absolutely not!" He bent to refasten her bodice, anxious to cover the delectable breast which peeked at him enticingly. "I must have been insane, letting myself even *touch* you! First I offer you my ear and my shoulder, but clearly I can't be trusted to draw the line at neck level!" Damon's fingers whipped the cravat into precise folds. "Get your hat! Where are those goddamn horses?"

Somehow, Courtney wobbled to her feet, trembling with waves of painful emotions. "B-but, Damon . . . I don't understand."

He raked a rough hand through tousled raven hair. "I'll tell you all you need to understand, Courtney, and I suggest you listen well and remember my words. You just came dangerously close to losing your virginity to the worst possible man, so take heart at your narrow escape. Now—and I'm deadly serious about this—I'm going to leave you and your horse at the edge of the woods, and I want you to ride quickly and get home before dark. After we part, I intend never to be alone with you again. If you have half the sense I credit you with, you'll pretend this afternoon never happened!"

Chapter Seven

June 8, 1814

Courtney was numb for three days. Grateful to be spared what would surely be throbbing pain, she tried to prolong the absence of sensation. Carefully, she practiced shutting the door of her mind on thoughts of Damon Sheffield and discovered that this was most easily accomplished by staring at a fixed, meaningless point or, better yet, by going to sleep. Unfortunately, dreams had a way of squeezing in where conscious thought would not be allowed. During Courtney's frequent daytime naps, she learned to wake up if a dream about Damon began, but in the black, silent depth of night, escape was not so easy. Like a swimmer who has dived too deep and is struggling toward the surface, Courtney would be tormented by long minutes of Damon's too-realistic company—amber eyes just inches away, a skeptical eyebrow that cocked into a question mark, tapered fingers that brushed the pulse inside her wrist, warm lips that parted hers again and drew her into the irresistible magic that was Damon

Sheffield. By the time Courtney was released by the dream, she would awaken to solitary darkness and scalding tears. Weeping until her pillow became soaked and cold under her cheek, she would eventually drift back into a slumber that was colorless, foggy and bare.

Meanwhile, Lisabeth spent three days trying to explain her sister's behavior to her parents, Timothy and herself. On the second evening, when the four of them dined without Courtney because she was still asleep—continuing a nap begun in midafternoon—they all concluded that she must be ill. Her odd actions of the past week must have been a prelude to this "fever." Lisabeth agreed, trying not to reveal her own uneasiness that whatever was wrong with Courtney was better kept from Timothy Lamb and her parents. For now, she kept up a running stream of distracting conversation, designed to keep their minds off Courtney.

It proved especially difficult to divert Timothy's attention. The two of them enjoyed the hours Beth spent substituting for her sister, but by the third day the situation had grown awkward, and he was voicing his questions more loudly. Finally Lisabeth confronted Courtney as the two girls lingered alone over luncheon.

"Look, Courtney, don't you think you might feel better if you got out and took some air? Mr. Lamb is coming today for tea, and I promised him I'd try to talk you into an afternoon stroll with him. He's terribly bewildered by your—"

"No. I just don't feel up to it." Courtney pushed a bite of pound cake around her plate. In spite of her listlessness, she looked enchanting; sunlight struck sparks on her hair, which she had merely brushed and left down, and her features were poignantly lovely in their sadness.

"Why don't you try to think about someone else for a change? Perhaps it would do you good!"

"What is that supposed to mean?"

"Only that Mr. Lamb has a great deal to worry about

these days, and you aren't being very kind when you add yourself to his problems. If you care for him, you should try to help him! Men need good women whom they can turn to for reassurance and comfort, to confide in—"

"Timothy has known all along that I'm not that sort of person, yet he has stubbornly insisted on marrying me." Courtney couldn't resist adding under her breath, "Perhaps he'll come to his senses and change his mind."

"How can you be so utterly lacking in compassion? Mr. Lamb is a wonderful man, and I think you'd find a great deal more fulfillment and peace in your life if you'd stop struggling and devote yourself to the task of becoming the sort of wife he'll be proud of."

"Oh, please! You're making me feel worse!"

"Can't you stop thinking about yourself long enough to consider the war? The world doesn't end at our front door, you know! Mr. Lamb is plagued with concerns that could affect all our futures!"

Before Courtney could respond, their mother appeared, and she was able to slip away before long, pleading fatigue and a headache. But Courtney was curious about Lisabeth's allusions to the war. After Timothy had arrived and she watched him and Beth leave the house and start down Duck Lane, Courtney returned to the dining room. Instead of Amity, she found her father seated at the table, reading the mail as he ate a huge slice of pound cake.

"Well! If it isn't my older daughter!" He seemed to be teasing, but Courtney could hear the sarcasm in his voice. "I'd begun to think you'd left us!"

"Father—" She was furious with herself for letting him see her uneasiness. Now he would be convinced she wasn't ill at all. "I can't explain what's been wrong with me . . . I almost wonder if I didn't pick up a bit of some tropical disease."

"Well, of course! That must be it!" One bushy brow was cocked high in disbelief.

"At any rate, I'm feeling better, and I heard Beth say something that made me curious. Has there been some new development in the war these past few days? Some news I've missed?"

Gerald chewed his cake thoughtfully, then took a long drink of tea. His blue eyes unnerved her, all the more because she knew he stared so hard for that very reason. "If you are well, you ought to take a little more pride in your appearance and pin up your hair," he advised. "As for the war, yes, there is news. Several days ago—on the first, I believe—Commodore Barney made a daring, secret attack on the British. He was aboard his flagship, the *Scorpion,* with only its eight cannonades and a long gun. He chased a British schooner and seven other ships, which action many have called foolhardy, but others—including me—are convinced could have been successful. Sheer determination and courage should have driven them down— the British, I mean—but it was as if they hadn't been surprised at all. As if they'd been prepared for the attack. Their biggest ship, the *Dragon,* had six dozen heavy guns and managed to drive Barney back into the Patuxent River."

"Well, really, Father, it sounds as if we were terribly outnumbered and overpowered."

"How do you explain the appearance of British reinforcements right at the moment of crisis? They blocked our gunboats, so that Commodore Barney had to take them into the shallow waters of St. Leonard's Creek!"

"What are you saying? How do *you* explain it?"

Gerald's eyes skipped upward to trace the corniced ceiling. "I don't know, except it has people worried. The whole affair doesn't smell right."

Courtney started back toward the stairs, pausing en

route to her room only to remark, "It 'smells' to me as if the Americans should stop believing this foolish notion that the British navy can be overcome solely by Commodore Barney's determination and courage!"

Still, she couldn't help thinking about it. The suspicious undercurrent in her father's voice conjured up an image of a wind-burned Damon Sheffield who'd refused to tell her where he had been. It would be just like Gerald Ashton to invent some wild fantasy about Damon . . . and if her father did, how could she tell everyone that she *knew* what sort of character Damon possessed? He might be inconstant in love, but she was convinced he was incapable of anything so spineless as trading information with the enemy. It was impossible.

Sitting in her window seat and thinking of him, Courtney let the waves of melancholy wash over her body. A piercingly vivid imagination made her feel the touch of his hands, see the warmth of golden eyes with their irresistible sparks of mischief, even hear his voice, tart with irony.

Instinct straightened Courtney's back. She looked out her bedroom window, down at the dusty ribbon that was Duck Lane, and saw Damon Sheffield standing directly in front of her house. He was facing south, engaged in conversation with Lisabeth and Timothy.

How splendid he looked! Courtney's heart jumped, then turned a somersault. He wore no hat, and his hair was as sleek and ruffled as a raven's wing. She saw the wicked flash of teeth when he laughed, impossibly white against the deep tan of his face. Eagerly, Courtney devoured every detail of his appearance, from the expertly tailored gray frock coat to the handsome dark blue vest and spotless white of both cravat and breeches. She loved the elegant strength of his booted legs, remembering their steely contours against her own body. . . .

What were they talking about? The idea that Damon might be coming into the house, that she might speak to him and feel his hand holding hers, sent a shiver of powerful excitement through her. Just then Damon moved his head almost imperceptibly and glanced upward, amber eyes flickering over Courtney. She held her breath as his attention returned to Beth and Timothy; his dark head was shaking in a negative gesture while he spoke. Lisabeth turned pink when he bent to kiss her hand. Courtney could see Timothy's mouth forming the word *goodbye,* and she watched in despair as he and her sister entered the house without Damon, who continued down Duck Lane.

Courtney's numb pain was dissolving rapidly, giving way to indignant rage. She thought about how he had looked up at her window before deciding not to come inside. Until now, Courtney's fragile defense system had been trying to cope with the way Damon Sheffield had caused her passion to blossom forth and then had dealt her a stunning blow of rejection. Suddenly she could see beyond the pain to an outrage that felt quite wonderful. How dare he treat her like that! After all, she didn't have two heads! He had humiliated her—used her!—and now he was adding insult to injury by avoiding her! Just who did Damon Sheffield think he was?

Her simmering indignation came to a violent boil when Courtney saw Damon stop near Cherry Alley and greet a young widow, Prudence Hatch, who was known for her beauty and her desire to make a new, magnificent marriage. Courtney's eyes flashed fire when Damon bent to graze Widow Hatch's eager lips. She recognized the teasing expression he wore as he glanced around with mock anxiety before allowing Prudence to snake her arms around his chest and snuggle against his shirt front. By the time they had disappeared down Cherry Alley, with Damon allowing his arm to be clutched possessively, Courtney was more furious than she had ever been in her life. If that arrogant, conceited scoundrel thought he could get her all stirred up and then proceed to tell her not to come near him again, he was in for a rude awakening if he believed she would stand for such treatment!

"Courtney?" Beth said from the doorway. "I saw you in the window earlier, and thought I would make another stab at persuading you to join Timothy for tea."

The older girl glared back restlessly. "Perhaps that's not a bad idea. Will you help me pin up my hair?"

Surprised, Lisabeth hurried forward and took the brush in hand. "You'll never guess whom we met outside."

Glad that her sister was standing behind her, Courtney replied, "I give up. Surprise me."

"That devilish Damon Sheffield. I pleaded with him to join us for tea, but he wouldn't budge." Beth laughed while putting in the last two pins. "I suspect he has other fish to fry . . ."

Courtney almost let out a scornful snort. "Come on. I want to get my share of cakes before Timothy eats them all. I'll need my energy for the ride I'm planning in Parrott's Woods today."

Chapter Eight

June 8–20, 1814

Flushed with excitement and daring, Courtney waited at the edge of Parrott's Woods, watching the horses and riders cantering north out of Georgetown. It was a lovely afternoon; High Street was more crowded than usual with people anxious to enjoy the sunshine. There was nothing like a hard ride in the country to dispel one's worries.

And there was Damon. Perfect timing, thought a calm Courtney, leaning farther back into the shadows and watching the stallion and its handsome rider approach. When he had passed, Courtney then nudged Yvette with her knee and clicked her tongue, so that they advanced slowly, smoothly, gradually picking up speed until the red roan was keeping pace alongside the gray stallion.

"Well!" she sang, slyly gay. "If it isn't Mr. Sheffield! Where *have* you been keeping yourself?"

His eyes pierced her like twin rapiers. "Good afternoon, Miss Ashton. You're looking beautiful as always."

"Have you missed me, sir?" She saw the stallion stretching its elegant legs just a bit farther and nudged Yvette to keep up with him.

"I've been very busy." Damon's tone was deliberately remote.

"Oh, yes, I'm sure." Courtney heard the words that came out of her mouth, but couldn't believe she was saying them. "I saw you taking care of some dull, pressing business today—where Cherry Alley meets Duck Lane. It's a shame you must work so hard."

Damon blinked in disbelief, then lifted an eyebrow into a sharp arch. "Please don't misunderstand, Miss Ashton. I may be busy, but I'm not complaining."

Oh! Her cheeks flamed as if he had slapped them. She opened her mouth, searching for a proper reply, but Damon spoke first.

"Courtney, I don't want to be rude to you, but I came out here for some time to myself. So I must bid you goodbye here, and I'd suggest that you do yourself a favor and take *your* afternoon rides with your devoted fiancé."

Stunned and humiliated, Courtney watched Damon ride off across the meadow, oblivious of the other horses and carriages milling around her. She had no intention of letting him brush her off like an irritating bit of lint, particularly when he chose that Widow Hatch, a lady of easy virtue, for her replacement.

During the next few days Courtney's frustration mounted. She learned that Damon Sheffield possessed a sly stubbornness to equal her own, combined with a talent for evasion that made her fume. After their clash on High Street, he lost no time in countering any further attempts on Courtney's part to join his afternoon rides. The next day, when she determinedly stationed herself in the woods, she was met by the sight of Damon and Prudence Hatch cantering up High Street, side by side. The Widow Hatch, clad in a fetching habit of fern green, was gloating over her public appearance with Washington's dashing man of mystery, and as she scanned the road for familiar faces, she spotted a tight-lipped Courtney amid the trees.

"Why, good afternoon, Miss Ashton," she trilled.

Courtney managed a sickly smile and a nod of greeting, barely fighting back a wave of nausea as she realized that Damon did not even mean to glance her way after hearing his companion's clearly audible words. So, instead of bursting out of the woods to challenge him, Courtney was reduced to cowering in the shadows, watching the straight, broad back of the man who haunted her dreams disappear over the crest of a hill. He hadn't even said "Good day." Courtney had been crushed when Damon had shouted at her to stay away from him, but this was infinitely worse, for he behaved as if her existence wasn't worth the effort of turning his head.

Still, her feistiness would always resurface, no matter how often Damon rejected her. The truth was, she was obsessed with him, and the thought of putting him out of her mind and her life was too depressingly final to consider. Each morning Courtney mustered enthusiasm to face the long hours ahead by convincing herself that this would be the day she would encounter Damon. This time, he'd kiss her hand and give her a rakish smile that would tell her just how much he wanted her. Flushing at the prospect of being held in those hard, sure arms she remembered all too well, Courtney would dress in a rush of optimistic energy.

However, the discouraging truth was that, for all her strolls past the Union Tavern, the *National Intelligencer,* and even Cherry Alley, Damon Sheffield was rarely to be found; and when she did see him, he was always with either an adoring female or a group of men.

If he had no other choice, he would give Courtney a distant nod or a terse greeting, but more often he pretended she did not exist.

Preoccupied and moody, Courtney refused to expend additional energy worrying about her family or Timothy Lamb. She airily evaded her father's questions, hinting that, as long as she remained engaged to Timothy, Gerald ought to be satisfied. As for Timothy himself, he continued to gaze at Courtney adoringly and to attempt to woo her, yet found himself turning more and more to Lisabeth for companionship and conversation. She was warm, sympathetic and reassuring when it came to the enigmatic Courtney. After their talks, Timothy's spirits were boosted; Beth insisted that Courtney's odd behavior of late had nothing to do with him personally. She had been acting strangely even with the family, but Lisabeth was convinced it was the strain of the war that upset her sister, and if Timothy would be patient, the unpredictable moods would pass. Certainly, as Courtney's wedding day drew closer, a glow of happiness would dispel these current tensions.

Indeed, during the last week of June, Timothy did have some rare good luck in his dealings with Courtney. In the midst of a steamily hot afternoon, Congress was dismissed early and Timothy strolled home along Pennsylvania Avenue. When he spied Damon Sheffield lounging against a poplar tree and smiling into the sparkling eyes of the sable-haired heiress, Rebecca Chilton, common courtesy prompted Timothy to pause and exchange pleasantries with the couple. Then, as he started on his way, tipping his hat to Miss Chilton, he saw Courtney. Half concealed by another tree in the line of poplars, she was staring past him with icy-blue eyes at some distant object.

"Courtney! Whatever are you doing out alone on Pennsylvania Avenue?" His brown eyes took in the pale lime muslin gown which clung damply to her warm body. A tremulous stirring began in his groin that both thrilled and shamed him. Honey-gold tendrils framed Courtney's face, setting off her incredible beauty, while, farther down, an emerald pendant seemed to point the way to mostly bare breasts that enticed Timothy alarmingly near the bounds of his self-control.

"I was hot. And restless." There was a petulant, angry note in her voice that baffled him. Abruptly, she turned away from whatever she had been looking at and began to walk in the opposite direction. "I should return home, I suppose. Will you walk with me?" Rage at Sheffield mingled with guilt for her ill-treatment of Timothy, and Courtney resolved to be nice to her fiancé, at least during this walk back to Georgetown. The poor man must believe his future bride to be quite deranged!

"It would please me immensely to escort you home, Courtney, as you well know," Timothy was saying, wondering at the enigmatic smile he had just seen flicker over her mouth. "Our moments alone together are so infrequent."

They discussed the war and the weather all the way into Georgetown. Courtney was careful to smile every so often in an effort to appear interested, but it wasn't until they were turning into Duck Lane that he said something that genuinely caught her attention.

"Would you care to attend the Madisons' levee this Wednesday night? It might prove to be an amusing diversion if this heat persists . . . and Mrs. Madison invited us herself, from her carriage this morning! Now that the regiments are beginning to be called, she is probably thinking that each levee might be her last."

Courtney's beauty shone like a light as she smiled radiantly, first at the sky, then at Timothy Lamb. "I'd love to attend the Madisons' levee!" Soft, slim fingers went out to find his. "As for Dolley, I think her worrying is only an excuse for an especially grand party. Nothing short of British troops arriving en masse as uninvited guests will stop the levees at the President's Mansion!"

Lisabeth, seated before her dressing table, couldn't help fidgeting as she waited for Mrs. Belcher to finish arranging her hair.

"There's no reason why you should fuss over my few mousy curls," she told the older woman. "I don't even know why I'm going to this levee. Without a proper escort, I shall feel a fool."

"I heard that!" Courtney's voice rang gaily from the hall. Moments later she was perched on Lisabeth's bed, but her sister couldn't turn to speak to her as long as Mrs. Belcher continued to labor over her coiffure. "You never know, Beth. This might be the evening when you meet your prince! Besides, a party will do us both good."

"Don't pretend to be so unselfish, Courtney. I think your motive for insisting I accompany you and Mr. Lamb is quite clear. If I am there to keep your poor fiancé company, you'll be free to dance and flirt with other men!"

"Well . . . as long as you've brought it up, I won't deny that the thought did cross my mind." Courtney's voice was clear and candid. "Just remember whose idea my engagement was. I never pledged to love Timothy through eternity! I like him very much, but beyond friendship, I can't force myself to feel something that simply isn't there! Since you and he are such great friends, he will doubtless have a better time tonight chatting with you . . . and I'll be spared the pain and guilt of pretending something I don't feel!"

Mrs. Belcher put in the last pin, then narrowed her eyes at Courtney and made several "tsks" of disapproval.

"Really, you are terrible," said Lisabeth sadly. However, when she stood to face her sister, the picture

Courtney made in her gown melted Beth's hard feelings. "Oh, my . . ."

"Do you like it?" Courtney's expression was hopeful as she crossed the room to take Beth's hands. "I'm sorry if I've made you angry, but I'd rather be honest than lie to you about my feelings. I'm still young, Beth. I want to have some fun before all of you send me into a rocking chair with a lapful of children."

It did seem a shame to keep such beauty from the rest of the world, or to deny Courtney the pleasure of blushing under the admiring gazes of attractive men. Her dress was exquisite, fashioned of the finest ivory satin and edged with gold-encrusted ornamental braid. The low neckline displayed high creamy breasts, while short, puffed sleeves accentuated the slim grace of Courtney's arms. Smooth gold chains, curving just below the hollow of her throat, and a striking gold armband were the only jewelry she wore. Her hair, caught up in a simple Grecian knot with a flurry of tendrils framing the classical oval of her face, seemed laced with spun gold as well. Never had Lisabeth seen her sister's eyes more vividly sapphire or her countenance more radiant.

Was there a man alive capable of resisting her tonight? Beth wondered with a strong twinge of anxiety.

Chapter Nine

June 30, 1814

The President's Mansion was often described as a palace, and its splendid elegance was even more impressive in contrast with the city that surrounded it. At night, Pennsylvania Avenue was almost menacing, particularly for those who were walking to the Madisons' levee on broken, uneven stretches of sidewalk illuminated by a total of only three lights for the entire street. Rising like a beacon out of this gloom was the President's Mansion, its one thousand candles sending out a warm welcome.

Courtney was always awestruck when she stepped into the bright, pillared entrance hall, but tonight she was fired with a special excitement. She was certain that Damon Sheffield would be in attendance. A myriad of different scenes had come alive in her imagination over the past few days; surely *one* of them would actually come true. Every time she thought of being kissed by Damon before the evening ended, Courtney felt faint. Now, as a liveried servant led her, Timothy and Beth across the hall to the corner dining room, Courtney stole a glance at the curve of her bosom and the line of her legs under the satiny concealment of her gown. In her mind's eye she could see herself being crushed against the hard-muscled length of Damon Sheffield—his wide chest, narrow hips, steely thighs . . .

"Why, Miss Ashton, you look positively ravishing!" Dolley Madison swept out of the dining room to greet them. When her twinkling eyes fell on Lisabeth, she almost succeeded in complimenting her with equal enthusiasm. Courtney took that moment's diversion to settle her thoughts; certainly no better distraction than Dolley Madison could be found. Vivacious and uninhibited, the First Lady loved people and was never at a loss for words. Tonight she wore a gown of light blue satin trimmed in ermine that set off her plump curves. The ostrich plumes on her velvet turban bobbed as she exclaimed to Timothy, "I hope you realize how fortunate you are, Congressman Lamb! Your fiancée is the most beautiful woman present tonight"—she turned a mischievous smile in Lisabeth's direction— "except, of course, for her sister and myself!"

The President came up then, beaming at his wife with longing admiration. The small, pale Mr. Madison was as reserved and somber as his wife was gregarious. For him, the high point of these social evenings was the sight of Dolley in one of her formal satin gowns.

"Jemmy!" she exclaimed. "I'm not sure if I should allow you to look at these gorgeous Ashton sisters."

"Then I suppose I must look at you instead," he replied with a fond smile.

Dolley laughed at this, then guided her newly arrived guests into the dining room. A splendid, life-sized portrait of George Washington dominated one wall and appeared to preside over the largest sideboard Courtney had ever seen. The piece of furniture groaned under the weight of dishes heaped with roast turkey and duck; fried eggs and fried beef; the newest dish from

Europe, called macaroni; whole rounds of beef; a variety of ices and a veritable mountain of cakes and tarts.

Too nervous to eat, Courtney waited until Timothy and Beth had filled their plates and were deep in conversation with James Monroe before she slipped through the door to Dolley's smaller sitting room. A portrait of the First Lady looked down over the gracefully elegant chairs and settees, now occupied by guests who were interested in quiet discussion. Courtney strove to appear preoccupied as she made her way across the room, smiling and nodding at acquaintances. There was no sign of Damon Sheffield, but her eyes darkened when they fell on Prudence Hatch. The lovely widow was fluttering her long lashes at a young fop whom Courtney didn't recognize. As she reached the entrance to the immense, magnificent drawing room, Courtney smiled to herself, realizing that Prudence had not arrived at the President's Mansion on the arm of Damon Sheffield. Courtney could cross *one* troublesome rival off her list!

The oval drawing room was radiant with golden light, music and the magic of beautifully garbed people who danced and laughed and flirted with one another. The war had never seemed more distant. As she scanned the crowd for Damon, Courtney admired the sumptuous room that Dolley Madison had decorated so cheerfully. The ceiling-high windows, elaborate mantelpieces and mirrors, and handsome oil lamps were all warmed by yellow satin and damask, imported from France. In front of the instruments, which were being played by somber, skillful musicians, stood the exquisite pianoforte that Dolley had been criticized for buying at the outrageous price of four hundred fifty-eight dollars. All along the side of the drawing room were painted chairs with red velvet cushions, divided into four arrangements by high-backed sofas, and it was on one of these yellow satin sofas that Courtney finally spied Damon Sheffield.

Her heart plummeted. He was sitting with Rebecca Chilton, the same girl she had seen him with on Pennsylvania Avenue the other day. Miss Chilton, looking winsome in pale pink velvet and with pearls encircling her bare throat, was earnestly imparting some information to her rakish companion. When he bent to whisper a response in her ear that elicited a rosy blush, Courtney felt ill. Why had she been such a fool to think he would come alone to this levee? There wasn't a single woman in the District of Columbia who wouldn't have forfeited a week's desserts to enter the President's Mansion on Damon Sheffield's arm.

To Courtney's horror, tears stung her eyes, and she tried desperately to swallow the bitter lump of disappointment. She leaned against the doorframe and looked down at the floor as she willed her composure to return. If there was one thing worse than feeling as if she wanted to die, it was letting everyone else at this party see her cry and make a fool of herself. A few heads had already turned curiously in her direction.

Summoning all her resolve, Courtney lifted her head and glanced, dry-eyed, around the drawing room. She was about to escape back to the sitting room with some semblance of dignity when an impulse made her gaze helplessly back at Damon. Rebecca Chilton was searching through her reticule, and he was staring directly at Courtney. The piercing light in his amber eyes stopped her heart before he abruptly returned his attention to Miss Chilton. Courtney knew he hadn't meant for her to see him look at her. Euphoria swelled her heart; by letting his guard down for one instant, Damon had negated all his efforts to appear indifferent, even contemptuous, toward her. Courtney wanted to sing. She couldn't have felt more triumphant if he had knelt before her and begged her hand in marriage.

"Here you are!" Timothy exclaimed, grinning at her. He was holding a plate that contained the last few bites of a delectable-looking cream puff.

Frustrated, Courtney asked, "Should you be eating in the drawing room? I don't see anyone else with food in here."

"When did you become so proper?" Timothy gave an affectionate chuckle. Clad in a new bottle-green frock coat, white trousers and a cravat tied à la Byron, he was feeling quite debonair. "Just to set your mind at ease, my dear, the President himself gave me leave to bring my dessert along in search of you. We were all beginning to worry that you had toppled off the terrace or had been abducted by some overeager dandy." He leaned closer and winked, unaware of the dusting of powdered sugar along his upper lip. "You know, you are all the talk back in the dining room, sweetheart. Everyone is agog over your beauty . . . and glaringly envious of me!"

Courtney managed a weak smile. If she weren't faced with the prospect of spending the rest of her life as Timothy's wife, she would think him rather cute, even sweet and lovable, in the manner of an earnest puppy. "You have an active imagination, Timothy."

"Oh, no. It's the plain truth that you're the most dazzling female in the President's Mansion tonight, Courtney. I am proud to say you belong to me."

Her smile faded. "I appreciate the intended compliment, but let us not lose sight of the fact that I do not belong to anyone, including you or my father or anyone else who imagines he can claim ownership of my person." She lifted her chin. "I belong to myself."

"You're beautiful," Timothy sighed.

"You've had too much wine."

"Brandy." He swallowed the last of the cream puff and stifled a contented burp.

"When did you begin to drink *brandy?* Really,

Timothy, use your common sense. That's too strong for you. You'll make a fool of yourself.''

"I haven't heard you scolding Damon Sheffield, and he fairly swigs the stuff!"

"Don't be ridiculous. He certainly does *not* swig it . . . and it doesn't cause him to behave like a drunken sot!" Sensing the uncalled-for emotion in her voice, she added hastily, "Besides, what Damon Sheffield does or drinks is no concern of mine. *He* is not my fiancé!"

"The way you act sometimes, I wonder if you don't wish he were!"

"Timothy!" Hot blood rushed unbidden to Courtney's cheeks. "How dare you?" Without looking, she could feel Damon's golden eyes turned on her from across the room, but somehow she resisted the urge to seek them out.

Timothy's lips were pressed together in a tense line as he pushed the blond hair from his brow in a nervous gesture. "Look, Courtney, I didn't come in here to quarrel with you. I'm going back to look after Beth, and when you are in a more congenial mood, please join us."

After he had gone, Courtney took a deep breath and tried to collect her thoughts. A liveried servant came along with a tray of champagne-filled goblets, and she impetuously accepted one, drank it, then took another when he passed by again. She refused three invitations to dance, but wished she'd accepted when Damon led Rebecca Chilton onto the polished floor and took her in his arms. It was torture to watch them. The sable-haired girl looked charming in his strong embrace, and if not for the memory of his gaze burning her from across the room, Courtney would have believed Damon's thoughts were all for Miss Chilton.

"*Bon soir,* Mademoiselle Ashton."

Courtney started at the sound of the silky voice at

her shoulder, knowing at once that it must be Louis Sérurier, the French minister. A thin, habitually melancholy man of forty, he had so far resisted all the matchmaking efforts of Washington's matrons, who insisted that a wife would cure his gloomy disposition.

"Bon soir, m'sieur." She smiled politely and took a sip of champagne when he lifted his brandy snifter to her.

"It is not right that a woman of such rare beauty should be alone. I shall watch over you until your fiancé returns."

Since she had been feeling rather awkward standing by herself, Courtney was glad for M. Sérurier's company. She watched Rebecca Chilton and Damon with one eye while pretending interest in the Frenchman's conversation about British spies in the capital.

"I was telling Madame Madison but an hour ago that I've heard rumors"—he paused to sip his brandy—"that one of these agents visited her disguised as a woman!"

Briefly, Courtney gave him her amused attention. "Sir, we have all heard a wild assortment of stories about the spies who supposedly swarm among us, but that is the most outrageous of them all!"

Sérurier raised an offended brow. "Americans should not laugh so readily. While they laugh, the British will steal this city away. America should look to France's experience for a valuable lesson!"

"I take it that Mrs. Madison also doubts the truth of your rumor?"

"She waved her snuffbox at me and cried out, 'Ludicrous!' I cannot help telling you, mademoiselle, that I am not impressed with Madame's etiquette!"

Courtney half listened to the rest of his tales, gathered from sources at a recent Dancing Assembly, from servants on his staff at Octagon House and from fellow gamblers at Major Baily's suite in O'Neill's Tavern.

Across the room, Damon pivoted to the music with

effortless, masculine grace. He had never looked more devastatingly handsome, clad in an expertly tailored fawn coat, an oak-colored silk vest and a spotless white shirt and cravat that emphasized the bronze of his cynical face. Remembering how sunburned he had appeared the day of their encounter in Parrott's Woods, Courtney decided that his tan was even deeper now. What caused him to spend so much time outdoors? As her mouth curved dreamily, she thought that even his raven hair looked perpetually, irresistibly, windblown.

"Mademoiselle Ashton, I hope you will not think I am rude if I beg your leave to join Messieurs Armstrong and Rush in the sitting room. I am anxious to let them know what I have heard about the English spies."

Courtney could only smile, half amused, as the French minister bent to kiss her hand before hurrying off toward the Secretary of War and the Attorney General. She finished the last of her champagne, then turned her eyes back toward Damon Sheffield. When she saw that he was gone, Courtney let out a short, hot gasp that continued until she spotted the distant outline of fawn-covered shoulders disappearing through the French doors leading onto the terrace.

What was he about? Did Damon mean to take that little tart outside—alone? Was Miss Chilton such a fool that she'd toss away her reputation in full view of Washington society—at the President's Mansion, of all places? A worse thought intruded on Courtney's outrage: Damon would hold that girl in his arms, bewitched by the stars and the light, and kiss her. Worse yet was the alarming possibility that he might fall in love with Rebecca Chilton, as he hadn't with Courtney. That easy-virtued wench looked so sweet and beautiful, Damon might not readily perceive her true nature!

Distraught, Courtney twisted the fingers on one hand, then on the other. While a charming tune tinkled from the pianoforte and the other guests continued to dance and gossip, she was inclined to pull out her hair.

One thing was clear: Damon mustn't be left alone for a moment longer at the mercy of the moonlight and that scheming little heiress.

Courtney didn't stop to formulate a plan, but strode out the French doors without a backward glance. Just then, Lisabeth came into the drawing room, her delicate face etched with concern as she looked for her sister. Beth had never seen Timothy angry before, or even slightly intoxicated, and she had tired of waiting for Courtney to display a measure of good grace and make the first gesture of peace. Since Courtney insisted on involving her in this matter, Beth was determined to find out what had transpired between her sister and the agitated Timothy. Then, once and for all, she would make Courtney see what she—

While the fire had grown under Beth's thoughts and resolve, her brown eyes had been scanning the sea of guests who danced and stood chatting in the drawing room. Suddenly her mind went blank.

Was that Courtney's figure she had glimpsed outside on the terrace? A moonbeam briefly illuminated the gold braid that edged the neckline of a gown, a golden armband and a honeyed haze of curls before the slight figure crossed the terrace and disappeared down the steps which led to the trees and gardens beyond.

Lisabeth barely hesitated, then started toward the French doors.

Chapter Ten

July 1, 1814
Midnight

Damon had to look away. It seemed that moonlight only intensified Rebecca Chilton's luminously adoring gaze. He, meanwhile, felt more and more uneasy. When first introduced to Miss Chilton at Elizabeth Monroe's garden party, Damon had been charmed by her soft beauty and shy serenity. She seemed a perfect decoy to discourage the persistent Courtney, and Rebecca's company afforded him a respite from the chatter and clinging of Prudence Hatch. However, this new light that had begun to glow in Rebecca's green eyes, as well as her frequent blushes, sounded the alarm in Damon's mind. The last thing he needed was another society virgin in love with him!

"Have I told you about Tawny, my horse?" Rebecca was asking. Her hand encircled his sleeve a bit more firmly.

"Why, no, I don't believe you have." Damon managed to release a quick smile at her. "Are you certain you aren't cold out here? Perhaps I should take you back—"

"No! I mean, I feel wonderful. It was horribly crowded in the drawing room, and more than anything else, I enjoy . . ." She blushed. "I enjoy being with you, Mr. Sheffield."

Oh, God. Damon smothered a groan. "Well, that is very flattering, but in light of my reputation, it might not be wise for us to separate ourselves from the other guests for more than a few minutes."

"Your reputation?" Rebecca echoed.

Seeing the confusion in her wide eyes, Damon was reminded of his sheltered ten-year-old sister. For someone on the brink of womanhood, Rebecca Chilton could appear alarmingly childlike and witless, and there were scores of men who sought wives with those very qualities.

"Miss Chilton, I really think it might be best if—" His voice stopped in mid-sentence. Over the top of her head he saw a slim figure approaching on the flagstone path that made a stripe across the lawn and gardens. The blaze of light pouring out of the drawing room's French doors sent its golden haze in the figure's wake, and Damon recognized Courtney. His heart gave an odd jump. The full-length halo lent her an ethereal—as opposed to angelic—air, and Damon's appreciative eyes moved from the cloud of honey curls to linger over bare arms and high, sweet breasts before tracing the ivory lines of the satin gown all the way down to the small satin slippers.

Rebecca Chilton turned, following Damon's stare, and saw Courtney just a few yards away. "Why, Courtney, how quiet you are! I didn't even hear you." She gave her a pretty smile. "Why are you outside all alone?"

Coming to a halt next to them, Courtney subtly lifted a delicate brow and smiled. "Rebecca, I was about to ask you the very same question! For my own part, I came out to tell you that your mother has sent word you're to come inside and speak to her."

"My mother?" Rebecca repeated in bewilderment. "She's not even here tonight!"

"Apparently she is now. All I know is what I was told. But if I were you, I'd go without Mr. Sheffield, just in case she's waiting."

"Well . . ." Rebecca turned doubtful eyes upon Damon.

Slanting a look of cynical amusement at Courtney, he abandoned his better judgment and said, "As much as I hate to agree, I think Miss Ashton may have a point. No doubt Mrs. Chilton is better apprised of my reputation than you are." Damon lifted her hand and kissed it, knowing that Rebecca would be rendered too speechless to argue. "I'll join you in the sitting room after you have placated your mother."

"If you're certain . . ."

Damon and Courtney both nodded soberly. Rebecca wandered down the flagstone path, up the steps to the terrace and inside through the French doors, too perplexed to consider that Courtney ought to have accompanied her rather than remaining where Courtney's own reputation might be compromised.

"Really, Mr. Sheffield, you should be ashamed—luring that innocent, trusting child out into the night." Courtney's lips curved in a saucy smile.

"How fortunate that she had someone like you to look after her," Damon remarked dryly.

Courtney tried to read his face, which looked even more rakishly chiseled than usual in the moonlight, and wondered if he guessed that Rebecca Chilton could search the President's Mansion for hours without locating her mother. He probably did; he wasn't easily fooled. And what about Miss Chilton? Was Damon taken in by her innocent act? The reasonable part of

Courtney knew she had no evidence that Rebecca was being devious or, in fact, anything but the picture of innocence she presented. Jealousy, however, brought out Courtney's fighting instincts and prompted her to furnish Rebecca's current status as the enemy with some negative traits.

"I wouldn't want Rebecca to end up with a broken heart," she said now, pleased with the enigmatic quality of her tone.

"I wish you wouldn't waste your precious time worrying about other people's love lives," Damon replied coolly. "Besides, Miss Chilton seems to be in admirable control of her emotions."

Courtney was reeling inside from the slap of his words when Damon turned casually and wandered down a narrow fork in the path. Hurt by his rudeness and his abrupt dismissal of her company, she wanted to return to the yellow drawing room and nurse her wounds. That was obviously what he wanted her to do, but she was damned if she'd allow Damon Sheffield to crush her dreams for tonight so effortlessly! Narrowing starry-lashed eyes, Courtney lifted her satin skirts and hurried after the shadowy figure making its way down the cobbled path. Coming up behind him, she realized there wasn't enough space for them to walk side by side, and she was forced into the embarrassing position of peering around Damon's steely arm while stumbling in an attempt to keep pace at the same time.

"Have you enjoyed the levee?" he asked after a silence that left Courtney with cold, wet palms. Now, hearing the astonishingly impersonal inflection of his voice, she had even more trouble breathing.

"Not very much." When he made no response, did not even turn his head, she went on. "I can't enjoy myself if I'm not happy. You know how I feel about Timothy." She stopped, closed her eyes and blurted, "And how I feel about you."

"So you took matters into your own hands and came after me, disposing of Rebecca Chilton along the way, of course." He had stopped as well, turning to face her, and one dark hand roughly caught her arm. "You would do well to stop concentrating on Miss Chilton's reputation and spare a moment's worry for your own!"

Courtney stared up at Damon in the moonlight and had to take a deep breath to subdue the dangerous mix of desire and love that swelled in her heart. With his ruffled raven hair, brandy-fire eyes and dark, cynically carved features, Damon exuded an irresistible magnetism. Even if she made an idiot of herself and he despised her, it was worth it just to be near him and be the focus of his attention.

"But, Damon, I thought you didn't care about reputations. We agreed, in the woods, that a person can't go through life always worrying about what other people think. Don't you remember?" Feeling his grip relax on her arm, Courtney leaned close enough to breathe in his familiar scent—soap, wind, the starch in his snowy shirt, the lingering aroma of his last cheroot, the masculine undercurrent that was as unique as Damon's fingerprint. Words spilled from Courtney. "You must remember! You said it yourself—that we only get one chance at life, that we must be true to our own convictions and emotions and not live to please others."

"Courtney." He wished he'd never come tonight, never brought Rebecca Chilton, never met Courtney . . . and especially that the day in the woods could be wiped from their pasts. He'd been a fool to believe that any of the usual, easy solutions would work in this tangled case; that a complex creature like Courtney Ashton would abandon her "convictions and emotions" just because he paraded a series of different girls under her nose. Of course, she must realize, instinctively, that she cast every other female miles into the shade, and she knew him too well to think him blind enough to prefer either Miss Chilton or Mrs. Hatch to Courtney herself. He tried not to look directly into her eyes as she caught a coatsleeve in each hand and stood on tiptoe; tried to put a wall between himself and the silvery tear that trickled down a soft, delicately curved cheek.

"I felt so close to you that day," she whispered. "Closer than I've ever felt to anyone in my whole life, and—no, let me say this! Just let me speak, and then give me an honest answer if you want me to stop sneaking around after you! That day, when you kissed me . . . I was so filled with joy I was dizzy. I never knew a man could be strong and tender, understanding and masculine, all at the same time."

Damon winced, thinking, I just *had* to give her a glimpse of the perfect man! "But, Courtney, compared with your father and Lamb, any man would—" He stopped, aware that the sentence was not ending gracefully.

"There is much more to it, and you know it!" She swiped frustrated tears from her violet eyes. "Also, I was so certain you were feeling something for me . . . as a person, an individual, not just another girl to charm. Damon, look at me. Be honest. What did I do to change your feelings?" Courtney paused, then added almost inaudibly, "Was it because I let you kiss me . . . and touch me? I swear that never before—I mean, if you imagine I've been dispensing favors all over Georgetown and Washington—"

"For God's sake, Courtney!" The despair and bewilderment and anger in her beautiful face were combining to drain his resolve. The thought of telling her, explaining everything, skittered across Damon's consciousness before she interrupted.

"You probably won't believe me, but Timothy hasn't even kissed me!" She laughed, a bit crazily. "I don't blame Beth and everyone else for wondering if I've lost my reason. It all sounds rather insane to me as well! If Lisabeth had any inkling—" When Damon gathered her into his embrace, Courtney relaxed a little. Leaning her wet cheek against the clean, spotless shirt front, she continued softly, speaking to the cadence of his heartbeat. "I used to dream about the things we shared that day. I mean the conversation and the exchange of confidences and the understanding as much as the . . . other. I truly felt there was a bond between us. Was I wrong?"

Reason told Damon to say yes, to thrust her away and put as much distance between them as quickly as possible. He compromised with silence. Refusing to let any expression creep over his face, he stared over Courtney's head at an anonymous, distant star.

She ignored her own question and pressed on. "I wouldn't have let you kiss me, at least not more than once, if I hadn't felt that bond between us. I know girls have been fooled by men before—"

"You'd do well to reread *Charlotte Temple,*" Damon said tersely.

"But I don't consider myself just any girl, so eager for love that I believe the first sweet words whispered in my ear, nor do I consider you one of those 'gay seducers' who drains the sweet freshness from young ladies before discarding them." Courtney sent blue fire flashing from her now-dry eyes. "Damn you, stop looking so uncomfortable and give me a straight answer! Was I only one more girl, the one in line before Prudence Hatch? Was your understanding—your talent for listening—all part of a well-polished act?"

Her accusation about his uneasy demeanor found the guilty part of Damon. His eyes met hers straight on, striking sparks on the challenge in her own violet stare. "No!"

From the current of emotion emanating from his tall,

hard body, Courtney sensed more than he was free to say. "Oh, please, tell me, then—something! Why? What caused you to turn away from me? It's as though I had leprosy!"

"I cannot—"

"Oh!" she gasped. "I think I know what it is!"

Taken aback, Damon groped for words as he searched Courtney's shocked face. "Well, then, please do enlighten me!"

"You're married!"

He blinked, then managed to smother a burst of laughter but not a wry, maddening smile. Now what? he wondered, realizing that this was his chance. Courtney had come up with the perfect excuse. He could already hear himself embroidering her sentence with sympathetic details guaranteed to melt her heart. Casting amused eyes on her, Damon thought he'd never seen Courtney looking so enchantingly fierce. Iridescent moonlight enhanced the defiant set of her fragile-boned face, the hurt that showed in the quaver of her lower lip, the magical transformation of her eyes from sapphire to amethyst.

"Stop looking at me that way—as though I were an amusing child," Courtney said in a low, bitter voice. "Just admit the truth—you have a wife hidden away in Maine. Children, too? You needn't worry that I'll let out your secret to Prudence Hatch or Rebecca Chilton."

"I wish the explanation were as simple as that, Courtney . . ." Damon took a breath, thinking, a clean slice is the best way. It may hurt more now, but she'll heal permanently, with hardly a scar. "There isn't any kind way of saying this," he continued, then paused again, barely resisting an impulse to feel the texture of her hazily made curls of honey gold.

"I've heard enough unkind words from you lately, Mr. Sheffield. A few more couldn't make very much difference. Please don't confuse me with unexpected compassion!"

"All right. The reason I didn't make love to you that day in the woods was not because I had a low opinion of your moral character. I liked you very much, Courtney, but that's all. When I sensed the strength of your feelings for me, I couldn't allow myself to take your virginity without giving you real love in return. I felt sorry for you, as a friend, forced into a betrothal with Lamb—"

"A *friend?*" Courtney echoed in disbelief.

"I admit I flirted with you. You're a lovely, passionate girl . . . but I've known scores exactly like you. I never wanted to say these things aloud, but you've pushed me to the end of my patience. The truth is, my dear child, you're better off in the arms of Timothy Lamb, who loves you, than in mine. If I hadn't *liked* you, it would've been the easiest thing for me to enjoy your sweet charms in full. And I doubt that I'd have spoken to you again."

"Are you implying that I should be grateful?" she cried incredulously. Feeling as if she were caught in a twisted nightmare, Courtney wished she could see Damon's face more clearly. In the blue-shadowed night, his cynical, dispassionate expression chilled her heart. It was a stranger standing before her, arching a cold eyebrow.

"Yes. Be grateful to escape with only a cracked heart and crumpled illusions. You'll mend." A muscle moved in Damon's jaw. "And the next time a man tells you to stay away and forget him, be good to yourself and listen. Some of the realities in life are easier to deal with if we accept them before they slap us in the face."

Nodding jerkily, Courtney rubbed her hands over the goose flesh that chased up her arms. "I see. Your advice to me is to stop questioning and stop listening to my heart. I should take lessons in blind acceptance from Lisabeth and Mother!'' Her attempted laugh sounded like a cry of pain, and a tear escaped, dropping to scald the bare curve of one breast.

Damon ached to gather her into an embrace that would erase all her anguish, confusion and disappointment. Unable to meet Courtney's shining eyes, he murmured. ''There really isn't any more to say—and we should have gone inside long ago. I think it'd be best if we returned separately, as if we'd taken solitary walks along different paths.''

''What would people say?'' Courtney mocked. ''Before you rush off, there's one small thing I'd like you to do.''

Damon raked taut fingers through his hair. ''For God's sake, Courtney! I—''

''Shh.'' Sliding her hands inside his frock coat, she ran them from lean hips up to the hard width of his back. A part of her marveled at Damon's body. In expertly cut clothes, he always presented an image of lithe strength, but hidden beneath this elegant cover were clear outlines of muscles that previously existed for Courtney only in her father's anatomy book. Damon's muscles weren't seam-splitting bulges, but were long and lean inside taut, golden-brown skin. Courtney thought he was like a panther—powerful and enigmatic —as opposed to an ox's brute strength.

''What the devil—''

When he tried to disengage her hands, Courtney took courage from the spark of emotion that burned a tiny hole in Damon's angry tone. She clung to his silk vest. ''I'm so confused! Please, just show me the difference between love . . . and what you felt in the woods that day. Is it called lust? Just one kiss. A demonstration! Is that so much to ask?''

Damon was furious at Courtney for pushing relentlessly at him, and at himself because he couldn't keep her at arm's length. When her fingers began to play with the crisp black curls that brushed his collar, a fiery tide of yearning coursed through him.

"Courtney . . ." Feeling her slim form press lightly against the length of his body, he clenched his teeth in an effort to regain control. Firm breasts seemed to sear through his vest and shirt, and he breathed in a tantalizing jasmine scent from burnished tendrils grazing his cheek. Somehow he managed to say huskily, "It would be against my nature to deny a lady a kiss . . . so I am pleased to grant your request, in return for your promise that, henceforth, you will leave me alone. Give Lamb a fighting chance to woo you, and if you still cannot bear him, break the engagement."

"But I shouldn't expect you to rescue me, because by then you'll be dangling four or five other eager, passionate females," Courtney purred sarcastically. "I give you my word, Mr. Sheffield. In the future, I won't bother to give you the time of day. But first I want to sample this heartless kiss of yours . . . and sweeten the memory *you* will have of *me*."

Courtney stood on tiptoe, touched the square line of Damon's jaw with petal-soft lips, then brushed them across the warm, firm mouth that had haunted her dreams, day and night, for weeks. She wondered momentarily about the low moan Damon couldn't quite suppress, before a whirlpool of exquisite sensation sucked her in. At first his slow, feather-light kisses sent hot sparks over Courtney's nerves, then she felt faint when his tongue gently parted her lips and briefly explored the sweetness beyond. Illogically, Courtney's mind searched for the word to describe the effect Damon had on her. *Tantalizing*. She melted into his strength, let her head drop back and gloried in the pattern his mouth scorched over her throat. Courtney was aware of the taut muscles in his arms close against her as one hand slid around to cup an anxious breast.

103

His dark head bent to kiss the exposed curves, and she shuddered unexpectedly.

Moments later, her feet were suspended above the ground as Damon's mouth came down to cover, then invade, her own. Courtney held fast to his shoulders, conscious of the pounding of her heart and the thrilling hardness of his manhood. She choked on a sob. How could Damon say he didn't care? The sparks that flew between their bodies could never be kindled by anything as commonplace as *lust*. As her mouth turned to liquid under a scorching, magical kiss, Courtney knew that he was lying, either to her or to both of them. What she could not fathom was *why*.

"That's enough." Somehow Damon managed to lift his head, then set Courtney a few feet away. "I'm all too human, Miss Ashton. It seems prudent that we end this 'demonstration' before it escapes our control."

She blinked in the inky-blue night. On the surface, Damon was once again the familiar essence of lazy, half-amused irony. "I . . . oh . . . well, of course." Heart pounding, cheeks flushed and thoughts churning crazily, Courtney wasn't up to his cool repartee.

"I'm so pleased that you agree." Damon's teeth flashed white in the darkness. "Goodbye, then, Courtney. I hope you'll reconsider about giving me the time of day and perhaps even grant me a smile and a nod if our paths should cross." Amber eyes piercing the night, reminding her of their bargain, making it clear that he would allow her no more. "I wish you good fortune with Mr. Lamb. If you could manage to redirect some of your passion in his direction, he might well be transformed into a new man!"

Watching Damon's splendid dark head and wide shoulders become less distinct as he walked back to the main path, then on to the President's Mansion, Courtney pressed a fist to her mouth and let the aching tears spill over. What was the truth? How did he really feel?

In fact, Damon Sheffield's inner turmoil was considerable, for he failed to notice the figure standing behind a tree a mere few feet from where he had turned onto the main path. Normally, Damon would have sensed the person's presence long ago.

Chapter Eleven

July 8, 1814

Courtney took a long drink of lemonade, then replaced the glass on the table with a sigh. She sat alone on the window seat in the music room, the casement thrown open behind her to invite any breeze which might be astir on this miserably hot afternoon.

Solitary interludes such as this had been few and brief since July had settled its sheen of perspiration over Courtney. Her world had altered considerably in just the space of the past week. The day after the fateful levee at the President's Mansion, Gerald Ashton had received word that his regiment should proceed without delay to Bladensburg, just over the Potomac's eastern branch from Washington. This was the seventh day since his departure. The knowledge that her father was in a position to lose his life in battle sobered Courtney considerably. After her frustrating encounter with Damon Sheffield in the Madisons' garden, she had resolved to be sensible for a change and try a more positive approach toward Timothy. When Gerald had bidden her a gruff goodbye and clasped her in a tight hug, Courtney had realized there was no returning to her dream world. Somehow she had to find a way to deal pleasantly with Timothy Lamb. There was no place for her in Sheffield's life; he had made that crushingly clear, even if his reasons remained a mystery. If it weren't for the war, Gerald's departure and her responsibilities to Lisabeth and her mother, Courtney wouldn't have dropped the matter so easily. But because of these considerations, it seemed that she had no choice.

"You are certainly looking pensive," Lisabeth observed from the doorway. Setting down her sunshade, she untied the ribbons of her chip-straw bonnet and crossed the room.

"It's difficult to summon up enough energy even to think in this weather," Courtney answered, making a face at the way her gauzy dress clung to the dampness of her back, arms and midriff. "Let's ring for more lemonade, and you can tell me where you've been."

Lisabeth deposited her bonnet on the Louis XIV console table before joining her sister. "I stopped to pay my respects to Mrs. Madison, and she persuaded me to accompany her to the Thorntons' for tea. I had enough lemonade to fill the Potomac, so please don't ring for more on my account."

With the sun shining on her slightly tousled curls, Beth looked quite charming, Courtney thought. Something about her sister seemed different lately, but she couldn't put her finger on it. "Is there any news about the army?"

"Only the usual round of arguments about the possibility of Washington being invaded by the British. Mrs. Madison was cheery, as always, and seemed to make light of the subject, but she did go on and on, repeating all the President's latest conversations." Beth's brown eyes were properly sober. "It's clear that she's worried, for all her wagers that the redcoats would have left Chesapeake Bay long ago if they intended to attack us."

"That was convincing logic before we heard of Napoleon's defeat and Wellington's newly available troops," Courtney said sharply. "If Mrs. Madison cannot manufacture any better reassurance than *that* old chestnut, the situation must be gloomier than I'd imagined."

"Poor Papa!" Lisabeth sighed.

A single high-pitched sob caused both girls to look around. The sight of their mother in the hallway, leaning weakly against the doorframe, brought Courtney to her feet. She went to lead Amity over to the curving window seat, her tone soothing.

"You mustn't pay any attention to us, Mother. We're just silly, hysterical girls, letting our imaginations run wild," she said hastily, realizing that Amity needed an explanation she could identify with. "Why, if Father could hear us doubting and weeping, he'd roar like a lion!"

Amity gave her daughters a wan smile. "I'd endure the worst of Gerald's temper, ceaselessly, if only he could be returned to us."

Eyes brimming, Lisabeth nodded in agreement and held fast to her mother's thin hands.

"Honestly, if the two of you are going to keep this up on a permanent basis, you'll drive me berserk!" cried Courtney. "Is this the way it's going to be until Father returns? Are we going to flail helplessly because we haven't a man in the house to tell us what to do, what to feel, how to behave? Are we going to sigh and swoon all summer, unable to form an independent idea or opinion?"

Amity's golden-brown eyes widened in shocked confusion. "Oh, Courtney, must you carry on so? This is such a difficult time for me. Why can't you try to help and cooperate instead of always stirring up—"

"I *am* trying to help! I want you to see that you are a

strong, capable person in your own right and can function perfectly well without Father's direction."

"How can you talk this way?" Beth whispered. "Don't you miss him?"

"Of course I do!" Frustrated, Courtney jumped up and paced over to the harp, then looked back at the bewildered faces of her sister and mother. It maddened her to see them wasting their beauty, spirits and potential in subjugation to the authority of Gerald Ashton. She knew there were women who withered and died when they lost the men who led them through life—like roses cut from their stems that dried up and crumbled into dust. With calm deliberation, Courtney knelt before the window seat. "Please, listen to me. I'm not trying to make trouble. Honestly, I love Father with all my heart, and if you'll hear me out, I think you'll find he would probably agree with me."

Amity wore the expression of someone preparing to endure painful news. Unable to help herself, Courtney smiled affectionately at her mother. Amity seemed more beautiful than ever, toffee-colored waves up-swept to accentuate her slim, elegant neck and dainty face with curly-lashed, sherry-gold eyes. Because she was so adept at blending into her husband's back-ground, people failed to notice her as a lovely individual. Courtney decided that her mother lacked the inner passion that would translate into fiery eyes and matchless charm and laughter. Perhaps by the end of the summer . . .

"Don't look so apprehensive, Mother!" she admonished, smiling. "Now, I want you two to keep an open mind. I think Father, being the dynamic person he is, would expect his family to summon all its resources in hard times. Do you suppose he'd be pleased that we were unable to function without him? That we went to pieces under stress?" She shifted in her damp, uncomfortable gown, wishing she could take it off and wear only her chemise. Amity, always the lady, seemed not to perspire at all. "I admit he wants us to follow him, since he is head of the household, but I don't think that wish applies to times of crisis requiring his absence."

Amity inclined her head ever so slightly and gracefully. "Do you know, darling, I believe your father would agree with you. I've always said that you're too much like him for your own good. I mean . . . to be a proper lady." She shifted a bit uneasily and cleared her throat. "Dear, what *do* you think Gerald expects of us in times of crisis?"

An unfamiliar warmth spread through Courtney as she realized her mother was *listening* to her for the first time in her memory. "I think he expects us to rise to the occasion and be strong individuals. Wouldn't he want to be proud of you, Mother? And of us, Beth? If Father were here right now, he'd tell us to struggle against sadness and despair, to represent the Ashton name to the rest of the world."

Lisabeth stared at her sister, wondering if Courtney had some ulterior motive for acting this way. Beth could have sworn that Courtney had tired of trying to change her and their mother long ago. What was behind this sudden, loving concern? It *did* seem that Courtney had been behaving more like an adult since Gerald's departure . . . but Beth was slow to trust and quick to suspect these days. Shocked disillusionment had washed over her repeatedly the night she had watched Courtney clinging to Damon Sheffield— kissing him!—in President Madison's garden. Since then, Courtney had been unusually friendly and warm to Timothy Lamb, a development that baffled Lisabeth. She was tortured by the sight of his hopeful, eager expression and the memory of Courtney's blatant unfaithfulness.

"I'm certainly intrigued by these noble ideas of yours," Lisabeth said aloud. She was unable to keep her voice completely free of cynicism. "I take it you have a grand scheme bursting with ways in which we can 'represent the Ashton name to the rest of the world'?"

Courtney's delicate brows arched slowly. If she hadn't known better, she would have said her sister was being sarcastic. "I can't say I've hatched many schemes lately . . . but since you mention it, why not begin with Mother's gloomy tendency to languish here in the house?"

"What do you mean?" Amity queried, nervously doubtful.

"You should go outside, accept invitations, see people, socialize! Father isn't dead, after all, and you're not in mourning! You're capable of walking and talking without Father's directions, and I think it would be healthy for you to keep yourself occupied."

Amity's mouth formed an open rosebud of astonishment. "You cannot be suggesting that I appear in public . . . on a regular basis . . . *alone?*"

"Oh, Mother!" Courtney couldn't suppress an exasperated sigh. "Can't you hear how ridiculous that sounds?"

"No, I cannot! I am a married woman, Courtney Amanda Ashton!"

"I'm certainly aware of that, Mother. Honestly! You behave as if those words should be accompanied by thunder and lightning! Did you cease to be an individual when you married Father?"

Lisabeth spoke up quickly. "This may be difficult for you to comprehend, Courtney, but perhaps Mama feels it would be disloyal for her to prance around to all of Washington's social gatherings without Papa."

"Have you lost your powers of reasoning?" Courtney cried incredulously. "She and Father are not Siamese twins! I'm not suggesting that Mother tumble into bed with other men!" Ignoring the chorus of horrified gasps, she hurried on. "For heaven's sake! She doesn't have to speak to anyone but women if that will allow her to practice the art of conversation with a clear conscience!"

Amity looked as if she might faint. "Oh, please, girls, don't let me be the cause of an argument! This is the reason why it seems so much simpler if I remain quietly at home."

Courtney wanted to scream.

"You look as if you're having a heat stroke," Lisabeth remarked acrimoniously to her sister.

Courtney was prevented from answering in kind by the unexpected appearance of Mrs. Belcher, followed by Timothy.

"You've a visitor, Mistress Courtney," the old woman announced. Somehow, in spite of the heat, she was able to wear her customary black, long-sleeved gown and remain as dry as a bone.

Courtney wondered, not for the first time, if blood ran through Mrs. Belcher's veins at all. Ice water, perhaps?

The housekeeper was pouring the rest of the lemonade, muttering that she would bring a fresh, iced pitcherful, while Timothy greeted his fiancée with a cheerful smile.

"Good afternoon, Courtney." He glanced politely at Amity and Beth. "Ladies."

"Timothy, I had no idea that you were coming. I must look a fright." Courtney scrambled to her feet. "Let me run upstairs and freshen—"

"Oh, no!" Catching her hands, he held them fast and gazed at her flushed face with adoring eyes. "I know it's rude of me, dropping in this way, but you've been on my mind all day and I thought I should see how this houseful of beautiful women was faring. I'm surprised you haven't a line of chivalrous men outside!" He chuckled at his own humor. "As for your looks, my dear, I can't allow you to change a curl. Warm dishevelment flatters you."

Courtney blinked dismayed sapphire eyes. Suddenly, Lisabeth rose. "I don't . . . feel very well. Excuse me."

Seconds after Beth was safely out of view in the hallway, hot, bitter tears spilled onto her cheeks. She managed to make her way up the stairs, one hand flattening innocent, muslin-covered breasts. Behind her bodice, the pain was so intense that Lisabeth thought her heart must surely be breaking.

Muggy twilight stifled afternoon's white-hot fire. Still perched on the window seat, Courtney tuned out the dull conversation between her mother and fiancé. Dreamily, her eyes surveyed the garden. Coral seeped over the horizon, while lavender shadows invited her to enjoy their cool, dry caress.

Timothy, hearing the sigh that escaped Courtney's lips, could have shouted with relief. For two hours he had listened to Mrs. Ashton ramble on about her husband, the war, the Madisons, the problem of finding a husband for shy Lisabeth. Obviously the poor woman was lonely, particularly in the absence of the dynamic Gerald Ashton, but Timothy ached to spend some time alone with Courtney. Lately, she seemed to have changed. Her manner was softer, more friendly and inviting than the distant restlessness she usually radiated. Still, Timothy hadn't been alone with Courtney for days, so he couldn't be certain his wishful imagination wasn't simply playing tricks. If not . . . the thought of Courtney melting in his arms, eagerly returning his kiss, brought a sheen of cold perspiration to Timothy's brow.

"Mrs. Ashton," he said with a smile, "it looks as if your daughter is yearning to go outside. The twilight must be refreshing after hours of hot sun! Would you be gracious enough to excuse Courtney and me for a few minutes?"

After exclaiming that she must seek out Mrs. Belcher to discuss the approaching evening meal, Amity insisted that the engaged couple enjoy the garden for as long as they pleased.

The moment Courtney stepped out the back door and inhaled the twilight air, her smile faded. Although relieved of the burning midday sun, the atmosphere remained stifling.

"This weather is utterly intolerable!" she cried. "There isn't the slightest hint of a breeze. How could it look so inviting, then deliver absolutely nothing?" She whirled around to find Timothy wearing a bittersweet smile.

"Courtney . . . I hope you are never encouraged and then disappointed by anyone or anything more personal than the weather."

At a loss for words, she meekly walked next to him as they wound deeper into wild, fragrant July garden. Ribbon grass trimmed the little moss roses Courtney had adored since childhood, and honey locust trees cast lacy shadows over the brick walkway ahead of them.

"I suppose you think I'm a tease," she remarked at length. When Timothy stopped walking but remained in profile, she cast a sidelong glance at his face. Was it possible that he almost seemed attractive . . . and not as a puppy, but as a young man?

"I wouldn't say I think you're a tease but I *have* felt that your heart has changed positions many times since we became engaged." He looked at her, dark brown eyes gleaming with emotions Courtney was unable to identify. "Sometimes you seem genuinely enamored of me, but more often I'm encouraged only to be abruptly deflated on our next meeting."

"I—" Discomfort and shame reddened Courtney's cheeks. "I admit I have my own moments of confusion. I'm sorry if you've been hurt because of them."

The sun was setting rapidly as she moved ahead of him, circling around to the fountain. Remembering her selfish, poor treatment of Timothy and the many disparaging remarks she had made about him, both in her mind and aloud, Courtney felt sick with guilt. Suddenly she realized this was the first time they had ever shared their feelings, and the first time she had felt such warmth toward her fiancé. Was it possible that Damon had been right? Had she simply been too stubborn to give her feelings for Timothy Lamb a chance to take root?

Leaning back against the bowl of the fountain, Courtney watched curiously as Timothy approached. Their eyes met, and he almost lost his courage to speak, so fetching did she seem to him.

"My mother has been anxious for news of yours," he announced after an uneasy minute of silence. "She reminded me twice today that I must beg you for an honest report."

"Mother is doing quite well, considering how truly attached she is to Father." Courtney nearly let a smile slip by, thinking that Mrs. Lamb was the last person with whom she'd share an "honest report." No doubt Mrs. Lamb would have rubbed her hands together in satisfaction if the news had been bad. "If my dear future mother-in-law is that concerned, she ought to come for tea one day."

"Well . . . today she's not feeling well. Her head is hurting, as I recall."

Feeling sorry for Timothy and bubbling with amusement inspired by Mrs. Lamb, Courtney caught his hand. "Truthfully, I am a bit concerned about Mother. I'd adore it if she would mingle more. I'm trying to think of a way to persuade her to have a party." Seeing his suddenly daring eyes on her lips, Courtney flushed, then added, "It would be the perfect project, and a wonderful means of showing people that, although Mother is alone, she's coping magnificently."

"I'd be happy to help you. Perhaps we can discuss the details . . . later."

Courtney strove to relax, waiting for goose bumps and a thrill down her spine as she saw that Timothy was about to kiss her. His face came closer, blurring before soft lips touched, then flattened, her own. Desperately, Courtney prayed for feelings even vaguely similar to those Damon Sheffield had sent shooting over her nerves, but not even the feeblest spark was kindled. Pity kept her from pushing Timothy away. For the first time, Courtney had regarded Timothy Lamb as a person with feelings and worth. She realized how callously she had treated him over the past weeks, as well as the amount of courage it must have taken for him to kiss her. His effort to sweep her off her feet seemed not lecherous, but guileless.

Beneath her reluctant hands, the back of Timothy's coat had grown damp with earnest perspiration. He was trying so hard, and smothering Courtney in the process. When she felt his lips press one final, moist kiss on her neck, Courtney shivered in relief.

"You are more beautiful . . . to be near . . . than I ever dreamed," Timothy whispered.

Touched, Courtney momentarily forgot her own physical revulsion. The sweetness in Timothy's eyes made her smile with sincere affection, and she reached up to brush back a pale, wayward lock of hair that had found its way across his brow. "No one has ever said such a thing to me. Your choice of words is . . . lovely."

Timothy thought he would burst with euphoric wonder. Ardently, he declared, "It's actually going to work out, isn't it!"

The instant his last word was said, Courtney's heart was pierced by a stinging needle of regret. Unable to speak or meet Timothy's gaze, she managed a smile but kept her eyes averted. It was then, through tangled, twilit branches, that Courtney saw the figure in the upstairs window.

It was Lisabeth. In spite of the distance, the trees and the dimness, Courtney was convinced that her sister was quite purposely watching them.

"It's all right, my sweet," Timothy was murmuring. "You don't have to say even one word. It's enough for me now just to know you feel differently . . . today."

When he covered her lips again with his own, Courtney opened her left eye. It was immediately apparent that her sister hadn't moved from the window. Courtney's stomach flipped once in confusion.

Why, she wondered, would Beth watch us kissing?

Chapter Twelve

July 23, 1814

As Courtney made her way down the stairs, a smile hovered at the corners of her mouth. A fortnight had passed since she had discovered Timothy Lamb as a person, and during that time she had grown truly fond of her fiancé. They were friends. He seemed to sense the wisdom of not pressing Courtney physically, and she was grateful for that understanding. In return, she made a sincere effort to learn about the subjects which interested him. The fact that Lisabeth was more attuned to his interests, and ever present with a comment, wouldn't have bothered Courtney in the least if she hadn't seen Beth watching her and Timothy kiss that day.

After a brief glance at her gown, Courtney shook off whatever dark feelings hovered nearby. Within a quarter hour, people would begin arriving for a garden party hosted by the Ashton women. She was wearing her prettiest summer dress, a high-waisted, cream-colored thin muslin with a recklessly low neckline that revealed most of Courtney's perfect breasts. The hemline, puffed sleeves and bodice were trimmed with a narrow, celery-hued silk ribbon, two streamers of which were tied in back and floated after her. Another, wider piece of celery silk, embroidered with tiny pearls, encircled her slim neck and blended attractively with her midnight-blue eyes and honey curls.

Courtney was feeling proud of the success Amity, and her daughters, had made of the weeks since Gerald's departure. A dozen days earlier, Courtney had begun to despair of ever convincing her mother to socialize, or even to invite friends to their home. Then Gerald had made a brief visit to Georgetown. After a late, boring evening of chess with Lisabeth and Timothy, a sleepy Courtney had excused herself, and mounting the stairs, overheard a snatch of conversation between her parents. Apparently Amity had barely mentioned Courtney's proposed party to Gerald, but he'd reacted with typical negative stubbornness. Courtney hadn't needed to hear the actual words to know that her mother hadn't cowered in surrender. In fact, from the tone of Amity's voice, it seemed she had displayed a startling impudence. At the end of three days, when Gerald had returned to his militia, he'd worn a stern expression that allowed a sliver of pride in his wife and daughters to shine through.

Also during the visit, the usually rebellious Courtney had been pleased by her father's reaction to the improved state of affairs concerning her engagement. After the first evening Timothy had spent with the family, Gerald had come to Courtney's room to say goodnight. The hug he'd given her radiated approval, and now that he was gone again, with a British attack expected any day, she was proud of the contribution she'd made to the stability of the family. Practicality had its rewards after all.

Reaching the foot of the stairs, Courtney gazed out onto Duck Lane. At nearly four o'clock, the heat was at its zenith, and she leaned against the narrow window that bordered the front door and allowed herself one soft sigh for Damon Sheffield.

Courtney had resolved, three weeks earlier, that thoughts of Sheffield were destructive—nothing more. She hadn't seen him in days, not since she'd turned away from the sight of him riding side by side with Prudence Hatch. Even more aggravating were the dreams that Damon invaded regularly, despite all her self-protestations before falling asleep. His appearances during her sleeping hours were not only frustrating but achingly real. Even in his total physical absence, he had the power to scramble all her well-planned emotions and reactions.

"So there you are!"

Startled, Courtney turned to see her mother, who had emerged silently from the dining room, standing behind her. In spite of Amity's rose Empire gown, its color did not soften the strained look on her face.

"You aren't nervous, are you?" Courtney exclaimed. "Don't be such a worrywart. A bit of frivolity is precisely what people need right now. As for Father's absence, I'm positive everyone will admire the way you've taken hold of life."

"I can't help feeling strange, but perhaps you're right." Amity paused, and the corners of her mouth turned up doubtfully. "Dolley Madison is coming. I just heard this afternoon. Possibly the President as well."

"There, you see!" Courtney gave her a hug. She couldn't remember ever feeling this close to her mother. Amity's eyes were still more placid than fiery, but even a little progress delighted Courtney.

The afternoon sun burnished Amity's upswept toffee waves and enhanced her aristocratic features. The worries that pinched her inwardly were concealed. "One of our guests has already arrived!" she chirped.

"Oh, my, it must be later than I thought! How are the flowing punch bowls? Have you tasted them? I don't trust Mrs. Belcher to see that enough rum is added—" Courtney broke off with a rueful laugh. "Listen to me! I sound as if this were your first party!"

"It's the first without your father, and you're doing a passable job filling his place, darling." Amity sighed. "He always wanted to supervise—"

"And he was more bother than help!" Courtney laughed. She stopped abruptly, her eyes drawn to a sudden movement inside the library. Lisabeth and Timothy were seated next to each other on a deacon's bench. They held a large book between them, but all their attention was directed at Courtney.

She wondered why the memory of Beth's observing her kissing Timothy was the first thing to invade her mind. Was it something in her sister's expression? But the moment Timothy stood and Courtney met his utterly innocent eyes, she smiled. Her husband-to-be wouldn't know *how* to be a cad; the differences between Timothy Lamb and Damon Sheffield were beginning to seem like advantages.

"Here's Courtney already, Beth!" he exclaimed, then rushed forward to kiss her cheek.

"So she is," Lisabeth agreed.

"Are you surprised?" Courtney inquired lightly, glancing at each of them in turn.

"Well, Beth told me you might be de—"

"I was," Lisabeth interrupted, "keeping Mr. Lamb company while we waited for you. He brought along a newly published book that chronicles the foremost silversmiths of Colonial America. It's *very* engrossing!"

Timothy smiled at Beth over his shoulder. "You must keep it for a few days and peruse it at length."

She beamed. "Oh, thank you! That is so kind."

Observing this exchange, Courtney bit her lower lip. Why was Timothy calling her sister "Beth," especially if the informality wasn't reciprocated? And what if it was . . . in her absence? Lisabeth had been acting strangely for weeks. Was there more to her sisterly affection for Timothy than Courtney had guessed? The idea was ridiculous. Even if he filled Beth's every waking thought, her sense of propriety made her more the type to do nothing about it.

Compliments were exchanged regarding everyone's wonderful appearance. Timothy looked his best in a coat that matched his chocolate-brown eyes. Someone had helped to negotiate his intricate cravat, while a tailor had worked miracles with a previously ill-fitting pair of tan trousers. As for Lisabeth, she wore, despite the heat, a royal blue spencer over a slim gown of spotted white muslin. The short spencer emphasized her tiny waist, and Courtney realized that her fawnlike sister looked more attractive, in spite of the severity of her costume, than Courtney had ever seen her before.

As the quartet started toward the parlor to await the guests, Lisabeth felt her stomach knot at the sight of Courtney smiling up at Timothy. Remembering the complete spiritual and intellectual harmony she had shared with him minutes earlier, Beth knew that tonight she had to learn the truth, for Courtney's and Timothy's sakes as well as for her own.

"How could I have forgotten to tell you all?" she exclaimed suddenly. The others stopped and looked back expectantly. "Courtney, do you remember remarking on Damon Sheffield's recent disappearance? Well, I met him today in Cherry Alley, and he admitted he's been away from Georgetown."

Timothy looked chilly. "I'm not surprised."

Beth was gauging Courtney's reaction, memorizing the intensity of her silent, wide-eyed stare. "Since Mr. Sheffield is such a colorful figure, and such a favorite with the ladies, I took the liberty of inviting him to attend tonight." Innocently, she glanced from her sister to Amity. "I hope no one objects . . . ?"

By ten o'clock, some of the guests had said good night and taken their leave. A tense Courtney was certain that Damon Sheffield would not be making an appearance after all. Relief and disappointment mingled in her heart, but she was beginning to regain her appetite. Excusing herself from a conversation with James and Elizabeth Monroe, she threaded her way through the crowded, torchlit garden and went into the hallway. It felt good to be indoors, away from the insects and the anxious gossip circulating among the guests. A few people were in the parlor, and she could hear more voices from the richly aromatic dining room. Pausing to survey her reflection in the Hepplewhite hall mirror, Courtney smiled as she thought of her mother. After a tentative first hour, Amity had begun to relax, like a slow-blooming flower. When last seen, she had been exchanging war news in a group of six or more guests, seemingly quite unconcerned about her role as hostess without a host.

Courtney smoothed her gown and the rebellious curls that had slipped from their pins. Since now she was free of the threat of Sheffield's arrival at any moment, she could spare a thought for Timothy . . . and Lisabeth. When was the last time she had seen them? On an impulse, Courtney turned and glanced into the parlor, then froze before one slippered foot could cross the threshold.

There, seated together on a sofa, were her sister and her fiancé. Lisabeth's head was bent close to the Chinese export bowl Timothy was holding as he described it in the kind of detail that made Courtney yawn. The picture they made was all very innocent, and yet . . .

Perplexed, Courtney wandered up the hall a dozen steps. She wanted to clear her mind of Timothy and

Beth entirely. There wasn't room in her life for one more problem. Then Courtney heard a lively, familiar peal of laughter and knew she had found her diversion. Without a word of warning, she started into the library, ready to greet Dolley Madison.

"Mrs. Madison, how ill-mannered you must think us—" Her mouth went dry. The First Lady stood in front of the bookcase, smiling expectantly, but Courtney could see only Damon Sheffield. Amber eyes, warily cynical, met her own, and she was shocked by the explosive effect he had on her body.

"Miss Ashton, are you all right?" Damon was immediately at her side, full of concern, although the irony in his tone was all too clear to Courtney.

Somehow, she composed herself. "Why, of course! I . . . just felt dizzy for a moment." Her hand, inside Sheffield's, was icy. "It's been a busy day."

A voice in Courtney's mind sarcastically complimented her own dazzling entrance and witty repartée as she allowed Damon to escort her back to the bookshelves. The First Lady waited there, resplendent in lemon-yellow satin embroidered with flights of butterflies. Under a yellow turban that hid her black curls, Dolley's rosy-cheeked smile helped Courtney to relax.

"You Ashton women can never know how welcome this party is to the rest of us!" she exclaimed. For a moment, worry and strain showed around her eyes and mouth, then disappeared. "The summer has been *so* warm, and people are preoccupied with such serious subjects. Even in wartime we all need to laugh and enjoy the company of our friends." After beaming at Courtney and Damon, she looked between them toward the doorway. "Why, there is your sister, the charming little Lisabeth." A quick squint was followed by, "And Representative Lamb!"

Her plump hand waved them over, and more pleasantries were exchanged. Standing between Sheffield and Timothy, Courtney felt a bit ill and was unaware of

Lisabeth's eyes—almost fawn-colored tonight—quietly scrutinizing her.

As always, the subject of the war came up. Recently, more and more stories had begun to circulate through the District of Columbia about the atrocities being committed by the fleet of Admiral Sir George Cockburn. During Cockburn's two years as commander in the Chesapeake blockade, coastal towns had been raided and pillaged with barbaric cruelty, but it seemed that lately he had outdone his own harsh record. Timothy announced that, over the past four months, Cockburn had destroyed well over a million dollars' worth of tobacco. Dolley Madison nodded sad confirmation.

The Ashton sisters gasped. Courtney had been watching Sheffield from the corner of one blue eye, wondering how he could listen with such nonchalance to the horrifying acts being committed against his own country.

One broad shoulder braced against a row of gold-embossed books, Damon had been sipping rum while Timothy grew flushed with outrage. Now he offered quietly, "Cockburn is a swine."

"What do you mean by that, Mr. Sheffield?" Lisabeth prodded.

His chiseled, sardonic countenance betrayed no emotion. "Like all of you, I deplore Admiral Cockburn's crass, uncivilized behavior, but I try not to put his label on every other Englishman." Seeing Timothy's face growing redder, Damon held up a hand. "Please, *don't* challenge me to a duel, Mr. Lamb. I agree vehemently that Admiral Cockburn should be stopped."

"If you will excuse me, ladies," Timothy muttered, "I find it uncomfortably warm in this room."

After he had stalked out of the library, Dolley Madison spoke first. "The subject needs changing." Opening her satin reticule, she withdrew a jeweled snuffbox and offered a dip to the others. Taken aback,

Courtney and Lisabeth declined, but Damon flashed a sudden grin and shared a pinch of snuff with the President's wife. Then Dolley produced a large bandanna from a hidden pocket in her gown. She put it to gusty use and hid it away once again, flourishing a dainty lace handkerchief in its place. Seeing the two girls' stares, she laughed. "Don't let it bother you. I only keep the one for heavy work, and this bit of lace is my polisher!"

Damon chortled with rich delight. Was this the same man who had been coldly laconic a few minutes earlier? Courtney couldn't take her eyes off him. It was one thing to put Damon out of her mind in his absence, to reshape her opinions about him and about Timothy, but to be so near the breathing, laughing, charismatic, *real* man and remain detached was asking far too much.

"Mrs. Madison," Lisabeth was saying, "let me take you into the garden so that Mama can greet you before it's time to say good night."

"I'll be glad to see Amity, but I'm pleased she was *not* at the door to meet me. With your father away, it's much more important for your mother to enjoy herself tonight than I."

As Dolley Madison and Lisabeth left the library, Damon slanted a gently satirical look at Courtney. "Please don't stay on my account. As hostess, you might be obliged to give me the time of day."

Color flooded her cheeks. "I had completely forgotten that."

"Completely?"

In spite of Damon's mocking tone, Courtney felt a warmth radiate from him that he couldn't conceal and she couldn't classify. It burned off some of the ice on her nerves. "Frankly, Mr. Sheffield, it has been so long since our last encounter, I have forgotten *most* of it."

"Really?" Damon took a long sip of rum, one black brow arched high above laughing gold eyes. Obviously he was relishing Courtney's every word. "Dare I hope you remember me at all?"

"It would be rude for me to claim otherwise, Mr. Sheffield." Knowing that flushed cheeks were giving her away, Courtney smiled wryly. "Actually, you're looking very well. Attractively battered by the elements." She could see that he had been away again, traveling in the sun and doubtless sleeping outdoors as well. An indigo-blue coat, a dull gold brocade waistcoat and champagne trousers combined to deepen the bronze of Damon's skin while accentuating the fire in his amber eyes. Why weren't other men's shirt fronts quite so fresh and snowy, their cravats tied with such casual precision? Against the lean, brown line of Damon's jaw, the starched cravat was a masterpiece. Beau Brummell himself would have been envious, Courtney thought.

"You are looking lovely yourself," came Damon's soft reply.

"Well, since Father's militia was called, we've all been under a great deal of strain, but you'll be happy and relieved to hear that Timothy has managed to win my heart after all."

Both dark eyebrows flew up in surprise. If it were any other female, he might suspect some strategy at work, but Courtney was too elementally frank. "Are you serious?"

"Mr. Sheffield, it has been weeks since I've found my situation a source of amusement." Momentarily, she was able to disconnect her longing. Gazing at the warm pecan grain of a nearby wall, Courtney was unaware of the exquisitely pensive profile she showed to Damon. "The advice that you gave me in the Madisons' garden has proved to be valuable. I put a sincere effort into my relationship with Timothy, and the results have been encouraging."

When Courtney looked over at him, Damon's right

nostril flared as if he'd caught a whiff of badly aged cheese. "You sound like a medical professor I once knew!"

"That was not my intent," she replied, gathering all her dignity.

"Shall I infer, rather, that Lamb has taken his rightful place as the grand passion of your life?"

Courtney stared. She sensed that Sheffield had spoken those words against his own better judgment. "If you insist on finding a pigeonhole—yes."

There was a hot pain in Damon's chest. Shocked, he strove to keep his face blank and cursed himself for coming here tonight. He had justified his attendance by telling himself he was bored and curious and that Courtney couldn't upset him. After all, he had spent nearly a month without her spicy, addictive company. Courtney, he had decided, was a simple flesh-and-blood woman, and therefore resistible.

Now, as the pain receded, leaving a tingling sensation in its wake, Damon realized that his mind and will had been overturned by emotions he could neither understand nor control.

"That's splended news, Courtney. You . . . all must be overjoyed to have the situation so neatly resolved."

"I suppose that's one way of putting it." She tried to match him, stare for stare, but suddenly had to drop her eyes.

The sight of the caramel-gold froth of curls encircling Courtney's high Grecian knot, the starry lashes brushing dusky cheeks, the tempting curve of her lower lip, melted Damon's heart. "So all's well that ends well, hmm, Courtney? Those reservations you used to have about Lamb—they all must have turned out to be nonsense, is that it?"

Jealousy had pushed out the first dozen words, but real concern gradually surfaced when she didn't respond. Although Damon had urged Courtney to give Lamb a chance, he'd never really expected her to change her mind about her fiancé. He'd made the suggestion in order to furnish an interval during which she could forget him and prepare herself to meet new men. The thought of Courtney trapped in a bad marriage because of him, the war and Gerald Ashton's will made Damon feel sick.

"Courtney . . ." Warm cognaclike eyes flicked around to make certain no one had come into the library, then Damon slid long fingers over the nape of her neck. When his thumb pushed gently at her chin, Courtney was forced to show him eyes stormy with a desperation she couldn't disguise.

"Why?" Damon hissed. He could hear the irritation in his voice and knew it was self-directed. "You don't have to marry him!"

"I certainly do!" Unsuccessfully, Courtney tried to separate herself from his touch. "Even months ago the argument for my marriage to Timothy was convincing, but lately it's become as much my duty as it was Father's duty to go to war."

Damon's other hand closed above her elbow. "What the hell are you talking about? Marriage isn't quite the same as the army, you know! It won't be over in a few months. Your father will fight and come home again, but *your* wartime duty would go on for the rest of your life!" His eyes shot gold lightning. "Is that what you want?"

"I *want* you to free my *arm*, Mr. Sheffield," Courtney whispered angrily. "I really find this conversation quite incredible—rather like a bizarre dream! The last time we spoke, you told me you wanted no further involvement in my life, and also urged me to put my energies into my engagement. You said I was much better off in the arms of Timothy, who loves me . . . and now that I've docilely done your bidding, and my family's, you behave as if I've lost my senses!" Her eyes were flashing amethysts set off by thick, sooty lashes. Her exquisitely molded cheekbones were stained pink with emotion. "Well, I'm sick to death of everyone telling me what's best for me. Save your advice for your next lovesick ingenue—Rebecca Chilton, perhaps? I won't be doomed to misery if I marry Timothy, so you mustn't lose sleep worrying about me. I'm deeply fond of him, and I've learned that trust and warmth and predictability can be infinitely more valuable than some transitory physical . . ." Courtney took a gulp of air, suddenly conscious of the strong male hand curved around her neck. Her own pulse, throbbing against Damon's palm, betrayed her.

"Desire?" he supplied. Only the barest hint of Damon's usual sardonic amusement flickered over his chiseled features. "Yearning?"

"Mr. Sheffield, I really must be getting back to my guests. I would appreciate it if you would remove your hand from my neck and keep your distance for the remainder of the evening." Courtney's icy veneer almost succeeded in covering her internal storm of emotion. If she hadn't completely forgotten to whisper, Damon might have believed that her heart had frozen against him.

"I don't blame you for being bitter, Courtney, but please don't throw your *life* away to spite me." Complying with her request, he removed his hand from her neck, sliding tanned fingers over a short puff of muslin sleeve, then down the slim, satiny length of Courtney's arm. She shivered involuntarily and bit her lower lip as if smothering a sob. "I agree that you deserve trust and security, but you can have those and passion, too. There's no reason—"

"Stop!" Angry, aching tears shone in her violet eyes. "Don't say another word. And if you touch me again, I shall slap you so hard that your face will bear a mark for all the world to see! Now, Mr. Sheffield, I must ask you to leave my home. Kindly do not return unless I personally invite you!"

Damon knew it would only increase her rage if she

saw his amusement, but he was unable to stop the corners of his mouth from twitching irrepressibly. "Do you truly hate me so much?"

"Sheffield!"

Courtney's eyes were huge, even frightened, as she and Damon turned to see Timothy walking toward them from the doorway.

"Miss Ashton has asked you to leave her home," barked Timothy, more pale than ever in his rage, "and now I am *telling* you! It's possible you may desire to take shelter somewhere besides the Union Tavern, because after I have ascertained just how grievously you have insulted my fiancée, you might very well find yourself on the receiving end of a challenge!"

Chapter Thirteen

July 24, 1814

Standing on Duck Lane just after midnight in the warmth of a new day, Damon Sheffield could look south, past the waterfront thoroughfare called West Lane Keys to the shimmering black expanse of the Potomac River. Georgetown was mostly asleep now. When he had gone to bid Amity Ashton good evening, he'd discovered nearly all the guests had disappeared while he and Courtney had been alone in the library.

Suddenly weary, Damon raked tense fingers through his raven hair and loosened the deftly tied cravat. His body reminded him of the long days he'd just spent on horseback, under a merciless July sun or in shadowed but stifling woods.

Sleep, he thought. That was what he needed, especially if he were roused at the crack of dawn by Lamb's second with a challenge.

The bemused smile Damon had managed to suppress in the library curved his mouth. For Courtney's sake, he'd pretended to take Lamb very seriously in the hope of placating him. If word spread through the entire Distric of Columbia that Damon Sheffield was an unprincipled lecher, it wouldn't matter for very long anyway. His days in Georgetown were numbered, which seemed a good thing. In spite of all his efforts to remain emotionally unencumbered, Sheffield knew he had come perilously close to a web of involvement that might never have set him free. As it was, other lives had been complicated because of him.

The bittersweet sting Damon associated with Courtney returned to surprise him again, and the cramp in his chest made breathing an effort. When he forced his thoughts away from her, Courtney's image kept up a tenacious pursuit and painted itself vividly in his mind. God, but she was enchanting! Raising a hand to rub an aching temple, Damon stopped, groaned and allowed himself to inhale the fragrance of Courtney that remained on his fingers. Violets. Her neck had been like satin to touch, while the baby curls along her hairline had grazed Damon's forefinger like downy feathers. It was odd how keenly pleasurable the time he had spent with her had been, just drinking in her expressive, lovely face and the sound of her voice, no matter what it was saying, and simply touching the scented softness of her neck . . .

"Jesus Christ!" Damon muttered disgustedly. "If I keep this up, I'll be ready for Bedlam!"

He'd been walking north, toward Falls Street, which led to the Union Tavern, a good distance to the east. Now Sheffield reversed his direction. Passing the Ashton house again, he glanced at it and noted that the library windows were still ablaze with light, although the garden had been given over to silent darkness. Golden eyes flicked away, searching out the street lamp that marked the narrow entrance to Cherry Alley. Thank God for Prudence Hatch, thought Damon with acid irony. She was one woman who wouldn't mind an unannounced visit at midnight. Better yet, Prudence knew some absolutely foolproof ways to clear his mind of troublesome thoughts.

In the Ashton library, Timothy paced to and fro beside the gaming table. The candles that fitted into the table's four corners had been lit earlier, and as he passed by, they flared and flickered dangerously. From her calmer pose in the Sheraton reading chair, Courtney worried that Timothy might knock one or all of the candles over and set himself, perhaps the entire house, afire.

"I'm going to ask you once more, Courtney," he blurted suddenly. "What did Sheffield do to prompt your outburst?"

"Imitating Father won't help, I'm afraid," she retorted evenly. "I don't care to discuss my conversation with Mr. Sheffield."

The look in her eyes deflated Timothy. "You *have* to tell me!" he cried.

"Why?"

"Why! Because we are betrothed! If— Well, I'm supposed to protect you!"

"I'll let you know if I need protection, Timothy," she said patiently. "In the meantime, I must demand my privacy. I cannot be obliged to repeat every conversation to you."

"Courtney! This is insanity! I have a right to know! If you don't tell me"—Timothy waved a fist, narrowly missing a candle—"I shall simply have to assume the worst and challenge Sheffield to a duel!"

"If you did such a foolish thing, I would never marry you," Courtney countered in the same firm tone. "But if it will help to calm you down, I'll say that what occurred between Mr. Sheffield and me was purely verbal. Just an impulsive argument."

Timothy stopped and stared at her with perplexed eyes. "It sounded like much more than that to me!"

Somehow, she fought the guilty blush and the urge to

look away. "He wasn't trying to lure me into his bed or take unseemly liberties, if that's what you mean."

"Courtney! Your choice of words wasn't very maidenly!"

"I'm exhausted. I don't have the patience to sit here speaking in circles all night because of my maidenly modesty!"

Sighing, Timothy crossed the room and sat limply on the sofa opposite Courtney's chair. "I don't mean to be overbearing, but Sheffield rubs me rather the wrong way. I don't trust the man, especially with a girl as beautiful as you are."

As usual, Timothy's honest sweetness touched Courtney's heart. "How silly you are." Her words were accompanied by a warm smile. "I can take care of myself with overfamiliar men, Timothy. And, in any event, Mr. Sheffield is not as villainous as you believe. I mean, it's clear he appreciates a pretty girl, but he'd never be the type to force himself on a young lady. Rogue or not, I trust him . . . and even like him somewhat."

Something in her voice struck a dissonant chord in Timothy. "You *trust* him! Well, in spite of my intention to keep this to myself until I was able to offer real proof, I can see you must be told."

"Really?" Courtney waited, looking bored and dubious. Her expression fanned the flames of Timothy's outrage.

"Honestly, Courtney, you are a puzzle to me. Would it upset you to know that your great friend Damon Sheffield is a British spy?"

She swallowed a harsh gasp, refusing to give Timothy the satisfaction of seeing her react. "Oh, please. I never would have believed you the type to make up stories just to win—"

"I am *not* making it up!" he shouted. A vein stood out in his forehead.

"But you have no proof?" Courtney taunted. She

135

couldn't believe she was actually speaking coherently, even coolly, when her insides were a churning emotional cyclone.

"As I have already said, I do not. But surely you can see that all the signs are there! His charm may have blinded you ladies, but dozens of congressmen have echoed my suspicions. The mysterious past, the vagueness of his plans and particularly the strange, unexplained absences for days at a time. All these things combine to—"

"Stop it!" cried Courtney. Her icy mask had melted to reveal flashing eyes and flushed cheeks. "What do you know about Damon Sheffield? Absolutely nothing! You've taken a few circumstances and fashioned an accusation that I find abominable! The man is entitled to his privacy—just as *I* am and *you* are! I happen to know that Mr. Sheffield is slow to share himself with others, even reluctant. Wherever he comes from and why, and whatever he does during the days he is absent from Georgetown, are his own affair." Courtney paused, breathing hard in an effort to stop her rage from boiling over. "I cannot answer your questions about Damon Sheffield, but there is one thing I *am* certain of. He is not a spy! All the world may believe him a scoundrel, and I may agree, but he has very real principles. He is not a traitorous snake that would sell the secrets of his own country!"

Timothy was completely overwhelmed by her vehemence and afraid to wonder what fueled it. Never had he seen Courtney display such passion; not for him or for any member of her family. Even in the moments of her greatest indifference she hadn't seemed this emotionally elusive and distant from Timothy. Fear made him act on impulse.

"If you're so certain, then I believe you," he said, kneeling beside her chair and smiling nervously. All he wanted was to catch her, to stop her from slipping farther away. "I don't want to fight with you, darling.

Please don't blame me for being jealous. I never meant to upset you this way. What you say about Sheffield makes sense, and I had no right to accuse him of such a thing without proof."

"Well . . . I'm glad I made my point." Now that the storm had passed, Courtney felt rather numb. How could she have carried on so?

"I'm perfectly willing to forget the whole thing. Wouldn't it be terrible to allow our relationship to be marred by an inconsequential acquaintance like Damon Sheffield?"

Courtney barely had time to recover from the impact of his offhand remark when Timothy was suddenly leaning closer, upward, until his face filled her vision. He spoke her name with hoarse urgency before closing in and covering her mouth with his. The library was warm, and Courtney felt the moisture on Timothy's face, tasted salt on the lips that threatened to cut off her breath. They were both overwrought, but in completely different ways. Courtney was in no mood to be touched, let alone kissed and pawed so repulsively. Timothy's body was beyond his control; physical need had broken free, forcing him to pull her closer, then down off the chair so he could press himself against her muslin-sheathed slimness. Dimly, Timothy was aware of her struggles, but it was as if his brain had been knocked unconscious by this overwhelming hunger. How sweet her mouth was! Trying to hold her still against the Kuba rug, he stole a clumsy stroke at one firm young breast. A groan rose aching in Timothy's throat, and he had to lift his mouth away. Courtney seized that moment to push wildly against him. Caught off balance, Timothy toppled sideways, and she scrambled to her feet.

"You must be mad!" Her eyes were great purple flames, her body frozen with anger. "How dare you?"

Timothy shook his head, stunned, and staggered to an upright position. Too ashamed to meet her accusing gaze, he stared at the rug and murmured, "I'm so sorry . . . so sorry. That wasn't me. Something I've held inside for so very long seemed to get the upper hand." The sight of the bulge in his trousers made him burn with humiliation.

Courtney saw then that Timothy was as much a virgin as she, perhaps more so. She had learned in Parrott's Woods what it meant to be swept away on a tide of physical craving. Momentarily, she imagined her wedding night with Timothy, and tears pooled in her eyes. If only there were some hopeful spark in his kiss that promised magical pleasure in the future. Sighing, Courtney slipped an arm about his back.

"Don't berate yourself. I know how you feel. "It's part of life, after all." She tried to meet his eyes, smiling. "Isn't it? I know that, Timothy. I'm not some shrinking violet who pretends that babies are acquired in the manner of a new harpsichord!"

In spite of himself, Timothy was shocked. Not once in all his life, including the adult years spent living at home, had his mother even hinted at any knowledge of the carnal relationship between men and women. He had assumed, after learning how babies were made, that his mother must have been asleep during his own conception. It had never occurred to Timothy that a female of breeding could feel even a twinge of lust or desire. "Part of life?" he repeated now, certain his ears were deceiving him.

"Didn't you know?" Courtney laughed softly. "Honestly, Timothy, you couldn't look more startled if I'd put a knife into you! Everyone feels what you felt, sometimes, to some degree, and I think it's silly for all of us to go through life pretending differently." Now that she had reassured him, Courtney couldn't wait to get away. In one instant of quiet, all that she had been through since first entering the library came back in a punishing flood. Her defensive system had somehow erected a dam, but Courtney knew it would never hold if she didn't get away from Timothy, this library, Lisabeth, the entire house. . . .

Stepping back, she tried to smile. "Now that we have straightened everything out, I believe I'll take a short walk. After such a wearing evening, the fresh air seems delicious."

Timothy was right behind her as Courtney started for the library door. "I'll go with you."

She whirled around, inches from his face. "No! That is . . . I appreciate the offer, but I'm certain you must be ready to go home to bed yourself, and I truly crave a bit of—"

"Privacy?"

Courtney didn't like the way he was curling his lip. "Exactly!" In the next instant she had opened the door and stepped into the hallway.

"Courtney! I cannot allow you to go out alone at this hour!"

"Fortunately, I don't need your permission."

Timothy was halfway along the hall with her when his arm was grasped, and he turned to look into Lisabeth's sympathetic, concerned face.

Courtney closed the front door behind herself. Timothy cried, "Wait!" but he made no move to pull free of Beth's gently restraining hands.

"Let her go," she whispered. "Courtney never listens, never stops once she makes up her mind. Why don't you come into the parlor and let me fix you a nice brandy? Then we'll sit down, and, if you'd like, I can keep you company until Courtney returns. It shouldn't take her long to cool off and come to her senses."

Timothy laced his fingers through Lisabeth's. When she was with him, he felt like a normal, even fascinating, person. "Beth, I'm beginning to fear I shall never understand your sister. In fact, I sometimes worry—"

"Yes?" For a moment, Lisabeth couldn't breathe.

"Nothing. I think I could use that brandy you offered, not to mention the pleasure of your company."

Timothy smiled, but when Beth turned toward the parlor, his expression clouded over again. He and Courtney were to be married in a month. What would their future hold? How could he ever make her happy?

Moonlight streamed across the huge, high four-poster bed in which Prudence Hatch lay naked under a filmy sheet. An anticipatory warmth crept over her body as she watched Damon Sheffield strip off his fine clothing, the silvery beams highlighting his lean, muscular strength. Prudence, drinking in each detail, found herself thinking of her late husband, Arthur. Less than two years ago, he had sat on the edge of the bed to pull off his boots, just as Damon was doing now. Sheffield was incredibly skilled in the art of lovemaking, but her husband had done something that left her as much aglow: he'd told her he loved her. Prudence wondered, not for the first time, what it would be like to hear those magical words from Damon. She knew full well this was one of those fruitless dreams that would never come true, yet she gave in to it all the same, just as she abandoned her pride and forgot about Arthur whenever Damon turned his magnetic gaze her way.

Arthur Hatch had been a wealthy sea captain of only thirty-five when he was blown overboard during a hurricane en route to the West Indies with his cargo of tobacco. Prudence had been left with a great deal of money, but she soon became aware that what she really needed wasn't for sale. Remembering, she touched herself under the sheet. Love would be wonderful, but in the meantime, what Damon gave and took in this bed would leave her as warm and satisfied as the plump cat asleep on her hearth. Prudence was proud of her body; it was juicy and ripe, ivory-skinned and warm. For her, celibacy was the equivalent of starvation. If that meant she had ruined her reputation, then it would be a price worth paying for the incredible moments of bliss Damon was able to draw from her unsuspecting body. After one shuddering climax Prudence always begged him to stop, and gloried in his soft, laughing refusal.

Now a pang of arousal spread up from her thighs. Damon was settling himself under the sheet, and she snuggled closer, trying to read his golden eyes. Leaning over to crush out his cheroot, he appeared completely relaxed, one brown arm crooked on the pillow, yet Prudence was no longer fooled. His hooded, indolent gaze was as alert as an eagle's.

"Are you really here?" she whispered. Barely a quarter hour ago, she had awakened to the sound of his key in the front door. Elation, rather than fear, had swept over Prudence. Spending the evening at home, hoping that he'd come and feeling more despondent with each passing hour, she'd been absolutely ebullient over this late call. Despite the midsummer heat, Prudence's bed seemed invariably cold. Perhaps *empty* might have described it more aptly.

Damon was gazing distractedly at a point in space. "Hmm?"

"Where are you?" Prudence whispered, trying to keep the hurt from her voice. The sensation of her breasts against his hard, muscular arm stirred her further.

Slowly, Damon looked over at her, almost forgetting where he was. Prudence's luxuriant chestnut hair shone in the moonlight, as did the eyes she turned up to him, eager as a child's on Christmas Eve. He sighed harshly at himself and turned to allow her to mold her lush curves against his unyielding flesh. What irony! Damon had come here to force Courtney out of his system, but the fire he felt seemed to be deflected toward Duck Lane. No sooner had he settled back into the pillow, ready for Prudence's able distractions, than Courtney leaped lightly into his mind and continued to dance there, making it impossible for him to concentrate on anyone else.

Prudence was running warm fingers through the dark hair covering Damon's chest, tracing the line it made down the ridges of his belly to the part of him she loved best. She had heard women sigh over Damon Sheffield's handsome face, well-made hands, gleaming raven hair and the lean muscles outlined against expertly tailored clothing. Gloating, Prudence nibbled on Damon's lower lip and worked her tongue between his teeth. If those silly virgins who flirted with him—Courtney Ashton or Rebecca Chilton, for instance—ever touched what she was touching right now, they'd swoon!

Damon grew and stiffened in Prudence's hand, but the response was automatic. He felt oddly detached and had no burning desire to make love to her. The Widow Hatch, on the other hand, was a glutton who didn't wait for Damon to make the first move. Usually, he enjoyed her aggressiveness and the knowledge that he could come to her house at any time. Prudence was as anxious and hungry as he usually was, so the pleasure they exchanged was mutual. If Damon had used her, then the reverse was true as well.

"Damon, are you simply going to lie there, stiff as a board?" After the words were out, Prudence realized the inadvertent pun and giggled.

Sheffield began to kiss her slowly while she took his hand and boldly shaped it over one lush breast. Damon's body responded sharply, but his mind and heart were far away. Briefly, he caressed Prudence's breast and ran his fingertips along the swell of her hip. Then, to her utter astonishment, he swatted her derrière lightly and swung long, tanned legs over the side of the bed.

"What on earth?" she cried.

"I'm sorry, Prue, but I have to leave. I shouldn't have come at all tonight." Damon couldn't explain it even to himself, but some keen instinct told him to sleep this night in his bed at the Union Tavern.

Watching him pull on champagne-colored trousers, Prudence wanted to scream. Instead, she scrambled across the bed, praying that the moonbeams on her naked body would change Damon's mind.

"Please," she purred, "stay with me."

As Damon pulled on boots, muscles played over his chest and arms. "I wish I could." To cover the lie, he bent and kissed a swollen nipple. Prudence's gasp burned his cheek before he straightened and shrugged into a snowy shirt.

"Damon!" She grew desperate on seeing him cross the room and gather the rest of his clothes. "You can't leave me like this!"

Ignoring the last outburst, Damon looked back from the doorway. "I forgot to mention I may not see you again for a while—a few weeks, perhaps. Please take care of yourself, Prue. You're one hell of a woman." Before closing the door, he flashed a wicked, heart-melting grin and stared openly at her aroused body. "Do you suppose you can save that for me?"

The door closed quickly as Prudence sent a little vase flying in Damon's direction. In spite of herself, she was smiling, even after the vase lay smashed on the floor and she was alone.

Chapter Fourteen

The Union Tavern was famous in Georgetown for its Pompeian ballroom, for the arched colonnade opening on the courtyard and for a stable that could accommodate fifty horses. The great men who lodged there were taken to the capital and back in the tavern's coach, The Royal George.

For three months Damon had lived in a charming corner room on the third floor. He particularly enjoyed the abundant morning sunlight which poured through four large windows. As a child, he had never been able to understand why his mother slept with her drapes drawn, waking to late-morning gloom. That was only *one* difference between them.

His indigo-blue coat slung over his shoulder, Damon climbed the candlelit tavern stairway. He didn't want to imagine the time, dwelling instead on the splendid Hepplewhite mahogany four-poster that awaited him. A servant girl would have plumped the pillows, turned back the linen sheet and left an oil lamp burning on the fall-front desk standing between the garden windows.

Pausing outside his paneled door at the end of the hall, Damon fished in his waistcoat pocket for the key and yawned. A moment later he was inside, puzzled a bit by the darkness. Had the lamp burned out? Too tired to be concerned, Damon shed his clothes, folded them over the back of a Windsor chair and, guided by moonlight, poured water from a ewer into a matching bowl. The reason he had arrived so late at the Ashtons' was that he'd fallen asleep in a blissful, soapy bath. Still clean, Damon was nevertheless in the habit of washing his hands and face, then scrubbing his teeth with a special boar-bristle brush before he retired each night. The balmy summer breeze plied his naked body with soothing caresses as he stood near the window, rinsing away soap and running wet fingers from his brow to the tense base of his neck.

Now, sleep. Damon turned toward the bed, thinking there was little danger of Courtney's keeping him awake any longer tonight. His bare feet were silent on the ocher, brick and blue Persian rug as he approached the big four-poster, cast in shadows even though its drapes were tied to the posts in summer.

Abruptly Damon froze, blinked, then blinked again. "What the hell?" he breathed.

Impossible as it seemed, there was Courtney Ashton, curled sweetly under the linen sheet, her exquisite face and flowing honey-gold hair resting on Damon's own pillow. At first he was certain his mind had gone, broken at last by his preoccupation with her. This would be his fate—the chit's ghost would follow him even after he'd left Georgetown far behind.

Stunned, he stared at the lashes sweeping her cheeks, the delicate translucence of her eyelids, the slight telltale pulse in her neck that suggested she wasn't really asleep at all. This was no ghost or product of his imagination, but Courtney Ashton herself! And from the look of the collar and cuff that peeked above the sheet, the vixen was wearing one of *his* shirts!

Slowly, gently, Damon touched the sheet, then, just as deliberately, he whipped it back. A startled Courtney flinched to her toes, gasped and stared through the moonlight with wide-awake, incredulous eyes. Her shock was such that she failed to notice the most obvious feature of Damon's nakedness. For two hours she had lain in this bed, waiting for him, imagining a variety of sensuous, fiery scenarios. Unfortunately, this hadn't been one of them.

"God's name, Courtney!" he raged hoarsely. "What are you up to this time? And in my shirt! How in bloody hell did you get in here?"

Midnight-blue eyes pooled with tears as she sat up. The painstakingly stitched shirt billowed over her beautiful breasts, waist, derrière and arms, but revealed another asset Damon had seen little of in the past: slim, satiny, perfect legs.

"I was waiting for you," Courtney whispered. "I couldn't keep my eyes open any longer, and I didn't want to ruin my gown, so I put this on." Her voice trailed off uneasily. His cynical, suspicious stare seemed to penetrate all her secret thoughts. "I was so terribly upset when I came here . . . and I didn't want to ask the tavernkeeper about your room, so . . ."

"So?" One black brow rose sharply.

"So I climbed the trellis to your balcony."

Momentarily, Sheffield was uncharacteristically nonplused. "You did *what?*" Without waiting for an answer, he declared, "Really, I can't believe this is actually happening! Any second I'm going to wake up and shake my head over this most ludicrous dream. It must have been those oysters I ate at the party tonight!"

When Damon started to get into bed, Courtney caught a glimpse of one lean, bare hip and immediately averted her eyes, blushing. Had he been standing there naked all this time? Her heart thudded as she glanced sideways at the long legs within touching distance, outlined under the linen sheet that reached Damon's waist. He propped up some pillows to recline against, his bronzed torso contrasting startlingly with the moon-lit bed linens.

"Don't look so skittish, my dear Miss Ashton," Damon drawled. "I am not the big bad wolf that has lured you into bed . . . after disposing of your clothes to prevent your escape, of course." He craved a cheroot but settled for a glass of the cognac he kept on the bedside table. Pointedly, he refrained from offering Courtney a drink, although there was a second glass beside the decanter.

"Please, I wish you wouldn't be so sarcastic." Her frame of mind left no room for pride.

"Excuse me! Am I failing as a host? I can't imagine what's come over me, particularly in light of the unfailing courtesy you showed *me* just hours ago! Never shall I forget your gracious parting words."

Damon's caustic voice cut her like a sword. When she tried to move nearer, back to her pillow, he held up a dark hand, palm out.

"No, no! If you get that close, I might accidentally touch you . . . and then, as we both know, you'd have to slap me so hard that my face would 'bear a mark for all the world to see,' and I couldn't possibly endure the shame." His voice dripped with mockery and he paused, sipping a liberal amount of cognac, allowing his tone of voice to soak in. "The decision is difficult, but I'm afraid I shall have to opt for the chance that you might spread a rumor about my three A.M. rudeness rather than risk the fearful imprint of your hand."

"What do you mean?" Courtney quavered. Her emotions were so ragged she couldn't summon the necessary strength to deal with Damon's bitter humor.

"I mean, go home. Get dressed, leave and take with

you all my best wishes for a rapturous future as Mrs. Timothy Lamb."

In the darkness, his eyes were tiger-gold, burning through to her heart. All Courtney could feel was the fire in her breast; her mind was numb. She wasn't conscious of the tears that spilled down her cheeks, nor of crawling over to Damon and burying her face in the warmth of his chest.

Damon's resistance melted instantly, like ice in August. Closing his eyes against his own weakness, he groaned and allowed his arms to fold around Courtney's slight body. After the tears abated, she poured out the tale of what had transpired with Timothy in the library. On the brink of repeating the accusation that Damon was a spy, Courtney couldn't bring herself to say the words. Instead, she referred vaguely to "more of Timothy's usual nonsense" that had grated her temper to the exploding point. It was a relief to give vent to the feelings of frustration Timothy had stirred up in her; somehow she knew Damon would appreciate her inner turmoil as no one else would. He alone in all the world might applaud this night's tantrum without even knowing its theme.

"Mmm." Quietly, Damon seemed to mull over and sort through her avalanche of words. "So, am I to understand that you'd been feeling hopeful about your relationship with Lamb, but now your doubts and confusion have been revived by this argument?" His heart burned with jealousy and an almost irresistible urge to turn Courtney back into the pillows and kiss every inch of her body. However, and rather incomprehensibly, Damon was mastered by something that went beyond his own needs—a tenderness and concern for *Courtney's* well-being.

Damon's summary of her agitation left Courtney wondering if he thought her rather hysterical. One tiff with her fiancé, and here she was, waiting in Sheffield's bed at three in the morning!

"It isn't quite that simple," she said haltingly. "What you said was true. I did feel a renewed hopelessness listening to Timothy express points of view so different from mine, but I'm strong enough to weather an argument without—" Courtney swallowed, glad that her face was against Damon's lightly furred chest so she didn't have to make eye contact. "Without resorting to . . . this." She waved a tentative hand to encompass the room, the bed and their embracing bodies.

"I didn't mean to imply—"

"Please, don't say anything until I've finished. It's difficult for me to tell you, but I can't justify coming here unless I do."

"You should know by now that you can say anything to me. If you really need me, Courtney, don't let the verbal barriers I erect stand in your way." Damon smiled wryly against her brow. "I'll always listen, keep your confidence and . . . I *never* judge."

"I didn't do anything wrong, unless one counts my initial engagement acceptance. What galls me is that you're the last person I should share this with and, at the same time, the only one to whom I can speak frankly and trust to understand!"

Damon kept silent. The sweet curve of her hip and buttock molded itself agonizingly to his groin; her right breast swelled against his chest with each of her anxious breaths. The linen shirt separating their bodies only tantalized him further.

"I'm sure you can guess what I'm going to say," Courtney murmured, while a tiny part of her brain questioned why she was humiliating herself this way. Why should she feed his ego? What if he laughed at her? Still, the urge to talk was too great to suppress. "Timothy forced himself on me."

"He did *what?*" Damon's entire body tensed. Grasping Courtney's chin, he turned her face up to his. "Just exactly what do you mean by that?"

"After we managed to patch up our argument—

though I truthfully felt no better about it—he appeared next to my chair and started to kiss me. He . . . got a bit carried away." She couldn't betray Timothy with a detailed account. "I felt just horrible. Ill, really. I managed to deter him, but by then I wanted only to escape."

Damon was urgently trying to keep his mind from imagining what Lamb might have attempted, fearing that the potential existed within his own body for murder. Had Lamb hurt her? Damon's arms tightened protectively around her slight body even as he realized he had no right to object to anything that Lamb, as Courtney's future husband, might do. At the same time, Damon sensed it wasn't so much Timothy's actions that upset her, but her own damning response.

"Courtney, you've said nothing that surprises me. What *has* surprised me is your actually believing you could make a marriage with Lamb. I don't want to fight about what I've said in the past on this subject—but please tell me what made you see him in a different light!"

Courtney was silent for several moments, then let the truth slip free. "Your absence. That was the difference. I forced myself not to dream of you, and then I tried with all my strength to see Timothy as a real person and not in comparison with you."

Her body was so warm, so soft yet firm. There wasn't a woman in the world he desired as much as Courtney, or one for whom he would submit to this bizarre, late-night chitchat in bed when all he wanted to do was make love. Testing the words *make love* in his mind, Damon realized they didn't scratch the surface of what he longed to do with Courtney . . .

"Perhaps it was a mistake for me to come to your party tonight." Did she notice how hollow his voice sounded? Damon tried to get a grip on his conscience's reminder that the girl was virginal in every sense of the word, still lost in a cloud of romantic ideals. Courtney moved her head then, just enough to afford him a fresh dose of the delicate violet fragrance of her hair. Like a drug, it sent a chain reaction both physical and emotional coursing through his body.

"No doubt Timothy and my mother and sister would say you're right," she began, looking up at him with eyes that seemed larger and more strikingly amethyst in the shadows. "No argument, however, even from you, could convince me it was a mistake. I needed to be jolted back to reality as far as my proposed marriage is concerned. What if I hadn't seen you until after the wedding . . . when it would've been too late? Just thinking of it gives me chills. I believe I would have gone insane!"

Courtney shivered with revulsion at the imagined horror of sharing a bed with Timothy Lamb for the rest of her life, putting her entire body at his disposal forever. Damon's arms tightened around her like warm steel, and with a shock, she felt the thrusting length of his desire that seemed to burn her hip through the linen shirt.

"Courtney . . . I want you to go now." Husky yearning thickened his voice.

"No!" Stunned, she reacted instinctively, like a wild cat. "Why would you ask me to leave? Please! All I want"—Courtney gulped back sobs—"all I want is to be with you. I love you! I couldn't have admitted it to myself at the time, but I know I went through everything I did to get up here because I had to let out my love for you or else burst! Can't you sense the ache inside me? Is there something wrong with me, that you find me repulsive?"

"God, no!" Damon groaned. "I wish I could make love to you for days on end, but the truth is that I . . . care for you as well, Courtney. I've tried to discourage you for your own good, and at considerable personal pain." One side of his mouth quirked tightly.

"Do you really mean that?" Incredulous, Courtney

leaned back to focus more clearly on Damon's face while gripping his upper arms excitedly. "What can be so complicated in your life that we couldn't work out together? Is it your mother? If you're thinking you can't take a wife when your future is uncertain, I don't mind! Wherever you decide to live and whatever work you choose to do, I will happily agree to! I only want to be near you!" Something in his expression squeezed her heart with apprehension. "I love you!"

"Courtney!" The single word cracked the air like a bolt of lightning. "Jesus Christ, I wish you'd never come here tonight! Why can't you accept what I say and spare yourself the same pain over and over again? If you had heeded my words the day I sent you home from Parrott's Woods, we'd both be a hell of a lot better off right now!"

All the animation had drained from Courtney's face. "I can't accept it because I don't understand. And I've come after you so often because I feel alive when I'm with you, even when I hurt. And because I love you. Most girls would have meekly obeyed your orders upon being sent home from Parrott's Woods. But I'm different. I keep fighting for my heart's desires . . . even for lost causes."

A year earlier, Damon had taken a bayonet in his side during a battle, but he was sure it hadn't been as painful as this conversation. If only she had a bit more respect for authoritative men! Unfortunately, his most threatening commands only seemed to egg Courtney on.

"Look, this discussion is giving me a headache, especially since I know damn well the situation will never be resolved to the satisfaction of either of us. So I'm going to speak plainly. This will be my final word. I'm almost twice as old as you. I'm better acquainted with the harsher realities of life, and I know that the most fiery passions are frequently the first to burn out. I'm not in a position to marry you or any other woman, but even if I were, I can practically guarantee you'd find the reality of life with me far inferior to the sweet, romantic dreams that keep you awake these nights."

Courtney had been slowly drawing away from him, out of his arms, until only the silver-blue night connected them. Her heart felt like a cold, heavy stone.

"Mr. Sheffield," she said, dignity radiating from her diminutive body, "you have woefully underestimated me."

Chapter Fifteen

A faint, lilac-tinged stain was seeping into the sapphire night when Courtney stirred restlessly. Her foot brushed a muscular calf covered with crisp hair . . . not an everyday occurrence in her mahogany field bed at home.

Dimly, through a drowsy haze, she felt the warm pull of another body lying next to her under the sheet, and she remembered. Damon. Courtney snuggled in his direction and gloried in the pressure of a smooth, steely shoulder against her own soft face. Before sliding back into complete sleep, she tried to remember how it had ended. Why was she still here? Beyond recalling his cold, final words and her own consuming pain, Courtney was at a standstill. Exhaustion must have overtaken her, she'd fallen asleep and Damon had allowed her to remain, perhaps out of sympathy. Or had he inadevertently dropped off, too? When he awoke, would he be as surprised as she to find her still in his bed?

With a smile that blended contentment with mischief, Courtney relaxed and waited for sleep to wrap her in its dark, cozy embrace.

Through thick black lashes, Sheffield regarded the enchanting face of the girl who shared his bed. The sight of her lips curving with pleasure made him wonder what she could be dreaming about. Like silken honey, Courtney's hair curled back over the edge of the pillow, inviting the touch of his fingers and revealing the slim, sweet column of her neck.

Earlier, when Courtney had drifted off to sleep, Damon's better judgment had ordered him to wake her and send her home. His body and heart had not been so easily convinced, however, and he'd let her sleep, while barely dozing himself. The cravings of his body were almost keenly painful; the vixen's presence sent his thoughts chasing one after another in an endless whirl-pool.

What hurt the most was the knowledge that their relationship was near its end. Damon would probably never see her again, yet most of what he had wanted to say and share with Courtney would have to remain inside him.

Aching with regret and longing, Sheffield let his golden gaze examine Courtney's sleeping body: face, arms and tantalizing outline of breasts, waist, hips and thighs beneath the shirt and sheet that covered her. Could he leave her without making love to her? Perhaps more to the point, could he leave her *after* making love to her?

Desire's white-hot flame moved his hand. Courtney felt strange—lost in a fantasy world between slumber and reality. She sensed Damon's magnetic nearness and the heat of his gaze upon her. An excited chill skittered down her spine.

When lean fingers suddenly grazed Courtney's breast, they seemed afire, scorching her flesh through the linen. Somehow she resisted the instinct to flinch and open her eyes. A delicious, curious thrill made her heart thump with anticipation. Connecting her body to Damon's was a powerful current generated by timeless desire. Courtney surrendered herself to inexplicable needs that seemed destined to be gratified in this unreal time between night and morning when the rest of the world slept.

A half-dozen buttons were undone on Damon's shirt, which was now so provocatively draped around Courtney's torso. He stared at the creamy curve of her breast that showed above the first fastened button and was astounded to feel a very real burning deep in his gut. His mind allowed him to experience the warmth of her skin and the headiness of its fragrance. Swallowing a groan, Damon flicked another button open, then bent his head and brushed his mouth over the softness of one sweet breast. Almost reverently, he bestowed feathery kisses across Courtney's heart, collarbone and throat before nudging aside the linen to fasten his mouth on the pink rosette that puckered at his touch.

Courtney barely suppressed a shiver from head to toe. Never in her wildest fantasies had she imagined such excruciating pleasure could exist. Feeling Damon's tongue trace a flickering pattern over her taut nipple, she wondered how he knew exactly what she needed. A throbbing heaviness spread downward in waves through her belly, settling in the mysterious place where her thighs joined, the place that had made its existence known only intermittently and with much confusing tantalization. Even Courtney's fingertips seemed to tingle. She couldn't hold back any longer. Slowly, she opened eyes the color of deepest amethyst and met Damon's fiery gaze. He was kissing the hollow at the base of her throat, his raven hair adorably sleep-tousled. With involuntary abruptness, Courtney wrapped her arms around his wide back and felt his body shift slightly. Hard, warm lips covered hers in a blazing, consuming kiss that seemed to draw her heart into his. She heard herself whimper as he slid the shirt over her head, then hugged her against the length of him. Kisses that seared Courtney's unsuspecting flesh were pressed to the curve of her hip, the top of her thigh and the soft valley between her ribs.

"Courtney."

She was almost too overcome by wonder and love and acute desire to speak, but managed a soft "Yes, Damon?"

"Courtney . . . I shall probably say this only once, to you or to any woman, so pay attention!" Almost imperceptibly, his body yielded against hers as if in spiritual prelude to a more complete, physical union. "I love you. Don't doubt me and don't forget! I wouldn't say the words if I weren't positive. I don't need to lie to make love to women, Courtney . . . even to you."

Until now she had been too shy to meet his eyes, but sudden outrage lifted her head. "Your nerve is intoler—" Seeing the laughter in his amber gaze, her anger sizzled away. They were smiling as they kissed, her words smothered under Damon's insistent lips. By the time he entered her with deft tenderness, Courtney was not merely ready, but burning; she wanted nothing so much as a joining of their bodies.

She had been incredibly naive, but somehow instinct took over to guide her. As Damon's hard length moved within the sheath of Courtney's honeyed softness, the seal was set at last on their love. Slim arms, clinging to his lean-muscled back, betrayed Courtney's passion and ecstasy. When hot tears trickled over the side of Damon's jaw, he slowed and looked at her in alarm.

"Am I hurting you? Are you in pain?"

Courtney's smile glowed through her tears. "I'm in love. Don't stop!"

He laughed out loud. "Oh, Courtney!" And they continued to kiss, her legs twining around his hips, until, finally, Damon raised his head and let out a long, eloquent sigh.

She hugged him, glorying in the feel of his lips on her

throat, ear and temple. When Damon slowly withdrew from her warmth, Courtney whispered, "It was more wonderful than I ever dreamed."

Damon smiled. He kissed her again, then reluctantly got out of bed. "Sweetheart, I'm so happy you enjoyed it, but you have a great deal more pleasure to learn about. Complete satisfaction, as it were!"

He returned with a soft, wet cloth and gently removed the smeared spots of blood from between her thighs. A minute later Damon was back in bed, and they shared a cup of cold water. Courtney ran her hand over the crisp black hair on his chest.

"I'm ready to learn about complete satisfaction now." She grinned.

"Oh, you are?" Damon laughed. "Insatiable wench!"

"Mmm . . . yes, I am." She nibbled on one hard shoulder.

"Don't tempt me! You'd regret it afterward, when you tried to walk. Courtney, stop that!" He pulled her down under the covers with him and held her still against his body. "You should sleep. *All* of you needs to rest."

She giggled when he patted the triangle of hair below her belly. However, that part of her was beginning to feel rather sore, and the rest of her was beginning to feel rather sleepy.

Courtney snuggled against Damon and yawned. Soon she was asleep and purring like a kitten, but Damon's eyes were open, and pain had replaced laughter in their golden depths.

A gentle gust of cool air woke Courtney again. Without opening her eyes, she reached out for Damon and caught the steely curve that marked the merger of chest and back. After a slight pause, Damon moved downward, back into the warm feather tick and the delicate circle of Courtney's embrace.

"Don't leave me," she whispered, childlike, smiling drowsily. "Ever."

He pressed his mouth to her shoulder and watched goose bumps sprinkle down her arm. "Oh, love, you're so delectable that any man would be mad to leave you."

Courtney gave an involuntary start when deft, hot lips kissed one swollen nipple. She buried her fingers in his gleaming black hair and moaned when he moved over her body, kissing her with an urgency that took her breath away. It was incredible that she could glory in the feeling of her face being burned by the caress of his unshaved cheek.

"Damon . . . is it really true? Do you love me?"

Gently he brushed back the tendrils from her brow, thinking that she was more enchanting than ever in the peach-gold dawn. "How could I not?" Tender lips grazed her temple. Then, with a painful resolve, he moved back to his own pillow. "In spite of my own longing, I know you'd be sorry later if you welcomed my lovemaking now, sweetheart. Your mother may very well turn you away from her door as it is, but if you're unable to walk through it, I shudder to think of the consequences."

Courtney shifted her position to search out his elusive eyes. "I cannot imagine you shuddering in any situation."

Sheffield laughed softly. "Well, perhaps *Gerald* could draw at least a *shiver* of fear out of me!"

Something cold flowered in Courtney's breast. "I'm perplexed. You told me you love me. You admitted that what exists between us is not a product of my romantic imagination. What we shared here—" Tears glittered like diamonds in her eyes, but she blinked them back. "I don't need to describe what we shared and what it meant to me, and I could sense it was just as real for you. Now, for you to talk about my father's wrath! I don't understand why we should even be discussing such a thing!"

Damon couldn't bear looking at Courtney's anguished face another moment. When he swung long legs over the side of the bed, she reached for his arm, but he eluded her. "I have to shave, Courtney."

"Shave? Why do I feel as if I've suddenly fallen into a bad dream? Damon, answer me!" It took every drop of her courage to speak the next sentence. "Aren't you going to marry me?"

He halted in the middle of the room, muscles flexing from the tapered length of his back to his hard-sculpted calves. Slowly, one bronzed hand found its way to his face. For a long minute Sheffield remained thus, frozen in his private agony, then he turned and came back to the bed. "Oh, Courtney . . ." She was stiff with dread, even after he had gathered her up and kissed disheveled golden curls. "Why couldn't you have listened to me, believed me! I have said over and over that there can be no future for us. It's impossible."

"But *why?*" Her tone was keenly tragic and bewildered.

"There is more to life than the love between a man and a woman. I'm not free to form permanent relationships. Please, spare us both additional pain and accept what I tell you."

"Then you *are* married!" she cried.

"No," Damon whispered.

The intense pain in her breast made it impossible for Courtney to consider what she was saying. "Perhaps Timothy was right, then!"

Sheffield didn't answer but continued to caress her back, in the manner of an adult soothing a child.

Bitter tears scalded Courtney's cheeks. "The reason Timothy and I quarreled tonight—last night—was because he said he believes you're a British spy."

"Does he really?"

"He made a convincing argument and insisted that

many of his colleagues in Congress share his suspicions." Damon's nonchalant reaction made her feel foolish, but she rattled on nervously. "I was shocked, of course, yet some of his points—"

"So you agree with Lamb?" Sheffield's voice was laced with seeming amusement.

"No! That is—I certainly didn't! I told him—"

"Yes?"

"Well, I told him he was absolutely wrong! I said you may be enigmatic, but there's no crime in that. I said I trusted you because you have strong, honest principles underneath your cynicism!"

"Why, thank you." Damon was smiling against her hair. "Don't let me interrupt—go on!"

"You have certainly handled this neatly," Courtney remarked with a bemused laugh. "Somehow I've been maneuvered into showering you with compliments!"

"Personally, I'm having a much better time. Has my name been cleared, then?"

"Timothy did seem to be won over . . ."

"What Lamb or the Congress or all of Washington and Georgetown believe doesn't matter a damn to me as long as *you* believe in the quality of my character." Lifting Courtney's chin with a finger, Damon looked deep into her stormy eyes.

"I—" She swallowed. "I told Timothy I was positive you couldn't be a traitor to your country, that you couldn't possibly sell its secrets like some deceptive snake. I believed what I said last night, and I still do. If you can't marry me, you must have a good reason."

Damon's arms went around her like bands of steel, and the fire of his kiss blazed a trail straight to Courtney's heart. Only later would she realize just how deeply she'd been scarred.

Walking home on Bridge Street an hour later, Courtney was numb. Early-morning sunshine poured over her, and she basked in it, refusing to think or to feel or to acknowledge the curious nods of passersby who stared at her fancy cream and celery gown and the heavy man's cape she carried over one slim arm. Damon had given it to her to wear when she left the Union Tavern. He had put it on her himself, instructed her to keep the collar turned up around her face. They both had known people would stare at her and realize she was a female, for, after all, who would be crazy enough to wear a long cape in July? But if she could slip downstairs and outside quickly, her face hidden enough to prevent identification, the rest didn't matter. The escape plan had distracted her a bit from their goodbye, though she could still feel the imprint of Damon's lips on her brow and the tender place below one ear. Neither of them had had the strength for another real kiss or embrace; too much pain had mingled with exquisite pleasure.

Courtney had seen only three people on her way out: a fuzzy-eyed gambler heading for his room, and two servant girls who had been trained to keep their eyes averted. Once out the door, she'd paused behind a poplar tree and pulled off the cape. It weighted down her arm as she walked, but it was part of Damon, and that fact alone eased her suffering more effectively than any potion from the apothecary shop could.

In spite of the sunshine, it was still early. Several people trickled out of dignified brick houses, but she guessed most were still lingering over their breakfasts or dozing in bedchambers with the curtains drawn.

Upon reaching Duck Lane, Courtney circled around her house to the vacated gardener's cottage, which still contained a few sparse furnishings. Painstakingly, she folded the cape, then noted, with the pride of a girl in love, the expensive fabric and fashionable tailoring so characteristic of Damon. Before placing it in an empty drawer of the dusty bureau, she lifted it and breathed in the intoxicating scent that was Damon's alone. Tears swelled in her throat. Seconds later the drawer had been closed to hide its secret contents and Courtney was walking around the fountain. Just two months ago, on the star-strewn night of her engagement party, Sheffield had very nearly kissed her beside this fountain only minutes after their eyes had met for the first time. It seemed as if an eternity had passed since then.

Mrs. Belcher was pouring coffee in the kitchen when Courtney entered. She couldn't feel anything as trivial as embarrassment today, and suddenly it occurred to her that no one would ever imagine she had spent the night in Damon's bed, no matter how they might distrust her.

"Good morning," she said simply.

The housekeeper's eyebrows went up and down, but aloud she merely replied, "Good morning, Miss Courtney."

Unwilling to suffer through a confrontation with Beth or her mother, Courtney slipped off her shoes in the hallway and padded quietly toward the stairs at the front of the house. Then some contrary instinct prompted her to peek into the parlor. What she saw sent her thoughts reeling and left her stunned.

There, on the striped sofa, lay an innocently slumbering Timothy Lamb. He was fully clothed except for his jacket, cravat and shoes, and his tousled blond head was snuggled into Lisabeth's lap. They must have been awake most of the night, awaiting her return.

Now Beth's eyes were closed. Without waiting to discover whether her sister was awake, Courtney lifted her muslin skirts with her free hand and sped upstairs. She wished she could get into her Hepplewhite bed and hide under the covers indefinitely.

Chapter Sixteen

August 1, 1814

Fresh from a session with the dressmaker who was creating her wedding gown, a listless Courtney Ashton drifted up Water Street. What should have been a happy time had seemed like a nightmare, and even the dressmaker had wondered at Courtney's melancholy mood. She was in no hurry to reach home. Timothy would be there for luncheon, and his presence only intensified her feelings of entrapment and confused depression. What a snarled mess her life had become! Incredibly, Courtney had to force herself to remember that Washington and Georgetown were tensed, tormented by a darkening British cloud of impending danger. Were they really coming? Would they surprise the city before its citizens could escape? Tales of the atrocities perpetrated by Cockburn's plundering troops were repeated over and over in hushed whispers; tales of merciless killings, brutal rapes—often by many soldiers in turn—the burning of innocent people's homes . . . The fear and dread became more acute as the endless, scorching summer days passed without news. Would this be the week they would come? Or was it true that Washington would be passed over in favor of the more important port city of Baltimore? No one knew, not even President Madison, who was forced to wait helplessly, like everyone else.

Courtney found herself watching the woman who was walking ahead of her. Automatically, she quickened her pace to keep the slim, auburn-haired figure in sight. If her brain had been more alert, Courtney would have recognized the woman instantly. It was Prudence Hatch, her hips and her reticule swinging gently in the August sunshine.

Courtney acted completely on impulse. "Good day!" The other woman did not look back. "Mrs. Hatch! Excuse me!"

Prudence stopped and turned her head, wary and quizzical at once. Hurrying toward her was that Ashton girl, wearing an expression of sweet anguish. How enchanting she looked, clad in a soft white muslin morning gown, a white lawn tucker and a chip-straw bonnet that framed a winsome face trimmed with frothy honey curls. Her gown and bonnet were both tied with satin ribbon the color of heather. Whatever existed between this chit and Damon Sheffield, Prudence wasn't surprised. His taste was flawless, which she took as a personal compliment.

"Hello, Miss Ashton. How are you?"

Courtney searched the older woman's eyes, recognizing the glint of sadness in them. She had looked much different the day Courtney had seen her riding with Damon past Parrott's Woods. Then her face had radiated a shining joy and open pride, an expression that had filled Courtney with jealousy.

"I'm . . . fine, I suppose." She tried to smile. "You're looking well, Mrs. Hatch."

Prudence lifted a neatly plucked brow and readjusted her sunshade. "How kind of you to say so. Allow me to return the compliment, Miss Ashton. Is there word of your father? I'm certain your mother must be beside herself."

"No, there is no word of late. We assume he is well, particularly since the British have yet to make a decisive strike. As for my mother . . . her attitude and strength have astonished us all. I encouraged her to stand on her own two feet during Father's absence, but even I never imagined she'd come through so magnificently. I'm very proud of her." Courtney blushed slightly, realizing she had divulged more than Prudence Hatch's polite question required. Courtney would never say so aloud, but she knew that their common bond—Damon—made her feel instinctively closer to the beautiful widow. Where was the usual jealousy? Perhaps Courtney's depression had defused it or the worry that Damon might be gone for good . . .

Prudence smiled more warmly. "Please give your mother my regards." After an awkward pause she asked, "Was there something else you wanted to discuss?"

"Yes!" Courtney bit her lip. "I know I have no place—it's ill-mannered of me—but I can't help myself."

"Is it about Damon Sheffield?" Prudence's voice was filled with sympathy. "I won't scratch your eyes out. I have no claim on him, heaven knows, and I am well aware of the potency of his appeal."

Courtney's eyes glistened eloquently. "I—it's none of my business, but do you genuinely care for him?"

"Yes. I'd be an idiot if I didn't . . . after what I've shared with him." She put a hand on Courtney's arm. "That doesn't mean he cares back, at least in the same way. I don't have any illusions about making him fall in love with me. I know I'll never be Mrs. Damon Sheffield, but it was worth it, anyway."

Brushing away a tear, Courtney managed a quavering smile. "I—oh, I don't know how to say this, and it's so difficult on the street. . . . Could I come home with you for a short while? I promise not to take more than a few minutes of your time."

"Well . . ." Prudence sighed audibly. She had just begun to feel some of her own pain, brought on by Sheffield's absence, easing. "Yes, yes, of course. It's all right."

They were only a few steps from the east corner of Cherry Alley, so they turned and walked silently to Prudence Hatch's house. Within minutes they were inside, seated on a sofa upholstered in dusty rose satin. Courtney removed her straw bonnet and held it stiffly in her lap.

"Would you like something to drink?" Prudence asked kindly. "Lemonade or a bit of wine, perhaps?"

Glad to delay the uneasy questions she had to ask, Courtney replied, "Well, if you are having something."

Prudence rang for her maid, laughing softly, and requested two glasses of claret. When the drinks arrived, Courtney sipped hers, feeling that this must be the height of decadence. A sudden current of warmth swept over her, mixing pleasure with poignant heartache. Only with enormous effort was she able to refrain from weeping. "Thank you. This is delicious."

"Perhaps exactly what the doctor ordered?" Prudence smiled again, bending to meet Courtney's amethyst eyes. How young, and innocent, the girl was, she thought. It was one thing to be vulnerable to love, but quite another to be helpless to stop it from destroying one's peace of mind. Obviously Sheffield had had such an effect on this girl that she couldn't regain a hold on her life, and probably couldn't sleep at night either.

"I have to ask you . . ." A tear spilled onto Courtney's cheek, and she flushed, humiliated. "Have you heard from Damon Sheffield? Have you seen him?"

"Not for several days."

"Oh, please . . ." Her face crumpling, Courtney pressed a hand over her eyes. "Has he gone away, or is he in the city . . . and just keeping himself hidden from me?"

Prudence stared hard into Courtney's eyes. "Why would he do such a thing? You must know that whatever has passed between you and Sheffield, he is no coward. Nor is he a cad. He may not be for marriage, but he wouldn't hide. He'd take responsibility in the way of a true man." Her eyes opened wider. "Is . . . is there some particular need for Damon to take responsibility?"

"I don't under—" And then Courtney did. "No! No! Absolutely not! I just—"

"Never mind. I know what you 'just.'" Prudence paused to sip her claret, scrutinizing Courtney's rosy cheeks. What was it—a schoolgirl crush, a rebellion against her domineering father and an arranged betrothal? Or was it real love? Was this girl capable of a love more eloquent than her own—a love that Damon might return? "I can't be sure what to say to you . . ."

"Just tell me the truth. That's all I want—some factual report, something I can *know!* When did you see him last and what did he say to you? Do you know where he is? Is he coming back?" Courtney thought, If she knows these answers, I have a dozen more questions for her!

"All right. Yes. I'll tell you, but you must accept what I say as an adult woman. I cannot say more than I know to be true. I'm not in a position to dispense personal advice—"

"I know that! I don't need your advice! I have enough trouble dealing with the advice I get from my parents!" The dazed look disappeared from Courtney's face, and her eyes sparkled hopefully. "Don't you see? It's not knowing that is driving me mad. I can't stop imagining and wondering, but none of it gets me any closer to the truth. That's all I am interested in!"

Prudence debated whether to withhold the more

intimate details of her relationship with Sheffield. Since Courtney would almost certainly never hear from him again, it seemed that a few harsh realities might tarnish his memory and help the girl to get over him. If he were romanticized, Courtney might be twenty-five before she'd be free to love another man without reservations.

"I can't tell you where he is now, but I do know he has gone away. He told me that he'd be gone for several weeks, but in all honesty, I have a feeling it was goodbye and he simply wasn't at liberty to say so."

A shadow crossed Courtney's face, but she maintained her composure. "Mrs. Hatch—"

"Prudence, please!"

"Prudence, do you think he's involved in the war somehow? I simply can't conceive of another explanation for his mysterious comings and goings!"

"It has crossed my mind," Prudence agreed. "I'm as much in the dark as you on that one."

"Where did you see him last? And when?"

"Are you certain you want the truth?"

"Yes." Courtney winced, afraid to hear what was coming next.

"Let me think what the date was. . . . Well, it was the night of your garden party. I remember because I wasn't invited and Damon came here in his frock coat." She found it difficult to look at Courtney. Prudence felt like a monster, but the words came out anyway. "Very late, he arrived, but he left long before dawn. So, to be precise, the last place I saw him was upstairs." A pretty white finger pointed to the ceiling. "Upstairs in my bedchamber."

A low moan rose in Courtney's throat; she had to bite her tongue to keep it from escaping. So that was where he'd been while she'd waited in his bed at the Union Tavern! The cad! He'd made love to two different women in the space of just a few hours, in the middle of the night! When she'd given herself to him and felt his body fuse with her own, Damon had still been warm from Prudence Hatch! More than anything, Courtney wanted to scream.

"Thank you, Mrs. Hatch. You have been very helpful." Was that her own voice? Courtney lifted the wine glass to her dry lips and drained it. Somehow she stood and forced the corners of her mouth into a smile. "I must be going now."

"Miss Ashton, you're so pale! Perhaps you should rest for a moment. I didn't mean to upset you this way, but it seemed kinder in the long run."

"Of course. And I begged you to tell me the truth, didn't I? Don't worry about me. I'll be fine. I . . . I'll go somewhere and see if I can't manage a good cry."

Sympathy swelled in Prudence's breast. At the door, she squeezed Courtney's hand and told her gently, "If it's any consolation, I know how you feel. I've been there myself and I'd rather visit hell."

When Courtney quietly entered her house through the front door, she found Amity waiting for her a few steps away in the parlor.

"How was your fitting?"

Courtney could scarcely muster the energy to answer. Her heart throbbed terribly, and she was certain no simple physical ailment could cause such agony. "It was all right, Mother, but I don't feel very well. If you don't mind, I think I'll go upstairs and lie down for a while."

"Wait, my dear. Wait and talk with me." Amity took Courtney's cold hands and smiled into her eyes. "Beth is in the garden with Timothy, so we can be alone."

"She spends a lot of time entertaining him these days," Courtney replied listlessly.

"I know she doesn't mind. They seem to have a great deal in common."

For an instant, Courtney was alert. What was it about Amity that seemed so different? Was it possible that she was revealing depths Courtney had never seen before? There was a gleam in her mother's brown eyes and subtle shadings in her voice. "Yes, they do seem to get along quite well." Courtney let Amity lead her into the parlor, where they sat down on the striped sofa.

"Darling child, for a bride-to-be you don't appear very happy. I'm worried about you."

"Oh, Mama . . ." Courtney removed her bonnet to hide the tears that burned her eyes. "I don't know what to say."

"You can say anything to me. I won't tell your father."

Shocked, Courtney gaped in disbelief. "You won't?"

"Haven't you noticed a change in me since Gerald left? You encouraged it!" Amity laughed softly, confidently. "I've finally realized I can have relationships independent of him, and independent of my role as his wife. Your father may have my love and respect, but he doesn't own me."

"Mama! Heavens! How lovely to hear you say those words!" Courtney beamed. "But when Father comes home, how will he feel about this attitude of yours? Will he intimidate you all over again?"

Amity shrugged, her eyes sparkling like those of a young girl. "We'll have to see, won't we?" She grinned. "But I doubt it."

"Do you know . . . so do I!"

"How happy it makes me to see you smile! If only Timothy could bring about such a reaction. Please, Courtney, tell me what's troubling you. You don't want to get married this month, do you?"

Courtney swallowed, then shook her head. Golden lashes brushed her dusky cheeks as she looked into her lap.

"Can you tell me why?"

"I . . . I'd rather not. But I think I'll be feeling more myself before too long. I'm tired of sadness and discontent."

Amity smoothed back her daughter's curls. "I see. Well, if you ever want to talk to someone, I'm available. In the meantime . . ." Gently, she lifted Courtney's chin. "Let us see what can be done to postpone the wedding without alerting Timothy and the rest of the family to your state of mind, hmm? Just to give you time to sort things out."

"You would do that . . . for me?"

"Well, of course, darling! What are mothers for?"

Chapter Seventeen

August 24, 1814

Dolley Madison was framed by the rectangle of sunlight streaming through an upstairs window. Oblivious to the heat, and to the perspiration that glued her lilac muslin gown to her plump body, she stared through a long spyglass at the grimy tangle of people, horses and vehicles swarming over Pennsylvania Avenue. So many anxious faces! The city was choked by the news that the British, who had begun their thirty-mile-northward march on August 18, were truly coming to attack Washington. All the long months of speculation, worry and reassurances had ended with the abrupt appearance in the Patuxent River of English ships loaded with thousands of troops, and the explanation was appallingly simple. Wellington, having beaten Napoleon at last, had been free to send his battle-weary men to America so that they might win that war for Britain as well.

Like ostriches, the people of Washington had tried to ignore unpleasant realities for months; after all, Cockburn and his fleet had been hovering like vultures in Chesapeake Bay for nearly two years! Unfortunately, by the time Napoleon fell, Washington was too complacent to face reality. Dolley sighed, remembering that even John Armstrong, the Secretary of War, had insisted as late as yesterday that the British would strike at Baltimore rather than at Washington. As for the residents, there was no longer any place for them to hide. The pitiful fact was that few people had prepared for an efficient escape in case of an emergency. Dolley could almost smell the panic that churned in the hot, dusty air outside as the urge to flee conflicted with desperate attempts to find wagons to help salvage valued possessions.

The President's lady paused to rub her burning eyes, then returned her gaze to Pennsylvania Avenue. *Where* was James? He had assured her that he would return this afternoon for dinner. Several Cabinet members and their wives were due at three o'clock, as well as the officers James planned to invite today. Of course, considering the tumultuous state of affairs, Dolley could barely think of playing hostess, but it helped her to know that her husband had this appointment in his own home. James was the sort of calm, reliable man who would honor an appointment even if he had to excuse himself in the middle of a battle.

Through the spyglass she caught sight of a slim figure hurrying up the drive. The girl was clad in the plainest of muslin gowns, which she held high over pretty ankles as she ran, while a chip-straw bonnet hid both her face and her hair.

Dolley was surprised to feel a twinge of apprehension. Don't be irrational! she chided herself. But the thoughts still intruded, the same ones which had made anger boil up in her for weeks. As fear of a British attack had grown, many inhabitants of Washington had vented their frustrations on the President, going so far as to declare that if Mr. Madison attempted to move out of his house in the event of an invasion, they would see to it that he fell with it.

No, no, it wasn't possible that anyone could have so twisted a heart as to want to harm her—and furthermore, such a mean-spirited person would win disgust rather than fear from Dolley.

A knock at the door announced John Sioussat, the Madisons' French major-domo. There were only a few servants to help her in her hour of need: Sioussat, his assistant, a gardener, a coachman, the cook and, of course, Sukey, the First Lady's own maid. Yesterday there had been a hundred-man guard surrounding the President's Mansion, but by this morning all had disappeared without a word.

The Frenchman bowed, clad, as always, in an impeccable uniform. "Mademoiselle Courtney Ashton is downstairs. She begs a moment of your time."

"You are certain the young lady is Miss Ashton?" Dolley felt silly, yet it seemed wisest to quell her apprehensions as quickly as possible.

"Absolutely certain, madame."

"In that case, I'd be delighted to receive her." She paused as he bowed, then added, "I hope none of you are encountering any problems? I want to be told immediately if there is something wrong, particularly if you have news of the President."

"The situation is unchanged, madame. Paul is preparing the table for dinner. He has already brought the cider, ale and Madeira up from the cellar, as you ordered, and transferred the bottles into coolers." The Frenchman tried to smile. "I do not doubt for one moment that Monsieur le President will be here for dinner at three o'clock, just as he told us."

"Of course . . . you're right. Well, we mustn't keep Miss Ashton waiting, with the British nearly on our doorstep."

The instant Sioussat turned to leave, Dolley lifted the spyglass once again and peered through it in search of her husband. So complete was her preoccupation that she failed to notice Courtney Ashton's entrance.

"Excuse me?" Courtney whispered after an uncomfortable minute. "I feel terrible, disturbing you this way."

Dolley spun around in her chair, looking repentant, and held out plump arms. "How rude I am!" She embraced the girl. "Sit down, please, and tell me why you're here. My dear! You are positively bedraggled! Has something happened? Don't say it's Gerald, or your mother!"

"No! Nothing like that!" Courtney sank into the chair opposite Dolley's and wearily pulled at a bonnet ribbon. "I went with Timothy to help Mrs. Lamb pack. As you know, they live just a short distance from here. I truly wanted to be of assistance, but she is the most—"

"Crotchety." Dolley smiled. Her expression reflected both mischief and charity.

"Yes, crotchety!" Courtney exclaimed, relaxing visibly. "Mrs. Lamb is a difficult old woman. She wouldn't even allow me to fold a blanket into the trunk. My method wouldn't do. When she began whining for Beth, I couldn't bear another moment."

"I was just about to ask you, where *is* Lisabeth? Have she and Amity fled? Really, my dear, it is exceedingly foolish, even reckless, for *you* to remain. I know your heart must insist that you wait for your young Mr. Lamb, but I confess to annoyance with him for not prevailing upon you to go with Amity and Lisabeth—"

"Mother is ill," Courtney interrupted. "Beth was with her all morning, but apparently Mother was sufficiently improved by midday so my sister could leave her with Mrs. Belcher and come to the aid of the Lambs."

"How heroic of your sister." The First Lady took a pinch of snuff, her brows lifted in eloquent crescents.

"As for Amity, I am most alarmed. A *most* inconvenient time to fall ill! Are you certain it's nothing serious?"

"It's ague, of a sort that provokes misery and fever but, fortunately, nothing more permanent. Beth assured me she wouldn't have left Mother's side if she hadn't been considerably less feverish."

"If that's the case, you must bundle her up and leave Georgetown!" Dolley cried.

Courtney's eyes were calm, brilliant sapphires set off by starry lashes. "If I might be frank, I'd say that I believe Mother does not intend to leave. She could never pretend to be ill, but her mind could create a physical condition that would enable her to remain at home."

"But, my dear, what reason could Amity have—"

"The very same one that keeps you here in spite of the danger all around! Truly, dear Mrs. Madison, you are in much graver danger than my uncelebrated mother is across Rock Creek in Georgetown!"

"Courtney, has she not heard of common sense and self-preservation? My husband will arrive at any moment to attend to me, but the same cannot be said of Gerald Ashton, and I cannot believe he'd approve of the three of you flitting about a city on the verge of attack!"

The First Lady's pink cheeks were contagious. There was nothing Courtney would have liked better than to escape from the heat, fear and confusion. Many neighbors had offered to take them, but Amity had been strangely stubborn. The sudden attack of ague had come just in time to save her from more arguments, or the possibility of being forced to evacuate.

"Mother knows she *should* go, and, of course, she's aware that Father would insist if he were present. But, you know, she has changed recently. She's found independence, yet it will take some practice for her to learn how to channel it."

"And you think that somehow Amity's new, strong will has brought on this illness so she can stay where she is?"

Courtney nodded. "I can't prove it, naturally. Call it a daughter's intuition."

Dolley digested this in silence, turning her eyes automatically back to Pennsylvania Avenue. "It seems so unlike Amity. I find it difficult to imagine her choosing the likelihood of danger over safety. Surely she has heard the stories of the atrocities committed by British soldiers along the coastline! Independence is one thing, but I must wonder if your mother has lost some of her reason!"

"No. In fact, I would say she has discovered depths and possibilities within herself that were dark until now. It was easy to live in Father's shadow." Courtney's lovely face grew radiant. "We've talked more in the past month than in all my previous life. Honestly, Mrs. Madison, I never would have believed it, but we've grown exceedingly close."

Dolley's plump face crinkled into a warm smile. "War is horrendous, and yet even in the darkest chasms we can find unexpected lights that might not have shone without the spark of crisis."

Courtney removed her bonnet. "That is certainly true," she murmured, gazing reflectively at the dusty brim. "One tends to reevaluate so many areas of one's life." She paused and blinked, barely stopping her tongue from rambling on indiscreetly. "As for Mother, I sense it means a great deal to her to stay and defend her home. She's just gotten a grip on some self-confidence, and I think she's afraid her newfound enlightenment would disappear if she ran away like the frightened, helpless female she used to be. Mother never gave a positive yes or no on any subject without first consulting Father. It means a lot to her to prove to him *and* to herself that she is capable of taking care of their home in his absence."

"Well, I can understand that. I feel the same weight of responsibility in spite of the constant assurances I receive that, since I am a female, it is perfectly fine if I tremble witlessly in the face of danger." Dolley raised her eyebrows as a hint of cynical amusement touched her lips. "Frankly, that attitude galls me. Don't women have backbones the same as men? I have no qualms about using mine to stand up straight and face the British with courage and dignity if they should happen to arrive before James. Certainly men have no monopoly on courage! All the one hundred men who guarded me last night have since disappeared."

Smiling, Courtney touched the First Lady's dimpled hand. "I need no convincing, Mrs. Madison. I've argued that case for so long in my home, my family thinks me peculiar."

"And now your mother has suddenly glimpsed a light of truth?"

"Yes, but she couldn't have picked a worse time to agree with me!" Courtney groaned, turning midnight-blue eyes toward the dusty throng on Pennsylvania Avenue. "I suppose I should be going . . ."

"I'm sure Mr. Lamb is very concerned for your safety, dear," Dolley agreed, thinking of her own absent, tardy James.

"I doubt that. Besides, I haven't time to traipse all the way back to Timothy's house. He and his mother have Beth there to help them. Obviously, her heart is in *that* task, but I don't share her confidence about Mother's condition. I think my place right now is in Georgetown."

Dolley was too preoccupied to wonder at the peculiar pattern of relationships and emotions in the Ashton and Lamb families, but kindness came automatically. "Sweet child," she admonished, putting out a hand to stop Courtney from readjusting her bonnet, "I cannot allow you to leave without some nourishment. We are having several friends in for dinner at three o'clock, so I know there is an ample selection of food downstairs, not to mention coolers of cider and Madeira. I think we should go and investigate."

Courtney was momentarily bewildered. Did the First Lady actually believe people would arrive for a party as if this were a day like any other? Then Courtney saw something in Dolley's eyes that belied her cheery demeanor.

"You're very kind," Courtney said. If it was easier for Dolley to pretend that her afternoon would proceed as planned, including the arrival of her husband in time for the dinner party, Courtney would cooperate. If the British invasion kept invited guests away, the President might not arrive either. Suddenly she felt cold and shivered involuntarily in spite of the sultry afternoon. "I admit that a tall glass of cider would be wonderful."

The two women had taken no more than a few steps toward the doorway when John Sioussat appeared and made a tense bow.

"Madame," he said through tight lips, "a messenger has delivered regrets from Mr. and Mrs. Jones and their daughter, Lucy. Because of the present state of alarm and the bustle of preparation for the worst that may happen, Mrs. Jones feels it would be wiser to dispense with the pleasure of your hospitality today. She prays you will accept this excuse and adds that she is packing, though without any idea of where they might go."

For a moment Dolley's composure and ready smile eluded her. "Well . . . of course, I certainly understand." The smile flickered, then held steady. "No doubt it's to be expected. Have Paul remove three plates, French John, but leave the rest for now."

"Yes, madame."

Dolley held her tongue until he had turned to exit, but the question broke free. "There's—there isn't any word of the President?"

"No, madame, but rest assured that I will hasten to

bring you any message he might send." The French steward closed his mouth but did not move to leave. Courtney could see veins distend in his neck and brow before agitation got the better of him and incautious words spilled out. "Mme. Madison, won't you let me spike the cannon at the gate and lay a train of powder so those cursed British will be blown back to London if they dare to cross the threshold of the President's Mansion? It galls me merely to stand by, first watching the hundred who were sent to guard you disappear so cowardly while you display more courage than all of them—than all the army!—"

The President's wife answered Sioussat's emotion-choked outburst with hands that reached out to squeeze his firmly. "I appreciate your feelings, but even in war there are advantages not to be taken. Do not think you are simply standing idly by, John, because your presence means more to me than you can imagine. For now, however, we must remain calm and continue about our business until the President returns to say what our next course of action will be." Smiling as she felt the steward's fingers gradually relax, Dolley added, "Please ask Paul to remove the plates now, and warn him that Miss Ashton and I are about to inspect the foods he has prepared for this afternoon. We don't want to send her off to Georgetown without proper fortification!"

When Sioussat's footsteps could no longer be heard, Courtney blurted, "Mrs. Madison, perhaps there are other matters you need to attend to. I mean, I wouldn't mind at all going downstairs without you. I promise to eat something," she ended lamely.

"I have been awake since dawn. Before, if the truth were known. I may choose to behave in a manner many would deem unrealistic—waiting for my husband, or simply believing he will come home as he said—but my mind still continues to function!" The cheeks that were often rumored, in catty whispers, to be rouged now shaded naturally to a rich rose befitting Dolley's character. "Come with me, Courtney. Not only am I quite prepared to leave if I must, I have also found time today to write a detailed letter to my sister Lucy."

Courtney followed obediently through a connecting door to the spacious dressing room where a traveling trunk had been carefully packed with clothes. "But, Mrs. Madison, surely you plan to take more than this?"

"If we can find a wagon, I shall pack more. There are other things downstairs as well, which you'll see, but still and all, I must be realistic and take only what will fit into our carriage."

As they proceeded toward the stairway, Courtney pondered this and felt bitter pangs of sadness, anger and disbelief at the thought of the furnishings and paintings in the President's Mansion possibly being destroyed. How could this be happening? How could the British be so despicable and barbaric as to drive the President and his lady from their home and threaten their safety and that of the beautiful structure which belonged to all Americans?

"If those red-coated reptiles so much as lay a finger on you or Mr. Madison or this house," Courtney fumed, "we should go straight over, invade England and give the silly King and the Prince Regent a taste of their own medicine! Send them running out in their nightshirts and demolish the palace and Carlton House as well!" She gave Dolley a demonic smile. "Isn't that a lovely plan?"

The First Lady was momentarily speechless, then her blue eyes crinkled at the corners. "Your ideas are undeniably original . . . and appealing, my dear. I'll be certain to pass them along to James."

Just as they started down the stairs, a figure appeared at the bottom and rushed up to meet Dolley. It was the mayor.

"My dear Mrs. Madison!" he puffed. "You must pardon me for bursting in without warning, but today—"

"Have you news of my husband?" she interrupted sharply.

Before James Blake could reply, the faint thunder of cannon caused all three pairs of eyes to open wide. "Oh, Lord, listen to that!" the mayor moaned. "I've not come with word of the President, but I do know that his message would echo my own. You must flee, my lady! The British draw nearer by the minute."

Dolley resumed her descent. "Have you a wagon, Mayor?"

"I—why, no," he sputtered, caught off guard by her unexpected, no-nonsense question.

"I appreciate your concern, Mayor Blake, but the President will be here shortly, and it is my ardent wish to remain until his arrival so that we may undertake our journey together." Dolley delivered this short speech without stopping on her way toward the dining room. There was no hint of rudeness in her manner. On the contrary, she was as warm and pleasant as usual, yet it was plain that she had no intention of continuing the discussion.

After the official wished the two women Godspeed and took his own anxious leave, Courtney followed in Dolley's wake as they entered the state dining room. The table was set with fine linen and plate holders stood by the fireplace, filled with dishes, but it seemed that the actual food remained in the kitchen. Setting off again, the First Lady showed a twinge of nostalgia when she took her visitor into the Green Room. Courtney pretended to be ignorant of the circular shelves that President Jefferson had had built into the wall there. When one touched a spring, the shelves revolved into the pantry, where servants could fill them with food. Fondly, Dolley spoke of Jefferson and of the touches of genius he had left behind in the mansion for which he'd had such dreams.

"In the parlor, where President Jefferson liked to work at night," Dolley related as they continued to the kitchen, "he had a wonderful little hidden cabinet installed. About midnight, he'd touch the spring and the door would open to reveal a fresh plate of cakes as well as goblets of cold wine and water."

Emotion welled in Courtney. Impulsively, she reached for the First Lady's hand. "I understand why you don't want to leave."

"Well . . . I feel there is a responsibility, a trust that is in my keeping." Her voice trailed off, and for a moment tears seemed to be threatening.

In the kitchen, various joints turned on spits before the fire, dripping juices into the flames. Added to these aromas were those of the vegetables, sauces and potatoes that simmered in their pots on the fireplace grate. Courtney inhaled and felt her insides churn unexpectedly. Suddenly she was ravenous.

Welcoming the diversion, Paul Jennings filled a plate for the unknown girl from Georgetown, who was looking altogether delectable herself. The expression of guilty pleasure on her face made him smile. For a moment the crisis was forgotten, until a long rumble of cannon brought them all back to reality.

Courtney's eyes sought the First Lady, who was standing near the hearth. Flames sent flickering shadows over Dolley's face and accentuated the alarm that pierced too deeply to be concealed. Even in the fire's glow her face was bleached by fear.

"I'll just wager," Courtney managed to declare, "that we are hearing the evidence of *our* victory over the British! Our cannon are doubtlessly helping to chase those swine, and I hope they aren't able to run fast enough!"

Dolley mustered a wan, grateful smile even as tears

shone in her eyes. "At this moment I can only pray to God that James is safe. What is so difficult is the knowledge that he has enemies among his own people. Many blame him for what is happening . . . and sometimes have such shriveled hearts. So much hostility—" She broke off at the sound of new thunder on this sunlit afternoon. Looking in the direction from which it came, the President's lady's expression changed and her back straightened with fresh resolve. Softly, the usually gentle and generous-spirited Dolley muttered, "Lord, how I wish we had ten thousand men to sink our enemy to the bottomless pit!"

Courtney's eyebrows went up in surprise, and Jennings emitted a gasp, clearly stunned by his mistress's words. However, they were all distracted by Sukey, Dolley's maid, whom Courtney had spied earlier lolling in an upstairs window. The girl was running down the stairs, yelling agitatedly, and Dolley went to meet her, Courtney and Jennings hurrying in her wake.

"It's Jim! Jim Smith!" Sukey wailed. "He says we've surrendered!"

At that moment Smith burst in the front door. His horse was visible, tied unceremoniously near the door, and the young black man appeared thoroughly exhausted and upset. Sweat streamed over his brow as he pulled off his crumpled hat and approached the First Lady.

"You must tell me, is the President safe?" Dolley demanded. Jim Smith was Madison's freeman, and he had accompanied him to Bladensburg, the site of this day's battle.

"Yes, ma'am, he's safe, but he wants you to clear out! I mean right now! General Armstrong's ordered a retreat, so there's no time to lose. Before we know it, those slimy redcoats will be swarming over Washington like maggots!"

Courtney felt removed somehow, as if she were

watching the drama through the misty veil of a dream. Panicked voices rose all around her. Paul Jennings grasped Courtney's forearm as he wondered fearfully how they would escape with their lives. Sukey swooned, moaning, but Jim Smith braced her and fanned her with his hat. It was all too incredible to believe, Courtney thought numbly. They appeared on the brink of doom, and instead of being with her own family in her own house, she was in the President's Mansion with his wife! Courtney shook her head sharply in an effort to dispel the fog that cushioned her thoughts and emotions.

Dolley, meanwhile, conducted herself in a serene manner. If Jim Smith had told her that it might rain, her smile couldn't have been more benign. "I certainly appreciate your advice, and I suppose we must go, even if the President does not return in time . . . but there are a few matters I must attend to first." She glanced around. "Where is French John?"

"Right here, madame." Sioussat appeared in the hall as if on cue.

"I would like you to bring the carriage around and have the things loaded—"

"I have just finished doing so, madame. Also, I have some encouraging news." He smiled slightly. "We have a wagon. When I went to the stables a short while ago, I found one outside the entrance."

"But from where?" Jennings wondered for all of them.

"I haven't the slightest idea! It's rather like magic, *n'est-ce pas?*"

"Magic or not, as long as it's real, we shall put it to good use! I want to pack more clothing, the silver, as many books as we've time for, our clock—you know the one, French John—and . . ." Dolley paused, beaming. "And the crimson velvet draperies from my sitting room!"

"I don't think you should—" Jim Smith began, taking a few steps in Dolley's direction.

"I haven't time to discuss it now," she interrupted kindly. "Please excuse Miss Ashton and myself."

As they walked toward the reception rooms, Courtney remarked to the First Lady, "I've been wondering what items French John has already packed in the carriage. You said there was much more downstairs, and I assumed it was the silver and other valuables."

Dolley's eyes twinkled for an instant. "Heavens! Silver would never by my first priority, Courtney! I spent hours packing up James's papers—four cases full—and now that we have a wagon, I'll do my best to pack more." Suddenly she seemed to remember that Courtney was not usually to be found strolling at her side. "My dear, I've been so thoughtless! What shall we do about you? I cannot allow you to go off alone all the way to Georgetown, considering these new circumstances, and I don't want to have you wait and ride with me. That might be even more dangerous. If the British don't get here before we depart, they, or some hostile citizens of Washington, might capture my carriage while it is in flight."

"I don't want you to worry—"

"Well, I most certainly shall! I'll talk to John, but I believe the best thing might be for you to go with the wagon when it leaves. They can take you to Georgetown and then go on from there."

"I truly wish you'd leave now yourself, Mrs. Madison," Courtney implored. "As you said, the British could arrive—"

"Hush. My mind is made up, and it only spends our precious minutes to argue about this."

No sooner had they entered the dining room than John Sioussat appeared in the opposite doorway, holding a good-sized crate. "I'll start immediately on the silver, madame." He crossed to join them near the sideboard and added, "Jo Bolin has just left with the carriage. Unfortunately, there was a rather unruly group badgering him outside, but they were put down by three American soldiers, apparently in the act of retreating."

Dolley was piling silver into the box. "You'd think people would be too preoccupied with saving their own lives to bother about James and me. Well, I can't worry about it. We'll all simply say a prayer for Jo's safe arrival in Maryland, with the President's papers intact. Now, John, you leave this to Courtney and me. I have something else to occupy you." She turned dark blue eyes toward the painting of George Washington that dominated the room. Sioussat and Courtney followed her gaze and then stared at the First Lady in disbelief.

"No . . . you aren't thinking . . ." French John whispered.

"Oh, yes, I am!" Dolley retorted. The life-sized, magnificent portrait by Gilbert Stuart seemed to look warmly back at her as if they were old friends.

Courtney and the President's wife continued to pack the silver until Sioussat returned with Magraw, the gardner. Because the painting was securely nailed into the wall on all four sides, Dolley gave the men permission to remove it as quickly as possible by breaking the frame with an ax. Courtney tried not to cringe as French John mounted the short ladder, ax in hand. But before the first blow could be struck, they were interrupted by the arrival of Colonel Charles Carroll. He was the officer who had been charged with protecting the President's home and lady but had disappeared mysteriously a few hours earlier. Now, flushed and sweaty, he pulled off his hat and made a deep bow. In answer to the question in Dolley's eyes, Carroll explained that he and his men had ridden out to have a look at the battle.

"Ma'am," he puffed at last, "there isn't time for conversation. The British are closing on Washington City, and we must see that you are safe away when they arrive!"

"Of course, Colonel, I am aware that I have to leave the President's Mansion," Dolley replied distractedly, "but first I must see to it that this portrait of Mr. Washington is properly removed and placed in safe-keeping."

Courtney stifled a giggle at the sight of Colonel Carroll's eyes bulging incredulously. As French John's ax cracked the handsome frame surrounding the portrait of the first President, who was clad in black velvet and standing beside a scarlet-covered table, Carroll tried to reason, loudly, with Mrs. Madison. It seemed that James had sent instructions for her to meet him and the Joneses at Bellevue, which was Charles Carroll's own house on the northern edge of Georgetown. This was no time to bother with a mere picture!

Calmly, Dolley told him, "I shall do my husband's bidding, Colonel, but I am an adult and capable of thinking and walking by myself." She smiled slightly and added, "This painting is no bother to me."

Colonel Carroll fumed as the men continued to separate the canvas from its frame. Meanwhile, Dolley returned her attention to the silver. When the crate was filled, she simply opened her net reticule and used it for the overflow.

Courtney was in the midst of piling flatware on the sideboard when the First Lady surprised her with a question. "Courtney, my dear, forgive me, but have you had word of that indecently handsome Mr. Sheffield?" Dolley's eyes sparkled irrepressibly when Courtney looked up to meet them, her own face exposing the vivid emotions which had been kept at bay by the day's distracting string of crises. "I don't mean to be rude, but something told me that you two were more than nodding acquaintances when I saw you exchange greetings at the garden party last month."

"I . . . oh . . . well, what a time to mention Mr. Sheffield!" Courtney knew that her cheeks were blazing, yet there was nothing she could do. "Actually, I haven't seen the man since that night."

Dolley dropped a fork into her reticule. "Neither has anyone else I know." At that moment Sioussat and Magraw pulled the painting free of the frame and held it aloft triumphantly. "Ah! Well done!" she called. "Please, we mustn't separate the canvas from the stretcher. Just set it on the floor, and we'll attempt to move it in one piece."

Courtney felt the penetrating gaze return to her and realized that the subject of Damon had not been dismissed. "I don't know where he is, Mrs. Madison. I can see this isn't a time to mince words coyly, so I will simply say that yes, I was attracted to Damon Sheffield —partly because my father forced me into an unwanted betrothal—but matters never became . . . serious between us. I haven't the faintest idea where he is now or what he's doing."

Dolley smiled with enigmatic kindness. "This isn't an interrogation, my dear!" she exclaimed. "I am simply an advocate of true love, particularly since one is married for such a long time. I don't mean to sound unkind, but I never thought Timothy Lamb was a match for you."

Courtney's heart began to sting as if frostbitten. "Aside from my duty and responsibility to my parents and Timothy, there is the larger matter of Mr. Sheffield himself. As I have said, I don't know where he is . . . and he hasn't expressed a wish to be a match for me in Timothy's place—good, bad or otherwise."

"I'm sorry I mentioned it," Dolley apologized, folding plump fingers over Courtney's slim hand. "Certainly we all have enough to worry about today . . . and I am romantic to the point of obtuseness. I apologize, my dear, but a man like that seems to bring to the surface every romantic impulse that ever sparked in me!"

Before Courtney could respond, two men burst in. She was barely listening as they identified themselves as Robert de Peyster and Jacob Barker from New York Town. As if sent by God, they offered to help in any way they could, and minutes later were on their way out with the precious painting which Dolley had instructed them to transport to a certain humble farm. She went with them to the door. Magraw was securing the last of the valuables in the wagon, including the silver most recently packed.

"Gentlemen, if you cannot save these things, destroy them," the First Lady cautioned. Then she turned back to tell Courtney it was time for her to leave; the wagon would take her to Georgetown before doubling back. But the girl was not in the entry hall or the dining room, nor was she to be found in the kitchen, or in any other room that Dolley searched. As the wagon clattered off down the drive, the portrait safely fastened on top of the load, the First Lady's relief was mingled with very real apprehension. What on earth had happened to Courtney? Dolley herself would be leaving the President's Mansion within minutes, possibly for the last time, but all she could think of was Courtney and the danger which saturated the streets of Washington on this blackest of days.

Courtney's heart beat wildly as she picked up her muslin skirts and hurried down Pennsylvania Avenue at a near run. Upon slipping out the Madisons' kitchen door, her reticule stuffed with the remains of her interrupted meal, Courtney had intended to head for the stables, where she might disguise herself in boys' clothing. The risk of running about the city alone was great enough right now; it wouldn't do for her to bump into a redcoat if she looked to be a lost young maiden! Unfortunately, the disguise plan had been squelched by the presence on the mansion grounds of a crowd of hoodlums. Some had carried tools from the stables, apparently to use as weapons, and others had begun to chant, "Hang Jemmy!" and "String him up!" Courtney had hidden in a row of tall shrubs, trying to decide whether to return to Dolley's protection, when she'd seen a carriage pull alongside the portico. The driver had fought off blows from the mob while Sioussat had rushed Dolley Madison and Sukey into the carriage. Moments later they had barreled off down the drive, followed by a huge cloud of dust and Courtney's fading confidence. The wagon had already left, Colonel Carroll had disappeared again and Sioussat could not help her because he was taking shelter at Octagon House.

So, less than half an hour later, Courtney found herself alone on Pennsylvania Avenue, frankly scared. Although the evacuating crowds had thinned, these people with their broken-down wagons and wheelbarrows seemed less refined and more desperate. Worse were the drunken, hostile bands that searched for "Jemmy," and the haunted faces of retreating soldiers.

To take her mind off the dangers that lurked only steps away, Courtney thought about Damon. Where was he? The mere taste of his name was bittersweet, but that question stabbed deep. Stepping over ruts, she fashioned a daydream of distracting enchantment wherein Damon suddenly appeared on Pennsylvania Avenue, galloping alongside President Madison and a few prominent aides. He spied her, and his face lit up with love and relief. Then Courtney found herself scooped up and sitting in front of him, safe within the circle of his steely arms. Damon bade farewell to the President, saying that he must see to Courtney's safety now, and as they rode toward Georgetown, he begged her to forgive him for having disappeared. He explained that the missions he performed for President Madison were absolutely secret, and the last had been so dangerous that he'd feared he might not return at all.

The thought of her worrying or grieving tore him apart, so it had seemed best—

Courtney's romantic reverie was broken by a mangy dog's sudden dash across her path. Although she managed to avoid being knocked down, the daydream had split open, leaving behind only one chilling piece of reality: the true Damon Sheffield *hadn't* returned to rescue her. Was he, like so many hundreds of other young men today, wounded? Or worse?

Perspiration made rivulets between her breasts and shoulders. Courtney couldn't remember ever experiencing such heat, but under normal circumstances she would never drag herself through a scorching afternoon. Approaching a more densely populated stretch of Pennsylvania Avenue, she saw that a large number of local courtesans had not joined the exodus from the city. They were administering to the retreating troops in the ways the men needed most—with water, bread and damp towels. One of the soldiers, his eyes very bloodshot and with several days' growth of beard, leaned into a poplar tree's miserly wedge of shade and stuffed bread crusts into his mouth. As she drew near him, Courtney remembered the food inside her reticule and felt only a moment's instinctive panic. The soldier's eyes sharpened and his nose twitched like a rat's. Almost immediately, he located the perfume of a real meal.

A filthy hand snaked out to grip Courtney's arm. "Good mistress, would you have a bite of food to share with a starving soldier?"

Her conscience reminded her of Gerald, who himself might well be dependent on charity now, yet this man was truly repellent. Courtney began to reach into her reticule to give him a piece of beef, but he grabbed her and tried to pull it out of her hands. The foul stench of his unwashed body filled her nostrils, and she lashed out, kicking, struggling, shouting a plea for help.

Courtney felt her head strike the trunk of the poplar tree and realized, dizzily, that someone was attacking the soldier, who had released his hold on her arm and her reticule. Coppery curls and what appeared to be a cast-iron ladle swam before her eyes until the images and colors blurred together and disappeared.

Chapter Eighteen

August 25, 1814
1:00 A.M.

Amber eyes . . . champagne breeches tucked into knee boots . . . a hard-muscled body with broad, straight shoulders tapering into lean hips . . . a scent that blended brandy and tobacco with other intoxicatingly masculine elements . . . sun-bronzed hands with long, sensuously sculpted fingers . . . wind-ruffled hair as black and gleaming as a raven's wing . . . a dark pirate's face chiseled to accentuate both ominous moods and flashes of white laughter . . .

Courtney let her mind carry her along, luxuriating in the disconnected images of Damon Sheffield that, one by one, washed over her. Some part of her was aware this wasn't a dream; only a thin barrier held back wakefulness. Still, Courtney could hear Damon's voice, warm, husky velvet, without its usual caustic edge. It was too real to be part of a fantasy. Wasn't it?

"Say, there, are you ever goin' to wake up?"

A hand shook Courtney's shoulder in accompaniment to the grating female voice. Courtney moaned, then opened hesitant eyes, hoping against hope that Damon would be standing above her. Instead, she found that her companion resembled a gaudy, eccentric, good fairy. Perhaps I'm still dreaming, Courtney thought, blinking.

"My name's May Willing, honey," the woman said, leaning over to pat Courtney's cheek. Her breath smelled of rum, while the rest of her reeked of cheap perfume. "I suppose you're wonderin' how you came to be here with a tart like me." She presented an expansive derrière to Courtney as she brought her chair and jug closer to the sofa.

"Well, uh, Mrs. Willing, I *am* curious." Her head began to throb, and Courtney put a hand up, discovering a tender lump centered on her crown.

"If I'd had a bit of ice, I'd have donated it to that nasty bump you took off the tree," May declared, pointing a plump finger at the window as she lifted her jug with the other hand. "Put you right out, it did."

Courtney tried to concentrate. The tree . . . the bright copper curls arranged high above May Willing's painted face . . .

"That man!" she exclaimed. "The soldier who tried to take my reticule! I remember now. He pushed me against the tree. Were you the person who—"

"I bashed him good!" May bragged. "I was givin' drinks to the boys comin' through from Bladensburg—had my biggest washtub full of water—when I seen that scum after your bag. I just took after him with my ladle. It's good and heavy—cast iron." She took another swig from the jug to congratulate herself. "A couple of decent soldiers were happy to bring you upstairs in exchange for a peek up your skirts." May winked. "So here we are. I've just whiled away the evenin' waitin' for you to come out of your dreams and waitin' to see what those slimy lobsterbacks have in mind for the rest of Washington."

Fully awake now, Courtney sat up, wide-eyed. "The British! Oh, my God! What time is it? I have to go home!" The pounding in her head intensified. "This silly bump!" she cried, blinking back tears of frustration. "What wretched luck, and on today of all days!"

"Not so wretched, honey. Wanderin' about the streets alone like that, you could've easily had worse done to you by that lout, or by one even lower. Hard times like these bring out the animal in mean men. Here, you have a long drink of this. It'll fix the pain and raise your spirits."

"No, I couldn't." Courtney turned away in mild disgust from the proffered jug of rum.

One of May Willing's painted eyebrows arched, but she said nothing and fetched a goblet instead, checked it for smudges, then filled it with dark Jamaican rum from a fancy crystal decanter. "Now, you listen to May, my girl. A bit of this will calm you down. Think of it as medicine."

Reluctantly, Courtney accepted the glass and sipped gingerly. At first she gasped, certain the soft insides of her mouth and throat had been burned away, but soon a comforting warmth spread out from her center. The pain receded, along with her anxiety, as she continued to drink obediently.

"There!" May nodded approvingly, lifting her own jug for emphasis. "Now, about the redcoats. They're here in the city, so you won't be leavin' this place alone as long as I'm strong enough to hold you back, honey! Midnight passed better than an hour ago—"

"What!" Courtney cried incredulously.

"That's right. Frankly, I don't think you *wanted* to wake up—that bump isn't so nasty—and I can't say I blame you."

"But why did you stay? I hope not on my account!" Feeling the throbbing begin again, Courtney took another sip of rum.

"God's eyes, no! Where would I go? You think some kind Christian wife would give me shelter?" May shrieked with laughter. "I'm safest here, honey. Those damn British won't harm us fancy ladies. Burnin' down our places would do them more harm than good."

Courtney gazed despairingly around the garish parlor. Decorated with cheap furniture in the Sheraton style, the room fairly shouted with color: crimson and mustard-yellow stripes on chair seats and the sofa she occupied; crimson velvet drapes replete with silken gold tassels; brightly colored Turkey rugs; an elaborate mantelpiece carved in pink Italian marble; Chinese wallpaper covered by branches heavy with cherry blossoms above crimson and silver pagodas. May Willing wore a "round gown" gathered a short distance below her shoulders. It clung to every overblown curve, revealing more bosom than Courtney had ever seen, though some of it was hidden by the numerous gold chains May had wound around her neck. Her earrings and armbands were encrusted with cheap gems. It did seem possible that the British would hesitate before setting fire to this place, but on the other hand, was what they might have in mind for the inhabitants so much better? Courtney shuddered, realizing that any protests of virtue or stories about hitting her head that she might offer were sure to be met with disbelieving laughter. To make matters worse, Courtney imagined the reactions to her current predicament of her mother, her father, Lisabeth, Timothy and, as a final twist, Timothy's mother.

"That's a mighty strange smile, my girl," observed May Willing. "How did a girl your age manage to store up so much cynicism?"

Courtney blinked at the last word, then smiled more kindly and replied, "I was just imagining the reaction of my mother-in-law-to-be if she could see me here."

Abruptly, May held up a silencing hand. She cocked

an ear toward the window, then rose slowly and inched across the room. "I've a feeling you'll have worse worries before long," she hissed, pulling aside a velvet curtain.

Courtney was suddenly overcome with curiosity. Within this overly decorated room it had been easy to stay a step away from reality, but there was something about the glow she saw in the night sky that drew her from the sofa to join the other woman.

"They're comin' now," May whispered. Every harsh wrinkle showed on her face when she looked back at Courtney. "I was goin' to tell you before. They burned the Capitol first, and, just before midnight, they set fire to the President's Mansion."

Stunned, Courtney took hold of the crimson drapery and stared past May. The sight of the Madisons' home, only blocks away and aflame, squeezed her heart painfully. The tangerine fire seemed to lick the stars almost maniacally, as if taunting her, daring her to break down in despair. In the distance, the Capitol continued to burn less crazily, but the eerie, pervasive light in the sky indicated other buildings were smoldering.

"Why . . ." Courtney breathed. Her mouth was so dry she could barely hear the one plaintive word. It was as if she had fallen down a dark hole and into a nightmare world that was endless. Certainly this had nothing to do with her real life, with riding her horse through the woods, reading *Charlotte Temple* in secret, daydreaming of travels to every corner of the world and rebelling against her father's iron will. When had the atmosphere altered? "Damon?" She formed the name experimentally with her lips.

"Are you feelin' all right?" May demanded. She went to retrieve her jug, tipped it up for a long drink, then brought the goblet of rum along as she rejoined Courtney at the window.

"Perhaps I've just had too much . . . medicine," Courtney answered with a wry smile.

"Nonsense! More likely you haven't had enough! A little extra's in order at times like these."

Courtney complied. The tangle of prickly emotions inside her seemed to curl up in temporary retreat. "Do you know, I was there only a few minutes before I passed your . . . ah . . . building." Glancing at her hostess, Courtney saw a blank expression on May's pudgy face. "You know—at the President's Mansion. I was with Mrs. Madison. I helped her pack silver in the dining room, and I watched them take down the huge painting of President Washington. Dolley insisted it be saved, but everyone thought she was mad to waste the time. Of course, none of us really dreamed those monsters would actually *burn*—"

May Willing had been listening to this speech with growing skepticism, but when Courtney choked and a tear slid down her creamy cheek, May abruptly relieved her of the goblet. It was almost empty. "If you say so, dearie. Listen, it's not so bad. I saw your *friend*, good old Dolley, barrelin' along Pennsylvania Avenue in her carriage. And knowin' old yellow-livered Jemmy, he was long gone as well before those lobsterbacks got near the place."

A sudden commotion in the street drew both women's attention. Courtney held her breath as she watched a column of British soldiers come into view. For the first time, she noticed the dark silence that shrouded the rest of Washington; shutters were barred, street lamps were unlit and the only voices to be heard were the incongruous accents of the English invaders.

"Oh, this makes me ill!" Courtney moaned softly. "Don't you care? Don't you feel anything?"

"What a question!" May's tone was venomous. "I hate those villains! And I'll let them know that Washington, and America, won't just roll over and give up to them!"

"Good Lord!" Courtney cried, stunned. "What are those girls doing outside *now?*"

May Willing narrowed her eyes. From houses on either side of her own, as well as from many across Pennsylvania Avenue, her sisters of the evening had begun to emerge. Illuminated by the fire that set the darkness aglow, they were like figures in a tragicomedy. Tarnished smiles greeted the officers on horseback as they drew near; then the girls lifted their petticoats to indicate they were ready to do business with the new men in town.

"Goodness, and I'd been shocked to see some of those girls going off with *American* soldiers they'd never seen before today's retreat!" Courtney exclaimed, trying to break the tense silence in the parlor.

"Unprincipled sluts!" was all May could manage to say.

After a few of the officers dismounted and approached the women, they were joined by a crowd of anxious foot soldiers who had been marching along farther back in the darkness. Suddenly the street was swarming with red-garbed figures. Courtney had not imagined the size of this British contingent; apparently their marching steps had been muffled by Pennsylvania Avenue's thick, dusty surface. When she realized that more than one man was attempting to take possession of each available girl, panic stabbed her anew. What would they do when they found *her?*

"Well, this just makes me sick!" May declared. "I'll be damned if I'll stand by and watch those unpatriotic cows *welcome* the very devils who are burnin' our city all around us!" Throwing open the sash, she grabbed a nearby candy dish. "This ought to *really* make them feel at home!"

Courtney stared open-mouthed as May Willing drew her arm back, let out a diabolical cackle of glee and pitched the dish out her third-floor window straight into the mob of British soldiers. "Ah, that felt damned marvelous! I think I caught one on the shoulder! Don't just stand there gapin', dearie. Take hold of something and let 'em have it!"

"But is that wise? I hate them as much as the next person, but I'm not certain the satisfaction of bashing them with some crockery is worth my—"

"Virginity?" May finished sarcastically. "Don't say 'life,' because we know they'd have better plans for you!" She continued to speak while extinguishing lights and loading her skirt with bric-a-brac weapons. "Listen, my girl, the truth of it is, they'll be much likelier to abuse your little passion flower if you hide in the corner and beg for mercy. Men like that are hard on helpless, frightened girls who plead and cry. It's true, and I should know! Makes 'em feel manly to deflower terrified virgins." By now the parlor was in total darkness, so that the British would find it more difficult to pinpoint the source of the unorthodox attack. Apparently the flying candy dish had caused only a momentary stir; the soldiers were already turning their attention to more pleasurable pursuits.

The prospect of those twisted men making sport of her fear and vulnerability made Courtney's insides freeze, first with dread and then with outrage. The latter emotion helped to liberate her from the frustrating sense of powerlessness that had been tightening around her like a vice for days.

May Willing saw the change in the profile that was etched against the fiery sky. Angry resolve had replaced baffled indecision. "I knew you had it in you!" Elated, May poured their "ammunition" onto the window table, then paused. Her bleary eyes were suddenly sober as she regarded Courtney, so much finer, lovelier and younger than she. "I don't really think there'll be any trouble. I feel safer about these things when there's a big group of men, all official. But *if* any man gets out of line, for God's sake, don't whimper or cry! Give him a knee where it hurts, if you can, scream and curse like hell, and generally act mean and vicious. I know it sounds like that would only egg 'em on, but those kind of men are cowards. They avoid noisy rejections 'cause they feel even less manly afterward. All you have to do is remember how much better you are, then just ooze out Queenliness all over any redcoat who starts to leer in your direction!"

Impressed by the succinct wisdom of May's advice, Courtney glanced out the window. Many of the men, including one who seemed to be a general, had brought flasks of liquor out into the open. Apparently this was going to be a resting spot. Choosing a china figurine of Marie Antoinette, Courtney lifted her arm to test the weight and gave May a smile. "I think I'm going to enjoy this!"

"That's the spirit, dearie! Let's give 'em the welcome they deserve!"

May generously let Courtney fire the next shot. As the Marie Antoinette figurine sailed into the crowd, it was followed by a silver trivet. The women continued to pitch bric-a-brac into the mob of startled soldiers, and it wasn't long before their surprise turned to anger. Several men were hit, however superficially, before they began to gather their wits and dodge the mysterious, pretty missiles.

"Where the hell are they coming from?" one officer shouted after being struck by a porcelain bookend.

"Up there, sir! From that dark, open window on the third floor!"

May and Courtney went right on throwing things even as six men were chosen to hunt them down. Their last grand gesture of defiance came when they spotted a sergeant pulling down the bodice of one of the girls and leering at her exposed breasts.

"That dog!" May growled. "Hmm . . . I have a special gift we can send just for him!"

There was already a commotion on the stairs when she returned from the adjoining room. Courtney peered through the shadows in an effort to identify the large object; May drew closer, and she realized it was a heavy brass chamber pot. The two women's eyes met, and they burst out laughing. Together they hoisted their final, malodorous offering, took aim and sent the chamber pot flying in an arc across Pennsylvania Avenue. The sergeant's attention remained on the girl's humiliation, so he never knew what hit him. The pot made a loud *bonk* when it struck his head, and May and Courtney cheered to see a British soldier symbolically felled through their efforts. The fancy girl pulled her gown together, smiled gratefully in their direction and made a hasty retreat to her house.

Meanwhile, the six soldiers sent to capture Courtney and May had located the source of the cheering. When their knocks went unanswered, they set about breaking down the door.

"Oh, God . . ." Courtney whispered. Her elation was replaced by cold, prickly fear.

May reached for her hand. "Listen, dearie, I wouldn't worry so much about their bein' overcome by your beauty. Don't take offense, but frankly, you look worse than the things my cat drags in!"

Courtney touched her hair and discovered it was in riotous disarray, then looked down for the first time to see the smudged, ripped condition of her muslin gown. Not only was the hem nearly shredded, but one sleeve was torn to the elbow. "My slippers!" she exclaimed suddenly. "They're gone!"

May shrugged, smiling. "As I was sayin', you ain't exactly Cinderella at the ball. More like she was with the pumpkin!"

Glancing at the sweaty dirt that streaked her hands, Courtney laughed. "Is my face this bad?" She held her hands up.

"Worse!" May winked. As the door began to splinter, she kept talking. "I suggest that when those imbeciles come rushin' in, we go rushin' out! Why make it easy for 'em? Besides, we'll be safer outside with 'em *all* than up here with these six, if you take my meanin'." She led Courtney across the parlor, which was shrouded in coral-tinged darkness. They waited just inches from the latch, and at the last moment before the heavy door gave way, May held Courtney close and hissed against her ear, "Don't forget. You're better'n all of them, and me, too! Don't let *them* forget it!"

May's tone, so husky and knowing, instilled Courtney with new confidence. It had been a long time since she'd felt so sure of her own worth. She pressed a hasty kiss to one plump cheek that smelled of powder, sweat and cheap perfume, and whispered, "Thank you!"

Then the door cracked asunder, and shadowy figures rushed past them into the parlor. Without a word, May Willing shoved her young companion outside and into the hall. The two of them had clattered down nearly all the stairs before the British closed the distance between them. May kicked the nearest one in the groin, Courtney opened the front door and they rushed out into the smoky night.

It was easier for Courtney to run since she was barefoot. Turning west, toward Georgetown, she seemed to fly over the powdery dust that covered the avenue while May screamed, *"Run!* Keep running!" from behind.

When the familiar voice of encouragement fell silent, Courtney knew she should keep going, not look back. May would have scolded her for being so foolish. Still, she slowed, craning her neck to see what had happened. The sight of May Willing, kicking and scratching in spite of the four soldiers who attempted to hold her down, made Courtney grin. Then the other two soldiers caught her. She fought almost as wildly as her friend, and the three of them collapsed onto Pennsylvania Avenue. Courtney vaguely sensed that her skirts were up, for her bare legs and feet kicked the summer

air in search of a target. Her captors were about her
own age, she noted; one had apparently made contact
with some horse droppings when they had fallen.

"You could at least remove your coat!" she
screamed. "That shoulder is disgusting!" Wouldn't
May be proud!

Humiliated, the young man flushed and moved automatically to slip out of his uniform jacket. The instant
Courtney's right arm was freed, she thrust it, fist
clenched, into her other captor's face. He fell back,
caught off balance as well as off guard. Quick as a wink,
Courtney scrambled up, but the soldier she'd punched
grasped the hem of her gown and yanked fiercely.

"Bleedin' she-wolf!" he croaked, blood pouring from
his injured nose.

This time, no energy was wasted on courtesy. The
two redcoats pinned her down, face-first, while Courtney continued to struggle, choking on the dust. She
neither heard the hoofbeats nor noticed the horse until
a cold voice spoke from far above.

"For Christ's sake! I hope you two sorry excuses for
men don't expect any medals for *this* capture! Let the
lady up."

"Major!" gasped the young man with manure on his
coat. "I don't think you understand, if you'll pardon my
say—"

"This ain't no lady, Major!" the second soldier
interrupted.

"Let her up anyway," came the officer's reply, which
sounded cutting to Courtney in spite of the upper-class
English accent. "It was fortunate that I met General
Ross on his way to the naval yard and that he asked me
to look in on you *lads* in his absence. I could swear the
British military has lost its reason, not to mention its
inhibitions!"

The soldier whose nose Courtney had bloodied
pulled her to her feet. Suddenly exhaustion swept
through her—combined, perhaps, she thought ironi-

cally, with too much "medicine." There was dust in her mouth and eyes. Wearily, she perceived a black knee boot against the flank of a handsome horse. Above it was a white-clad, masculine thigh topped by a blur of predictable red—all very superior. Courtney searched for the last drop of moisture in her mouth and directed it accurately onto the major's fine boot, which made a perfect eye-level target. Expecting a proper scolding, she was startled out of her fatigue when a hand came down instantly to grasp her hair in a punishing grip, forcing her to look up.

"It would be interesting to know," the major commented caustically, "which of your charming qualities could inspire a man to *pay* for the privilege of—"

He broke off abruptly, and Courtney wondered why. She peered up through the darkness, registering impressions of a square jaw, swarthy complexion, black hair and golden eyes ablaze with shock.

"Oh, God," Courtney moaned, *"Damon!"*

Chapter Nineteen

August 25, 1814

"What the hell happened to you?" shouted Damon Sheffield. "You look wretched! Filthy! And what are you doing here?"

Courtney was too stunned to speak. She could only stare, trying to comprehend this impossible reality. Damon, her Damon, a British officer? Wearing that wicked uniform? Speaking with an English accent? Perhaps it was part of his role as a spy for President Madison! Yes, yes, that was it. There was no other conceivable explanation. It wasn't possible that he could have so completely fooled both her mind and her heart.

Courtney glanced around in a daze. There were more fires. It looked as if the naval yard, to the south, was ablaze, along with several smaller buildings that sent their tragic flames leaping above Washington's rooftops. Nothing could make her believe this Damon was so fundamentally different from the man who had made such warm love to her. She knew every hidden depth in his amber eyes. He was a man of integrity. It was simply out of the question that he could be one of those small-minded, merciless animals who had plundered farms along the coast for months—seemingly for amusement, to pass the time—and now burned a city that was still an infant. Washington had just been getting its balance; for all the mudholes and rickety boardinghouses, the federal buildings had been sources of pride and accomplishment. Damon knew that, felt it, as much as anyone! He simply could not have helped in burning them down!

The words *not possible!* rang in Courtney's ears. When she looked back at the white breeches and neatly cut red coat with gold buttons and epaulets, then farther up to Damon's achingly familiar face, the pain eased. Of course it wasn't true. This only proved, more than any previous evidence, that Damon Sheffield was an American spy.

The conversation Courtney had conducted inside her mind had lasted barely thirty seconds. Damon had seen the emotional war being fought in her magnificent violet eyes—practically her one recognizable feature—and his outrage and curiosity about Courtney's disheveled presence there were subdued by potent guilt. Just as she opened her mouth to speak, the soldier with the bloody nose interceded.

"If she won't say it, I will, but I think you know anyway, Major. Didn't the other men tell you? This one was up in a fancy madam's parlor . . . so I guess we know what that makes this wench!" He added a wink for emphasis. "Under the dirt, I'd wager she ain't half bad—at least what I felt of her bloody well wasn't!" Several snorts of knowing laughter followed. "The two of 'em started pitching rubbish at us, and that's why we went after 'em. Like wildcats, they were! Look what she done to me nose. If you ask me, both of 'em were soused. One whiff of this breath'd be enough—"

"That will be all," Sheffield muttered. "You may go,

but I would like the corporal"—he lifted a dark brow at the young man who had tried to remove his manure-smudged coat—"to remain. I may need some assistance."

Courtney glared at her accuser as he walked back toward the crowd milling in front of the boardinghouse. "Lies!" she cried, loudly enought for him to hear. "Lies and fabrications and unfounded conclusions!"

Sheffield had to fight back a grin. Good God, how wonderful it was to see her, even looking like an alley-prowling urchin! But why wasn't she lashing out at *him* instead of at a belligerent boy whom she'd probably never lay eyes on again? Was it true that she was drunk, or was there more, as usual, to Courtney Ashton's thought processes than met the eye?

"Well, I'm inclined to believe it," Damon replied with studied detachment. His grip on her hair relaxed as he flicked some ash from his sleeve. "After all, I *have* known you better than most . . ."

Courtney responded with a fresh burst of fury, which subsided when she detected the wry gleam in his amber eyes. Damon's eyes had always been an intrinsic element in the magic that had haunted her for so long; during the last month she had dreamed of them repeatedly, exactly this way. Today's many brushes with danger and death left her with little desire to argue for pride's sake. Just seeing him and experiencing the magnetic currents that flowed between them made Courtney feel as if she'd discovered an oasis in an endless desert. She had had a torturous month thinking she might never see him again.

"Oh, Damon." She tried to smile, but tears came more easily. "I know you are joking . . . and you know me well enough to expect me to have an explanation."

Sheffield nodded. His own smile was both wicked and disarming, but behind it was considerable curiosity about Courtney's demeanor. Why had she dismissed the stunning fact of his uniform so quickly? Whatever her reasoning was, he wasn't about to contradict it now, if humoring her meant he could transport her to a safe place. God knew he couldn't leave Courtney here with half the British army and nearly every prostitute in the city of Washington!

"You see," Courtney was saying, "I went to the Lambs' today—"

"Whoa! Don't begin this tale, which must be incredibly long, just yet! I'll take you home, and you can relate every lurid detail en route."

With that, he leaned over, knees hugging the horse, shifted his grasp to Courtney's sides and swung her up in front of him. She was in such a state of exhausted bliss that she didn't notice when Damon inclined a finger to summon the waiting corporal, nor did she think to strain her ears when he bent to whisper to the boy.

"Have the other woman put somewhere out of sight—in the outhouse, perhaps, for an hour. Then inform the ladies across the street that I want this . . . prisoner given a hot bath. I'll allow you two minutes to relate the messages before I turn my horse back down the avenue."

The corporal nodded eagerly and took off at a sprint. Damon straightened, vaguely worried that Courtney might have overheard, but he found her dreamily oblivious to any reality except that of their reunion. In spite of her ragged, grimy condition, the sensation of Courtney's body fitting into his own was as keenly pleasurable as it had always been. His arms encircled her; he could feel her heart thumping against his chest.

"Are you all right?" he heard himself ask gently. "You weren't hurt, were you?"

"If I was in pain a few minutes ago, it's all gone now." Courtney wondered at her own giddiness. Was it caused by elation, relief or the rum she had imbibed at May's? "Seeing you makes everything that happened today fade away."

"Courtney . . . I hadn't forgotten. In fact, I've been thinking of you a great deal this past month."

For a moment she couldn't breathe. Damon's simple, tender words meant more to her than a dozen flowery declarations of love. "I've been thinking of you, too, but I certainly tried not to!"

Though he knew he shouldn't, Sheffield could not help smiling, any more than he could help feeling a dangerous rush of warm desire for this smudged, disheveled waif. Her eyes were like silvery violets in the moonlight, and her tempting rose-petal lips looked even more delicious in contrast with their grime-streaked surroundings. One tear spilled and left a narrow trail through the dust on Courtney's cheek until Damon stopped it with a feather-soft kiss. Then, with a ragged sigh, he covered her mouth with his own. Slowly, tentatively, they kissed, shivering with yearnings that were far more complex than physical desire. Down the avenue, May Willing shrieked and fought as soldiers carried her off to be temporarily imprisoned in her own outhouse, but Courtney heard nothing except her own heartbeat. One slim, scraped hand found its way to Sheffield's face. She touched the hard line of his jaw, lost in a kiss that deepened and drew her into its dizzying vortex. It seemed as if she had tumbled out of her nightmare and landed on the cloud of a dream too good to be true.

The sound of approaching footsteps made Damon reluctantly raise his head. He glanced back to see the corporal bearing down on them. Courtney pressed a hasty kiss above Damon's lace jabot and murmured, "I know you cannot explain right now—about the uniform and all—but I think I understand nonetheless. I always suspected that something like this might be the case. I've never doubted you, Damon, at least not your loyalty to your *country*." She punctuated this last with a soft laugh.

Damon echoed it, looking around for the corporal at the same moment and feigning disappointed surprise when he was told, "Major, I have carried out your orders. Miss . . . uh . . ."

"Ashton," Damon supplied.

"I beg your pardon, Major. Miss Ashton will have anything she should need or want. Everyone is waiting for your command until the return of General Ross."

Turning his horse back toward the crowd, Sheffield thanked God for sending the skinny corporal when he needed him most. The truth would find Courtney soon enough.

May Willing might have her flaws, but her taste in rum was superior! Damon reached this conclusion as he swallowed the last drop in a glass procured from her parlor. He'd had some to drink on the way downstairs. Now, back on the avenue, he stopped to enjoy the warmth that spread over tense, aching muscles and eased his mind. God knew he had enough to worry about. Too much, especially at this devilish hour of three in the morning.

Courtney was due to emerge from the bordello at any moment. Who could predict what awaited them at her home on Duck Lane? Better to have her bathe here, where she could borrow a clean gown as well. Damon would never admit it, but his decision to deliver a scrubbed Courtney to her family had developed partly out of the thought that their contact tonight might go beyond conversation and breathless kisses.

Absently, Sheffield walked over and set the glass inside May Willing's door. Only a handful of soldiers remained now; the others had moved on after General Ross's return from the naval yard. For his own part, Damon had been excused from further duty until dawn.

A minor commotion from the yard behind May Willing's boardinghouse drew his attention. If she could only quiet her protests until Courtney was out of earshot. Sheffield had tried to stir up some antagonism toward the woman, but it was impossible. He had gone back to meet her, enduring the outhouse for a quarter hour, and had heard her own colorful account of the hours she and Courtney had spent together. It was easy to see what had driven Courtney to pitch knickknacks out the window and to fight the English soldiers with such aggressive abandon. May's enthusiasm was contagious.

"Oh, Major?" came a syrupy voice from the house across the avenue.

Sheffield's cynical guard went up as he strode over. "Is the lady ready to depart?"

"Well, almost!" The woman gave him an exaggerated smile. "I should introduce myself. I'm Blanche."

Dark brows arched skeptically. Damon sensed he wasn't going to be let off easily. Blanche, a woman at least his own age, was breathing deeply to make certain he noticed the considerable swell of her mostly exposed bosom. With blue eyes and chestnut hair, she might have been pretty but for the rouge and powder and paint that seemed to obliterate every true feature.

Approaching Blanche, Sheffield was uncomfortably aware of her admiring gaze. By the time he'd drawn close enough to sketch a mocking bow, he felt not only undressed but memorized in detail as well. "I am pleased to meet you, Blanche," he said, coolly courteous. What the devil was delaying Courtney?

"The pleasure's all mine, Major," cooed Blanche. "You're enough to give the redcoats a good name!"

"Thank you." Damon thought she was on the verge of drooling, as if he were dessert.

Blanche slid a hand under the crimson coat that was cut even with his hipbones across the front. Sheffield's flat, muscle-ridged belly, warm through the fabrics of a white waistcoat and shirt, made her moan. Boldly, she reached for one of his bronzed hands and placed it on her breast while letting her own caress slide down the lean contour of one white-clad hip and thigh.

"Now, Blanche . . ." Damon attempted to free his hand, but it was pressed fast to her swelling flesh.

"Oh, Major," she groaned. "I haven't been so hot in years . . . and we've hardly touched yet!" She swayed against his chest. "Oh, mercy, you even *smell* good! Since the war, I've had nothin' but sweat and stink from every man—"

"I don't mean to be rude, Blanche," Damon managed to interject, freeing his hand at the same time, "but I have another engagement tonight." He had felt her hard, pointed nipple through the muslin; the realization that she wasn't acting made him try to spare her pride.

"Wait! Listen! That's what I was going to say. Whatever you see in that girl, I've got more of, believe me! I can pleasure you in ways she's never heard of!"

"I'm flattered you're so eager to try, Blanche," Sheffield replied in a tone of amused patience. "I'm certain you are expert at your . . . ah . . . craft, but I've discovered there are other kinds of pleasure." He wondered briefly at his complete detachment from the lush and anxious woman. Not only hadn't he felt even a flicker of arousal, but the idea of spending an hour or two in bed with her struck Damon as distasteful and boring. This was all the more incredible in light of his prolonged state of celibacy. Usually he had no problem finding willing females to warm unfamiliar beds during his periods of travel. These recent weeks had been no exception, yet his normally keen appetite for sex had virtually disappeared. For a moment Sheffield wondered if he were ill; then the memory of Courtney in his arms on the horse jabbed sharply at his gut. No, there was nothing wrong with his virility. Obviously the complete, delicious satisfaction of making love with

Courtney had transformed his appetites to those of a discriminating gourmet. This past month, during rare times of quiet, Damon had thought back over that golden dawn. Every passing day covered the memories in another hazy layer of dreaminess, until eventually—

"Major, are you feeling ill?" Blanche inquired a trifle irritably. "Looks to me like the other pleasure you'd like to discover is a long sleep!"

Sheffield blinked, then chuckled. "I think you're absolutely right, Blanche. I appreciate the advice, just as I appreciate the generous . . . um . . . offer you made earlier. Truly, you're a person of rare consideration." Damon was feeling generous himself and reached for her hand. Only a trace of mockery colored the gesture as he bent to press a kiss of scandalous duration onto her white hand.

"Well . . . I . . ." Blanche tried to slow her heartbeat and stem the hot tide of color that rushed to her cheeks. "Fancy words are well and good—" Tingling sensations ran like lightning up her arm and down to more central locations. "Still, *I* could use some consideration myself!"

Damon lifted his eyes from Blanche's hand to find her staring boldly at his groin. Straightening, he laughed at her audacity. A flash of color distracted him, and he looked past Blanche to the doorway. There stood Courtney, uneasily voluptuous in a filmy gown of spring-green muslin, her hair swirling around her shoulders like thick, glossy honey. After the initial, pleasurable shock of her appearance, Damon realized Courtney wasn't smiling and that her eyes gleamed with tears.

Blanche's plump fingers squeezed his own. Sheffield started, having forgotten her presence, then pulled his hand free as if from a fire. Oh, Christ! he groaned silently. Courtney's seen me with Blanche! On top of the uniform, this I didn't need!

As Courtney stood in the doorway, watching Damon

kiss the hand of a woman she didn't know, doubt spread over her heart like a dark stain. The red coat, so expertly tailored with its gold buttons and officers' epaulets, looked unnervingly authentic. Sheffield wore the British uniform with easy, natural elegance. The Washington sky was still the color of coral under night's black veil, and acrid smoke stung Courtney's nostrils.

The women in the boardinghouse had provided her with a bath scented with rose petals, plus a goblet of soothing red wine and some cream that had left her legs as soft as satin. Then, clean and sleepily relaxed, Courtney had been presented with a tissue-thin gown the style of which had added to her discomfort. It was the type rumored to be the rage in England, even among more genteel women. She and Lisabeth had heard tales of dresses being dampened so they would cling against the wearer's bare skin, but the notion seemed too shocking to be true.

"Sorry, miss," the girl who delivered the gown to Courtney had murmured. "It's all we've got to fit you."

When Courtney had requested some form of underclothing, the response had been a ripple of laughter.

"You don't wear anything under a gown like that!" the girl had exclaimed, still giggling as she left the room.

Courtney had found the garment both clean and the correct size, though alarmingly snug. The bodice hugged and displayed the lush curves of her breasts, the tiny puffed sleeves nearly bared her shoulders, and the rest of the fabric, falling from the usual high waist, seemed to stick to her body all the more because of the humidity from her bath. Regarding her reflection in a full-length cheval mirror, Courtney had groaned. "I look like a worse strumpet than May Willing!" she'd whispered in horror.

The door had then opened to admit an older woman who wore an air of authority despite her painted face and low-cut gown. "How do you do, Miss Ashton? I am Madame Pontoise. I am sorry not to have met you sooner, but I was busy. It has been a bustling night, yes? And who can sleep on such a night? So, because I have great regard for M'sieur Sheffield, I am happy to accommodate you here tonight, and to supply you with a beautiful gown. *Mais oui,* but you do look ravishing! I have brought a few other items." She had crossed the room and set down a brush, a vial of perfume, two or three tiny pots of cosmetics and an assortment of gold chains, armbands and other pieces of jewelry.

Courtney had stared. "I don't believe this is happening."

"What did you say, *chérie?*"

"Oh, nothing. It's just that I'm not used to gowns quite as revealing as this one, or quite so much jewelry."

"Nonsense! We will use only what you like." Madame had set to work, brushing Courtney's hair to a high gloss but leaving it loose. Courtney had agreed to a topaz-studded armband, hoping it would distract any viewers from the scandalous gown. She'd allowed Madame to apply rose-tinted lip salve but had shaken her head when the older woman opened a jar of darker rouge.

"I think my cheeks are flushed enough, naturally. Especially after this wine . . ."

"Not for your cheeks!" Madame had scoffed. To Courtney's horror, she'd set down the jar and pulled one of her own breasts free of its minimal bodice. The nipple was cherry red. "You see? In a gown like that, M'sieur Sheffield can see what waits for him. It will drive him mad!"

Courtney had swallowed a gasp. "Please, Madame, I really don't have time for all this, and I'm not terribly interested in driving Damon Sheffield mad. I appreciate the bath and the gown, but now I have to be on my way home!"

So here she was—topaz armband glittering as her city burned.

"Courtney."

Damon had seen her and was closing the distance between them.

"I didn't mean to interrupt," she heard herself say in a tone that strove for coolness but came out jagged-edged with hurt and doubt.

"Don't be a fool," Sheffield replied curtly.

"Obviously that's one thing she's *not*," Blanche interjected. When Courtney glanced over, Blanche gave her a suggestive wink. "Have a good time, now, you two!"

After Blanche had swept back inside the house, Courtney shuddered. "I look at least as brazen as she is in this *costume!*"

"Brazen but beautiful!" Damon smiled. "Now, let's get you home without further delay. I worry that the men who are still about might see you and be overcome with desire and steal you at gunpoint."

Courtney, unwilling to give in so easily, stifled a giggle. Instead, she looked at Damon askance and arched a delicate, ironic brow. "It's amazing that I've lasted this long!"

He smiled, but did not reply. The gray stallion stood patiently as Courtney was lifted onto his back, then Damon hooked a boot into the stirrup and swung himself up behind her.

"It smells like rain," he commented as they started off down Pennsylvania Avenue. Sheffield's arms encircled Courtney to hold the reins. She sat securely against the crook of his right arm, conscious of the play of his muscles across her breast and midriff.

"All I can smell is smoke," Courtney said. She wanted to ask him how he could bear even to pretend to be one of those barbarians, how he could stand by and watch them burn this city that had been built out of dreams of freedom, but she didn't have the strength. It was much easier to let her head drift back until it touched Damon's chest. Oh, heaven . . . Unyieldingly masculine . . . The texture of his shirt and waistcoat caressed her, and the prod of one gold button was like a kiss behind Courtney's ear. Even on this hot, chaotic night he smelled the same—intoxicating. Nestled in the safety of Damon's embrace, she dozed, oblivious to the rhythmic jouncing of the horse as they progressed westward to Georgetown.

For Damon's part, it was all he could do to refrain from burying his face against the place where Courtney's neck curved into a bare, creamy shoulder. He could smell roses in her soft hair, while just inches from his hand were breasts that strained against gauzy muslin that would be ridiculously easy to tear away.

As they crossed the bridge over Rock Creek, Courtney stirred and awoke, blushing to find herself snuggled so trustingly against Sheffield. He put her at ease with questions about her parents and listened intently to her replies, particularly to her account of her mother's illness and her own last sighting of Lisabeth and Timothy earlier at Mrs. Lamb's house.

"I infer, from the tone of your voice, that there is more to this story than I've been told," Damon remarked at length. "Do you suspect that little Beth is romantically attached to your fiancé?"

"I . . . I don't know what's been said, or done, between Beth and Timothy, but yes, I think she fancies herself in love with him, and for all I know it is mutual. Heaven knows *I* haven't been playing my role as the lovesick fiancée very convincingly, so I assume that my conscientious sister is stepping in to carry on."

"How do you feel about that?" Damon probed.

"Fine! Frankly, it's a huge load off my mind, but I don't see how we'll ever straighten things out publicly . . ."

"And?"

"And I must confess that if Timothy had to transfer his affections from me, I'd rather he had taken them outside the family. I mean, Beth has been so insufferably proper, always telling me when I misbehave and warning me about this or that—although, in my heart, I do want her to be happy. And Timothy certainly deserves better than me. He's a fine person."

"There is one advantage to the arrangement," Damon said with amusement. "Your obligation to marry first would be ended. One solution for two problems!"

Courtney inclined her head, considering this, then laughed. "That's true!" She paused, turning luminous violet eyes up to his face. "Do you know, there's not one other person with whom I could discuss this, let alone share my laughter!"

He smiled. "In that case, I'm glad I appeared . . . if only for this night."

Apprehension tied a knot in Courtney's breast. "Damon, I don't—"

The flicker of a torch and the sound of laughter farther along Bridge Street caused Sheffield to rein in the stallion. "Shh!" he cautioned Courtney.

She peered into the darkness, barely able to discern several male shapes in front of the Union Tavern. Were they soldiers? Craning her neck around Damon, she could see flames still licking the inky darkness above Washington. What did the torch mean? Was Georgetown to be burned as well? More laughter drifted back to them, followed by a sharper voice, seemingly from inside the tavern.

"Damn." No sooner had the curse left Sheffield's lips than he was pressing his knees to the horse's flanks to quicken their pace. In moments they were close enough to see that the men were indeed British soldiers, apparently drunk and in the act of putting their torch to the door of the hotel.

221

"What the devil is going on here?" Damon shouted.

When Courtney heard the British accent return to his voice with such seeming ease, her heart froze.

"What the devil d'ye think's going on, guvnor?" the man who held the torch bellowed.

Sheffield swung down from the stallion and stalked toward the place that had been his home for weeks. When he was near enough for the men to see his uniform and rank, their demeanor shifted noticeably.

"I want you to extinguish that thing in the horse trough around back," Damon demanded. After the soldier had complied, looking considerably less cocky now, Damon continued. "As I was saying, what the devil were you reprobates about?"

"Well, uh, Major, they weren't letting us have rooms for the night."

Even from a distance, Courtney could see the tensed fury of Damon's body. Eyes blazing, he shouted, "You were going to *burn* the place down because the innkeeper didn't welcome you with open arms? I think you lads would do well to find a nice tree to lie under and become sober! When you've accomplished that, give some thought to civilized behavior! We aren't here to burn America to the ground and brutalize her people! I don't want to hear of any more aggressive acts that have been committed without the specific order of Generals Ross or Cockburn. Do you understand?"

"Yes, Major," they chorused.

"I will let the matter drop . . . this time. Good night."

"Good night, Major," the soldiers replied in unison.

Vaguely nauseated, Courtney tried to empty her mind and hide from the doubts that were growing larger and more menacing. She concentrated instead on Damon, on the wonderful sight of him walking toward her through the darkness. He would take her home and satisfy her cravings. They would kiss and kiss, and he would undress her slowly, finding every secret point of heightened sensation. Just the thought of touching his warm, bare skin again sent shivers from the nape of her neck to her buttocks.

"Oh, Major!"

It was one of the redcoats, coming after Damon. He was very young and seemed sheepish about taking any more of the coolly confident officer's time.

"Yes?" Sheffield turned back, trying not to betray his impatience.

"I simply wanted to say, sir, that I stood near you today during the battle at Bladensburg. Your calm and courage and steady aim inspired us all. You set a magnificent example for every British soldier."

A sickening tide of dread swept down through Damon's gut as he listened to the loud, stiff tribute. "I . . . uh, appreciate your kind words," he muttered, then shook the boy's hand to delay the moment when he had to face Courtney.

He heard her climbing down from the stallion's back and knew the moment of truth had come.

"Courtney—" Sheffield looked for her in the dark, then realized she was already halfway across Bridge Street.

"Courtney!" Anger added strength to his other guilty emotions. Her muslin gown and satin slippers were restrictive enough to allow him to catch her before she'd reached the opposite footpath. "For God's sake, you don't have to—"

"Don't you dare speak to me!" she screamed, struggling wildly in his iron grasp. "Don't you dare *touch* me! Let go!" A sudden flood of tears made her last words nearly unintelligible.

"You're hysterical! Let me take you home and we can talk."

"I wouldn't sit still for a conversation with you if you were the last man alive on earth! Not only that," sobbed Courtney, "I'd kill you before I'd allow you to set foot in my house again!"

Realizing that words were useless, Damon leaned down to grasp Courtney around her thighs, then tossed her over his shoulder as if she were a sack of feathers. "I'll not leave you here to be raped by the sort of men who are wandering the streets at four in the morning!" he told her through clenched teeth.

"Better them than a spying, lying, cheating, two-faced, slimy *Redcoat* like you!" Courtney shrieked, pummeling his back and kicking all the way across Bridge Street.

Sheffield deposited her face-down across the stallion's back, then swung himself up behind. Under his breath, he murmured, "We'll see about that."

Chapter Twenty

"Courtney? Is that Courtney?" The frightened, weak voice of Amity Ashton came thinly down the stairs.

Sheffield's arms were like steel bands around Courtney's waist and shoulders, one hand muffling the threats and curses she continued to shout.

"Will you still that shrewish tongue for a moment?" he whispered savagely. "Do you want to give your poor mother an attack?"

Courtney considered this and fell silent, breathing hard with exhaustion and rage. Slowly, the hand was withdrawn.

"Answer her nicely," instructed Damon. "Reassure her."

Courtney took a deep breath and called, "Yes, it's me, Mother! I'm home safe. Is Beth here?"

"Oh, my dear, what a relief," came Amity's faint reply. "Your sister went with the Lambs to Montgomery Courthouse."

"Mama, I'll be up in a minute and you can tell me about it."

"Yes . . . all right, dear."

There was not a light in the entire house, for even if there hadn't been the danger of attracting the enemy, Amity's illness kept her in bed. Mrs. Belcher, it would seem, had fled—at her mother's urging, Courtney supposed.

Now she turned ice-blue eyes up at Sheffield, who continued to hold her fast against the chiseled length of his body.

"Loose me now and leave my house." Each terse word dripped contempt. "The proximity of that despicable uniform makes me want to vomit."

"How fickle is woman!" Damon remarked, his voice soft but sharply ironic. "Barely a quarter hour ago you were melting against me, snuggling into this very same red fabric as though it were the finest velvet!"

"I hate y—!" Courtney spit, and felt the hand close hard over her mouth, cutting off the last word.

"The hell you do!" Easily, he lifted her, kicking, and carried her down the hall and into the library.

"Just what do you think you're doing?" Courtney demanded furiously. "You redcoats are all the same— rude, barbaric, totally blind to the needs and wishes of the rest—"

"God, spare me this character study," he drawled, pushing the door shut. "I brought you here so your mother won't be disturbed if you lose control of your voice again. Also, I crave a taste of your father's brandy." Nonchalantly, Sheffield removed his arms from Courtney but pretended not to notice when she fell, off balance, against the gaming table.

"How *dare* you?" Scrambling up, she followed him to the celleret, bumping into furniture in the shadows. "I will not allow you to do this!"

"Oh, really?" Damon glanced back. "Considering

226

the fact that I just took the trouble to see you safely home, not to mention obtaining this enchanting new gown for you, Miss Ashton—" To punctuate this aside, he lightly pinched one tempting breast. "—I must say I find your attitude alarmingly deficient in gratitude."

Enraged, she struck out at his hand but missed, which only raised her temper to a more furious boil. "If you ever touch me again, I'll kill you!" she railed.

Pouring brandy into a crystal glass, Sheffield made a small noise that betrayed sarcastic amusement. "How terrifying."

Nostrils flaring, Courtney looked around for a weapon. "Animal! Cad! Murdering, lying, coldhearted reptile!" The sight of his grin, irrepressibly white in the darkness, rendered her momentarily speechless with fury. "You . . . you are worse than a . . . a dog!"

Damon choked on his brandy. "Oh, please, not *that!*" he laughed. "You have a cruel tongue, Courtney."

She opened her mouth again but closed it when she heard her mother's voice calling plaintively from upstairs. As one last defiant gesture, Courtney poured brandy into another glass and swallowed fearlessly. Momentarily certain her insides were on fire, she remembered that May Willing's rum had had the same initial effect. Damon's watchful golden eyes goaded her, so that she drank the rest of the brandy without taking the glass from her lips.

"Well, you certainly showed me!" he exclaimed, pretending to be impressed. "You must have been practicing diligently this past month. It's reassuring to know you weren't idle in my absence."

Courtney gave him a last frosty glance and shook back her loose curls before sweeping toward the hallway. She forgot that the door was closed and walked into it, but recovered quickly and delivered an ultimatum while turning the handle. "If you value your life, you will be gone before my return."

Sheffield's only response was a smothered chuckle.

Clad in a fichu to conceal her borrowed gown, Courtney sat on the edge of Amity's bed. She was realizing that it had not been wise to drink so much brandy. The liquor combined with her lack of sleep to dull her mind, but it heightened some of the physical senses she would have preferred to forget. A tingly, yearning ache was centered in her loins, her breasts were swollen, and even as she listened to her mother's conversation, she caught herself imagining tanned, masculine hands uncovering them, slowly pulling down her bodice . . .

"I insisted that Beth go on with the Lambs," Amity was explaining. "They wanted me to go, too, but I couldn't leave in this condition—or without you, Courtney—and Mrs. Belcher's presence helped to convince them I would be cared for. Of course, Lisabeth didn't want to go—"

"But she wanted to be with Timothy," Courtney heard herself say in a matter-of-fact voice. Seeing the alarm in her mother's feverish eyes, she hastened on. "I don't mind! For heaven's sake, Mother, we've both seen it for a long time! Frankly, I'm rather relieved. I didn't love him, and if they are right for each other, doesn't that solve *all* of our problems?"

"What about the right person for you?" whispered Amity. "Have you any word of Mr. Sheffield?"

"What a subject for a time like this!" Courtney's voice rose higher with each word. "I insist we suspend all other conversation until tomorrow—but first tell me where Mrs. Belcher has gone."

Amity's face seemed even paler in the moonlight, so that her sudden smile was all the more incongruous. "I tricked her." She paused. "Do you remember a young woman named Prudence Hatch? A widow—lived in Cherry Alley."

"Yes. I remember her," said Courtney, her voice carefully neutral.

"Well, it was quite odd, I thought, but late this afternoon she came here, and Mrs. Belcher brought her upstairs to see me. She said something about—" Amity paused to sip the water Courtney offered her. "Something about not being able to wait any longer for someone. A man, I gathered. She had come here to offer us transportation in her wagon to Montgomery Courthouse, which is, as you know, very near the home of Mrs. Belcher's son. I managed to act very angry and ordered Mrs. Belcher to go with Mrs. Hatch. And I lied a little . . . I said you had promised to return at five o'clock with a wagon that would have a feather tick in it for me. I'm not sure she believed me, but I was so adamant that she eventually went."

A twinge of bittersweet empathy stung Courtney. Prudence Hatch had waited for Damon, yet in the end she'd come to her rival's house to offer her help in an hour of crisis. What would the Widow Hatch feel if she knew that she had taken a *redcoat* into her bed and heart? Sighing, Courtney tried to answer her mother.

"I . . . I'm relieved Mrs. Belcher is safe away, as well as Beth and Timothy, but I wish you had let them persuade you as well. What if I hadn't returned? Not that I would let anything stand in my way, but—"

It came to her that she was talking to an unresponsive form. Momentary panic gave way to amused relief when Amity suddenly let out a loud, rumbling snore. Smoothing back her mother's damp hair, Courtney smiled, kissed her cheek and crept out of the room.

Caught in a moonbeam, cognac swirled against crystal. Sheffield's tawny eyes followed it around, then he yawned and carelessly set the glass on a side table. It felt wonderful, even sinful, to stretch his booted legs and sink lower into the wing chair. Damon had slung the crimson jacket over the back of his chair moments after Courtney had left the library. Now he summoned the energy to raise one dark hand and unbutton his white waistcoat before untying the elaborate cravat with a few economical gestures. It had been a long, hellishly hot, frequently frustrating and incredible day.

Damon was nearly asleep when Courtney crossed the room to stop before his chair. For a moment she allowed herself the luxury of gazing at him, keeping the dark truths and resentments at bay. Without the red coat, which now seemed to taunt her as an emblem of Satan, the dozing Sheffield stirred Courtney in all the familiar ways. Moonlight silvered his dark, chiseled face and hands and bathed his white breeches, waistcoat and shirt in seductive blue luminance. Every muscle was outlined by shadow, while the tantalizingly revealed portion of Damon's chest drew Courtney's hand like a magnet. Trembling with needs that frightened her, she turned away and found the brandy decanter. When she squeezed her eyes shut and lifted the freshly poured portion of liquor, she saw instead *his* eyes, vulnerably closed, their thick black lashes like smudges of soot against lean cheekbones. Was there a scrap of boyish innocence left inside this deceitful, villainous, callous redcoat who had taken her virginity and broken not only her heart but also her illusions?

Courtney took a sip of brandy, savoring the fiery courage that coursed through her veins, and opened her eyes. No. No! Already he had used her, made a fool of her! Never again. The truth was plain, and she would not be distracted or blinded by some animalistic desire that he so cannily stirred within her naive body.

Damon, meanwhile, had opened one eye a fraction and studied Courtney's profile. What was she thinking? The sight of her slight, luscious form, completely revealed under gauze by the pre-dawn light, gave him a sharp, telltale ache. When she abruptly returned to stare down at him, he stole a glimpse through his lashes at her sweet breasts, straining against muslin, each nipple standing out to betray her desire as clearly as the hard bulge in his breeches betrayed his own arousal. Damon realized then that the weeks without a woman had served one purpose: to lend poignantly keen emphasis to this reunion with Courtney. His eyes closed completely as he tasted her name. Courtney. It was like ambrosia. He sighed, savoring it.

"Excuse me!" A distinctly unfriendly voice broke Sheffield's reverie. "I expected to find you gone when I returned!"

Damon resisted the urge to continue feigning sleep. "Well," he said with elaborate patience, slowly opening amber eyes, "I'm still here, aren't I?"

"Still drinking my father's brandy, too, I see!"

He cocked an eyebrow in the direction of his glass, then lifted it and took a long, slow drink. "Yes, that does seem to be the case."

Unsettling feelings churned in Courtney; outrage and longing made her want to weep. "I don't have time for foolish chitchat! I want you to get out of my house—immediately!"

"That isn't a very hospitable attitude toward the man who brought you safely home tonight," Damon replied, coolness replacing mockery in his voice. "You might allow me a few hours' rest before tossing me back onto the street."

"You can get your rest and pampering *somewhere else!*" she shot back sarcastically. "Besides, you want more than rest—" Courtney's unfinished sentence hung in the tense air between them.

"Please, do continue!" Damon's brows formed satanic crescents. "What else could I possibly desire?"

The taunt in his last word spurred her on. "Me! You want to use me again!"

"Again?" he echoed with heavy irony. "I have used

you before? Lured you into my bed? Broken your defenses with my heartless lies? And, of course, I must have forced you to submit to my kisses . . . caresses . . . and then, finally, I had to tie you down, or you would never have allowed—"

"That's enough!" The brandy let her lash out in an effort to slap him into silence, but his hand came up easily to capture her wrist.

Angrily, Damon straightened in his chair and pulled her closer. "You are absolutely correct, Miss Ashton. I do want you, but no less than you want me!"

"Liar!" Some inner sense of Amity's sleeping presence made Courtney whisper the word hoarsely while attempting to strike out with her free hand. "You slimy, stinking, deceitful, cheating, two-faced, coldhearted redcoat! I wouldn't sleep with you if you were the last man on earth! I hate you! You make me want to vomit! I am sickened to think that I ever wasted a minute of my valuable time talking to you or allowing you to make a fool of me!"

"What the devil are you babbling about? Vomit! Do you mean to say that this uniform has completely altered your view of me? You find me even less attractive than Timothy Lamb merely because my jacket is red rather than blue? What a lot of rubbish!"

Hearing the British inflection in Damon's last word lent fresh heat to her temper. "You bastard! What do you think I am? A whore like your simpering Blanche? Do you suppose I would fall into your arms in spite of the fact that everything I believed about you is a lie? Do you imagine that I am so mesmerized I would forget everything, including your part in burning my city and deceiving my President? For all I know, you killed my father today!"

"Oh, Courtney, shut up!" Sheffield held her tiny wrists in his right hand and reached over with his left to lift the glass of brandy for a long drink. "You're hysterical. Sit down." Roughly, he pulled her struggling body onto his lap and held her fast. "I'm the same person you have always known. Simply because I'm British doesn't mean I am a barbarian—"

"Stop! I won't listen!" She pressed her hands to her ears. "You disgust me! All I can think of is your raping some poor innocent girl along the shore of Chesapeake Bay!"

"For God's sake! I didn't rape anyone anywhere and I never have—not even you, you little bitch!" Gold lightning flashed from his eyes. "I have a country just as you do, and I love it! You were all for me when I was risking my life to stop Napoleon! Can't you see how ignorant you're being by generalizing—"

"I don't want to hear it! I don't want you to touch me! I want you to leave my house and never come back! I want to forget I ever knew you!"

"Courtney! Listen to me, *please*. It's not that easy. Not for you *or* for me. I won't be ordered out of your life, and I don't believe you find me disgusting. Fortunately, hearing is not my only sense."

Instantly, she began to struggle. "Let go of me! I demand that you release me!"

A long moment of silence hung between them. Sheffield stared into her eyes, watching them change from sapphire to amethyst. "I think it is time," he said tersely, "for us to discover just exactly what the truth is."

Chapter Twenty-one

Courtney's heart thumped wildly when she felt Damon's left hand wrap around her neck. He drew her nearer, slowly, until their mouths were barely an inch apart.

"No!" she managed to whisper.

"Be quiet," came his soft rebuke as warm lips gently grazed her own.

Courtney compressed her mouth, swallowing a sob. Her power to resist was pitifully weak, a fact which made her despise herself. When she attempted to struggle, Sheffield increased the pressure on her neck while testing the edge of his tongue against her lips. This slow, sensuous invasion melted Courtney's last defense.

"Oh, no . . . please," she moaned, shivering. It was as if every nerve in her body were exposed, raw and aching with the craving she felt for Damon. She could scarcely breathe, and when he entered her mouth with abrupt intensity, his hand's on either side of her head,

Courtney sobbed as their tongues met. The sensation was so acutely pleasurable that she wanted to absorb all of him into her body and never let him go.

Damon summoned all his self-control and drew back. The first blush of dawn lent an apricot glow to Courtney's already considerable, magical beauty. Her eyes were intensely violet and heavy-lidded with desire; disheveled, honey-rich hair curled against flushed cheeks and swirled over a sweet throat and taut, tender breasts.

. "I assume you're hiding your revulsion and disgust in order to spare my feelings," he heard himself say with frosty cynicism. "I deeply appreciate your consideration, but I certainly don't want to make you *ill*."

Speechless, Courtney, could manage only a shocked moan. When she made a feeble attempt to slap him, Damon easily intercepted her hand and pressed a scorching kiss against her palm, then heightened the torment by brushing his mouth over each trembling finger before moving to the throbbing pulse at her wrist.

"I know this can't be easy for you . . ." he murmured, amusement creeping into his voice, ". . . being touched and kissed by a slimy, stinking, disgusting, barbaric redcoat. It must be torture, and I'll be happy to vouch for your moral courage later on. Perhaps I could write a letter in your behalf?"

"Why?" Courtney's whisper was barely audible. "Why are you doing this?"

Damon paused, looking up from the trail he had been blazing along her sensitive inner arm. "I don't know." His amber eyes were serious; then familiar mockery crept into them. "I suppose it must be because I'm British. Bad blood, you know."

Courtney's conscience screamed at her to push him away, to kick him, kill him, but she was incapable of moving even one finger of her own volition. So humiliating was the situation that she forced herself to turn off her mind and ignore the warnings of her conscience, surrendering instead to the exquisite arousal of her long-denied physical appetites.

Damon reached the elegant curve of Courtney's shoulder and began to unfasten her gown. Slowly he slid the puffed sleeves down her arms until the bodice tugged at her breasts, then freed them. Instinctively, she raised protective hands, but Sheffield bided his time, kissing and then nibbling on a skittish shoulder. Courtney gasped for breath as he placed firm, sure lips on the hollow at the base of her neck.

"Oh . . ." she whimpered.

"Shh." Damon slid lean fingers into her hair and moved up to kiss a delicate ear, cheekbone, eyelid and finally her tremulous mouth. "You can't be cold!" he teased gently. "Why are you shaking? It's all right, Courtney, shh. You know I love you."

"No! No, you can't. I can't," she sobbed.

"Too late." He smiled, almost sadly. "The facts can't be altered even by this evening's dreaded discovery. You may believe my red coat has transformed your love to hatred, but don't forget that the two emotions are usually opposite sides of the same coin."

Afraid of the tide of sensation and need that was rising to untested heights within her, Courtney pressed her hands closer to herself. "It's not fair. I don't know how."

Damon was unable to repress affectionate laughter. "I have complete faith in your ability to adapt to this foreign body of mine. Even though I may have grown horns the moment you learned I was British, I assure you, my dear, that the rest of me is unchanged since our last . . . ah . . . encounter."

"Oh, don't laugh at me!" she cried. "Don't you think I already despise myself enough?"

"You don't really despise yourself. That's your father's voice telling you I'm slimy and therefore you're slimy as well for wanting to make love to me. You know me, Courtney—I'm still Damon. I was always Damon. I never lied to you. The only deception was my accent."

"I don't want to hear it!" Tears rolled down her cheeks. "I've been such a fool. A blind idiot! The worst is right now. I *know* what you are, and I vowed not to let you touch me, but look! I'm worse than May Willing! Here I am, half naked and shivering with desire like some animal who doesn't know better! At least May is smart enough to do it for money! And she wouldn't let a redcoat into her bed for a hundred dollars!"

Sheffield allowed himself a quiet snort of disbelief but refrained from arguing Courtney's last point. "Sweetheart, if you're worse than May Willing, I shudder to think what that says about my taste in women. Stop berating yourself. You're not an animal. You're aroused because you're in love. Your body never felt these things until your heart came alive, isn't that so?"

Courtney had buried her face in his shoulder to hide her shame, but now she glanced up hesitantly to see if Damon was serious. "Now that you mention it . . ."

"Of course," he added irrepressibly, "there is the matter of my intoxicating charm and good looks."

Trying not to smile, Courtney surrendered to relief and Sheffield's mesmerizing kiss. When his lips moved to her throat, then lower, she panicked anew. "But— but you're an Englishman! A redcoat! You're my enemy!"

"Not *your* enemy, you silly twit. I'm a man! And I'm at my wits' end with this conversation!"

Quickly and quietly, Damon cradled her in his arms and carried her into the hall and upstairs. Courtney couldn't cry out because her mother was sleeping at the end of the hall with her door open. If Amity were to wake and hear even one whisper, the damage would be irreparable. In spite of Courtney's telling herself to feel a horrified sense of outrage, an undercurrent of anticipatory desire rushed through her veins. All those aching, empty dreams in which Damon Sheffield had come to her like a ghost, teasing but never fulfilling . . . Now he was real, and, humiliated or not, Courtney would at least be satisfied.

He undressed her as if she were a child, aware of the conflict between conscience and love-fired desire. The curtains were closed to shut out the sunrise, and the field bed was densely shadowed. Courtney was grateful for the concealment but remained tense as she sat on the feather tick and felt Damon's fingers unfasten the remaining buttons on the back of her gown.

"Don't be nervous," he whispered from behind. "Christ, but you're stiff! And cold! You're not locked in alone with the devil himself, you know. It's only me, and I don't bite . . . as you are well aware."

Firmly, Damon pried her hands from her breasts and replaced them with his own. His touch was exquisitely gentle as he cupped their taut, curving warmth; then his fingers began to act independently, drawing fiery circles that came closer to, but never touched, Courtney's aching nipples. Finally he lifted long, dark gold curls and slowly kissed the nape of her neck.

Courtney felt as if her bones were melting. Damon's lips seemed to scorch the length of her back, then moved leisurely over each sensitive shoulder, smiling just a bit as he felt her relax. Obediently, Courtney bent forward to facilitate the removal of the muslin gown. Sheffield inched it down over her hips, then bent to taste the pretty curve where her back ended. Hearing Courtney's moan, he went on to kiss derrière, waist and thigh, turning her and feeling small hands grip his shoulders when his mouth touched the satiny surface of her belly.

"Oh . . . oh, my God."

Damon sensed the undercurrent of panic in Courtney's voice. With any other woman he wouldn't have hesitated to assert himself, to master her the way he knew the deepest part of her would love to be mastered, but this girl was another matter. He didn't need to conquer her . . . and tomorrow would be hard enough for Courtney to deal with. Regretfully, he expelled a warm sigh against the soft curls that hid her womanhood from view.

Courtney shuddered. "I—oh, I hurt," she moaned.

"I know. That's good!" Damon whispered, hands supporting her waist as he moved higher. Courtney knelt unsteadily. "You are a woman and your body hasn't forgotten. Don't worry. This is one problem I can solve." He covered the rosy peak of one breast with his skillful mouth while his left hand caressed nearby and the other strayed downward.

Courtney was awash with yearning; it was like one of her frustration-filled dreams. Her fingers felt Damon's firm, suntanned shoulders, and she could see the gleam of his ruffled hair in the shadows, but still, the situation couldn't be real. What was he doing? The most exquisite sensations were traveling from the tip of her breast to the place between her legs. When he suddenly touched her there, she flinched sharply.

Sheffield's fingers moved against the hot wetness, finding the spot where Courtney's torment could be eased. His own body was tense, throbbing with desire, but he waited, carefully biding his time, touching his tongue to her other breast while gently bestowing magic with one fingertip.

On fire, Courtney gasped for breath. She pushed him away, quivering as a surge of spasms spread its tingling fever higher and higher through her loins. Shuddering, she collapsed against Damon. She felt as if she'd lost all control of her limbs; composure had never been less attainable. Somehow Courtney's hands found their way to the throbbing between her legs, covering the area defensively.

"Shh . . . just relax," Sheffield whispered, cradling her across his lap.

"What . . . what happened to me? Never—I never felt—"

"My love, you don't know what you've been missing!" He laughed quietly. "The little explosion that just occurred inside your beautiful body marked the gratification of all those carnal desires that have been plaguing you these past months. You're a bit alarmed by it right now, but I assure you it's perfectly normal—necessary, even, for one's mental and physical health. Otherwise, women go through life with a nagging yearning which their inhibitions won't allow them to seek satisfaction for." Damon kissed the elegant curve of her throat. "That's why so many proper ladies are so ill-tempered and sour!"

"Rather like not being able to sneeze?" Courtney ventured, feeling more at ease.

Sheffield laughed and pulled the gown free of her ankles. He was dying to get out of his own clothes so that he might seek some gratification for himself. It seemed he had been hard for hours. . . .

Seeing herself completely naked as the cloud of muslin sailed toward the window, Courtney stiffened. *What* was she doing in her own bed with a *redcoat*, and letting him touch her that way?

"Since I have . . . uh . . . sneezed, so to speak," she faltered, "will it be years before I feel that need again?"

Damon choked, looking at her innocent face with dancing amber eyes. "Years? Not quite. In fact, if you're with a skilled and patient lover, it can happen all over again within minutes, even seconds." He kissed her temple, feeling the pulse quicken there. Was she afraid? "Sweetheart, you should be elated! Think of all the pleasure you can look forward to. It's better than pastries or wine or even the scent of spring's first flowers."

"How can you say that? I feel terrible, like a strumpet with no control over her body. Like an animal! I'm so ashamed of my own weakness."

In spite of the tear that trickled down her cheek, Sheffield's patience had begun to ebb. "That's your father talking to you again. Listen to your own heart! What you're doing is an honest, wonderful aspect of love—*human* love!"

"Love!" A chill ran down Courtney's spine when she saw brown fingers against his white shirt, unfastening the remaining buttons. "I don't love you, and you certainly don't love *me*. You have used me, just as you used Prudence Hatch the night of the garden party and then used *me* when you were still warm from her bed and body! I don't love you, I hate you, and I hate all you redcoats for causing so much misery and destruction—"

"Shut up," Sheffield said tersely. He watched her scramble toward the pillows, then stood to remove his clothing. "You're a fool, my love, but that doesn't change the fact that you've stirred up a roaring fire within *my* body. It'll take a hell of a lot more than a sneeze, or a few nasty words from you, to cool it down now."

He moved like a panther, eyes golden in the shadows, alert yet burning with barely suppressed passion. The twinge Courtney felt at the sight of his splendid body only made her despise herself more. How broad Damon's shoulders were above the muscled, tapering chest as he bent to pull down the white breeches of his British uniform. Crisp black hair glinted on bronzed arms, chest, belly and lean legs. Even in the dimness his arousal was evident, and as frightening to Courtney as a weapon.

"Don't come near me," she commanded shakily

when he started toward the bed. "I want you to dress and leave my house!"

"Don't make me laugh at such a dramatic moment," Sheffield begged sarcastically.

The flash of white teeth was all too ominous, as was the sinking of his knee into the feather tick. "I'm warning you!" Courtney inched backward, hoping she wouldn't fall off the other side. "I'll cry rape if you go on with this!"

"Is your sister hiding under the bed, coaching you on what to say?" Damon pretended to peer toward the floor. "Lisabeth, you sly kitten, are you under there?"

His light mood put Courtney off guard. In the next instant her wrist was encircled by the iron ring of Sheffield's thumb and forefinger; then his mouth was branding hers with an insistent kiss. The sensation of his arms holding her bare back thrilled Courtney. No longer exquisitely gentle, Damon sought his own satisfaction with a roughness that was not painful but exciting. First, he crushed her breasts against the mat of hair covering his steely chest; then he gripped her buttocks and pulled her into contact with his hard, throbbing masculinity.

Sheffield smothered Courtney's gasp with a scorching kiss. He turned her easily into the pillows, felt her small fingers guiding him into the snug, warm passage. Slim arms held fast to his shoulders while her body answered his in perfect rhythm. It was as if they had endlessly practiced their lovemaking to succeed in reaching this sublime blending. Not only their bodies were coupling, but their hearts and spirits as well.

When Damon felt himself shudder in release, the sensation was incredibly intense, not his usual distracted satisfaction of a basic need. Layers of emotion rushed together all at once from both of them like the meeting of two separate oceans. Over the thudding of his heart he heard Courtney weeping, and felt the wetness against his shoulder.

Sheffield kissed away her tears, then, holding her carefully, leaned over with one hand to pull up the linen sheet. It billowed over their entwined bodies. Almost immediately, they were alseep.

Damon and Courtney were so exhausted that neither of them heard, just minutes later, the tread of familiar boots on the stairs.

Chapter Twenty-two

August 25, 1814
Dawn

"I ought to fire this pistol right now," rasped a voice that shook with shock and rage.

Sheffield awoke instantly and reached for his own weapon. Damn his fit of lust! To be so stupid as to leave everything in the library! A metal cylinder was jammed into his temple. Warily, he opened exhausted amber eyes to find the bed hangings pulled apart. A thin beam of grayish daylight drizzled over the haggard figure of Gerald Ashton. Wearing his American officer's uniform, he held the pistol to Damon's head with his right hand while brandishing a red coat in the other, trembling hand.

"Courtney!" Ashton shouted horasely. "Don't lie there like an imbecile! Run while you can and grab the sword on the table behind me!"

Courtney froze, clutching the sheet over her naked breasts. Her other arm was trapped beneath Damon's warm, tense back. "Father," she breathed at last.

"I'm no phantom, girl! Move!" Gerald was turning beet-red with frustrated anger.

"But . . . I'm not dressed!" She felt caught in an insane dream from which she desperately craved to escape.

"Sweet Jesus!" Gerald ejaculated. "If that's the only thing bothering you, I'll keep my eyes on this lobster-backed rapist while you leave the bed. I'll see to it that *he* keeps his lecherous eyes closed!"

The power of her father's will seemed to surround Courtney. She almost obeyed him until she realized Damon was staring—no, glaring—at her from the corner of his eye. Truth spilled out. "I don't want you to keep that gun at Damon's head, Father, and I won't get up until you take it away. Obviously he doesn't have a weapon in this room, and I know he's too honorable to—"

"Honorable?" Gerald cried incredulously. "Honorable? Honey, he must have addled your brains if you can use that word in the same breath with his name—"

"I'm perfectly lucid, Father. Damon didn't rape me. What I feel is difficult for me to understand myself, so I don't expect you to, but if you are condemning here today, you may as well include me." She reached around to touch his hand holding the gun. "Please put this down. Damon means us no harm."

"Have you turned traitor in my absence, daughter?" Gerald demanded.

"She didn't know," Sheffield said evenly. "Not until it was too late. Put the gun away."

Seething, Gerald lowered the weapon but kept it aimed at Damon's head. "You've plenty of explaining to do, Courtney Amanda Ashton, and I'll have all afternoon to listen. You and your mother and I are leaving within the hour for Montgomery Courthouse."

"Father, please let me put on a robe and then we'll talk. This situation is so humiliating!"

"Damn right! And I'd say you deserve to be humiliated, child!" Muttering, he flung white breeches at Damon, ordering him to put them on and leave the room while Courtney slipped out of bed. The two men stood together in the hall, Ashton glaring at Sheffield, who refused to leave until the matter was resolved. They were inches apart as they reentered after she'd called out that she was properly covered.

"Father," Courtney began, staring out the window to avoid his accusing stare, "I must ask first if you have seen Mother and if you know about Beth."

"I have spoken with your mother. I went straight to our room after I found that satanic red coat in my library!" he barked.

"Then you know she isn't well . . ."

"She . . . um . . . mentioned she felt a bit under the weather, but she certainly said nothing about real *illness*. In fact, Amity was overjoyed to see me, of course, and was elated by my news that we would be going away." He paused, coming up behind Courtney. "Why? There's nothing wrong with her, is there?"

Courtney tried to smile at her father. "Nothing that the sight of you couldn't cure, I'm sure." Sapphire eyes clouded. "What about you? Are you healthy? Where have you been all these weeks? We've been worried sick."

A wind had come up outside, rattling the windows and sending a gloomy darkness over the bedchamber. Gerald told his story in an equally gray tone, frequently turning hate-filled eyes on Damon as he spoke of the British and the efforts to stop them from reaching Washington. Gerald was tired and hungry, but most of all seething with rage and hostility toward the army that had humiliated and beaten his own, driven it back from the capital and then burned every building of importance or meaning to the American government. Finally, Gerald spoke of meeting Lisabeth, Timothy and Mrs. Lamb on their way out of town, and his eyes shone with tears.

"There is no time to lose, Courtney," he said tersely. "You and your mother and I are to join them in Maryland. Apparently the Lambs have a relative with a great deal of land and a large house." Pain flickered over his eyes. "I'd made up my mind, coming home, that you and Lamb would be married as soon as we arrived there. Now"—Gerald gestured at the bed in disgust—"what do you propose to do? Shall I simply pretend I didn't walk in on my betrothed daughter who had a redcoat spy warming her bed? Frankly, the way I feel now, I'd as soon kill you both!"

"Look," Damon put in softly, "I think there's a simple solution—"

"Father." Courtney seemed not to hear Damon. Her eyes were wide, the delicate brows arching with anguish as she stood before her father. All the old patterns fell back into place now that he was home after so long an absence. The progress she had made in breaking the controlling bonds between them seemed to evaporate. Perhaps if he hadn't burst in on such a disquieting scene . . . "Father, please . . . don't despise me. I already despise myself!"

"Courtney!" Sheffield caught her arm. It was cold through the silk robe she wore. "What the devil are you saying? You don't mean that rubbish! You can come away with me—leave all this madness behind once and for all!"

"This is my family!" she shot back, pulling free of his grasp. "What would I get from you? Marriage?"

Damon opened his mouth, but the words wouldn't come.

"I thought not! You'd rather go on playing with me until I began to bore you like Prudence Hatch did!"

When Courtney flung herself against Gerald's chest, he folded his arms around her. "I can see you were misled, daughter. You always were hotheaded, rebellious. Perhaps you needed a hard lesson like this one to shake you into responsible adulthood."

"Courtney, for Christ's sake, don't listen to him!" Damon cried angrily. "Don't throw away the rest of your life because of childish fear!"

"Stop. Stop it! You don't care. You don't!" Convulsively, Courtney brought her palms up over her ears.

"I suppose," Gerald murmured, patting her back the way he had when she was a baby, "I wouldn't have to say anything about this to anyone else, not even to your mother. Obviously it would destroy her. As for Timothy, why not go on as before? You can think of this past, dark night as a growing experience. Better to learn hard lessons now rather than after your marriage. You'll be a more mature wife and mother because of it."

Courtney was weeping. A hundred conflicting, bittersweet emotions churned in her heart, but somehow the strongest seemed to be one of relief that her father was forgiving her. She felt as if she were a little girl again and thought of all the times she had yearned for his understanding, for a warm hug and his hand patting her hair.

"It's been the longest, most awful day . . ." she sobbed.

"It's over now, honey. In a couple of hours we all will be on our way to join Beth and the Lambs. We'll stay together and support one another until this chaos is over and we can live here safely and peacefully again." He threw a poisonous glance at Sheffield. "As for you, I knew you were bad blood from the first. I could sense the evil in you. I regret ever having extended the hospitality of my family to you . . . particularly in view of what you have done to us in return! It was a dark—"

"Oh, for God's sake, Ashton, spare me the dramatics!" Damon interjected. "If you and your mesmerized daughter would grant me a few minutes of your time so that I might explain my side—"

"You must be joking!" Gerald broke in with a loud but unamused guffaw. "You entered my house as a spy, used my family's friendship and repaid us with treachery. You flirted with my daughter, doing all you could to come between Courtney and her honest, loyal fiancé, and finally you take her virginity by force—"

"Now, just a minute—"

"No, Mr. Sheffield—or whatever your real name is—I don't have even a minute to spare you. In fact, I still have a mind to shoot you before you do any more harm to my country!"

"No!" Courtney cried suddenly. Hearing the raw emotion in her voice and seeing her father gape at her, she flushed. "That is, it just seems we've had enough horror and death for one day. For forever, I think."

"Oh, Gerald . . ." It was Amity's frail voice, threading down the corridor.

"I'll spare you, Sheffield, but only for Courtney's sake and because her mother is ill and needs to have me nearby." Ashton held his daughter at arm's length. "Will you see this man to the door?"

Horrified, Courtney watched him leave the room. He paused, glancing back as if to say, I am testing you; do not let me down. Damon, meanwhile, sat down on the edge of the bed, the site of so many exquisitely shared magical moments. He pulled on white stockings and black knee boots with a vengeance, tendons standing out in his neck, forearms, even his shoulders. Courtney felt a familiar twinge and hated herself anew.

Without a glance in her direction, Sheffield scooped up his shirt and waistcoat on his way out. Telling herself that her father wanted her to make certain this spy didn't steal their silver, Courtney followed him down the stairway. She watched him shrug into the shirt with the grace of a panther, his step never slowing, and tried to keep her stare remote and frosty when he found his cravat in the library and tied it. She had brought along the evil red jacket.

"No doubt you'll be needing *this,*" Courtney said, her tone carefully disdainful.

Damon's black eyebrows quirked above mocking gold eyes as he accepted the coat, slinging it over one arm rather than wearing it. "Thank you so much . . . for everything. I hope you will understand if I don't kiss you goodbye."

Courtney had secretly been expecting a last, angry, passionate kiss, and disappointment pinched her heart. Inexplicably, she felt like crying again.

"What's the matter?" Damon taunted, gathering up his sword and pistol. "Were you hoping that I'd give you another excuse to cry rape to your papa?"

When he brushed past her into the hall, Courtney followed helplessly. She was numb. Everything seemed scrambled—emotions, thoughts, the day and even the weather.

"I . . . I'm sorry about Father," she told him softly as they faced each other by the large front door.

"Oh, Courtney, you know I don't give a damn about him! Only about you. It makes me angry and sad to see you listening to him again, trying to please him instead of *yourself.*" He paused, sighed and touched her pale cheek with a sun-bronzed hand. "If you should come to your senses before—"

"Courtney!" roared the summoning voice from above, and for that moment she thought how splendid it was to hear it. Considering all the terrible, disillusioning events of recent days, there was one reason to rejoice: her father was alive, unlike so many other men who had fought in America's army.

Damon's fingers left Courtney's cheek and moved to turn the doorknob. A powerful blast of wind struck her like a slap.

"Never mind," Sheffield said. "Goodbye," he

added, already on his way down the stone steps that led to Duck Lane.

"Your mother needs you," Gerald informed her, "and I have to inspect the house and the stables to see if the British did any damage while your mother was sleeping and you were off gallivanting with that redcoat!"

Courtney bristled but refrained from defending herself. Either her father knew better, or he wouldn't believe whatever story she offered anyway. "I haven't noticed anything out of place, but I haven't been outdoors, so your plan seems wise."

"Daughter, would you have me believe your concentration was on our *house* last night?" Gerald replied sarcastically.

"No, obviously not, Father, but I certainly was aware enough to notice if things were amiss!"

He gave a snort of incredulity and pushed past Courtney. She watched him start downstairs, feeling wronged and resentful. How dare he presume to pass judgment on her? Was this to be a repeat of the episodes during her childhood when she'd spent hours in her room alone, waiting for him to allow her to return to the family circle? Suddenly her happiness over his safety dimmed. The happy emotions were replaced by others that were less pleasurable and more bitter. Why did he have to behave this way? Would it ever end? Would he ever see her as a person rather than as a female copy of himself?

Sighing, Courtney went into her room and washed quickly, then clothed herself in a candlelight muslin gown with a golden-yellow sash. While dressing, she looked back at her bed. The linen sheets were rumpled, and it seemed that she could see the imprints of her and Damon's bodies. After stepping into satin slippers, she crossed the room and picked up the pillow upon which Damon had slept. Courtney pressed her nose to the soft fabric and inhaled the wonderful scent of the man she loved, aching inside but refusing to think. Perhaps after speaking with her mother, it would be easier to consider more difficult questions.

In the hall, Courtney glanced out the window, shivering at the gray clouds that boiled up from the southwest. There seemed little doubt that a storm of nasty proportions was approaching. Her parent's room, only a few steps away, was flooded with gloomy darkness. Amity was dozing, pale wisps of hair clinging damply to her forehead. Her lips looked very dry.

"Mama," Courtney whispered, and the brown eyes opened instantly.

"Oh, my dear, sit down."

"Let me bring you a drink first." She poured water from the pitcher on the bureau and held the glass to her mother's lips. "After we talk, I'll fix you a nice breakfast."

"Gerald was going to see to that, dear, though I'm not very hungry."

Courtney perched on the bed and held Amity's cold hand. "I'm worried about you! I thought you would brighten up knowing that Father is safe and home with us."

"You must *not* worry. It's only the ague, and I *do* feel better. Truly, it seems that God has sent Gerald home to us . . ."

Courtney wanted to say that God had a strange sense of timing, but she only smiled and nodded. "There's no doubt it's a blessing."

"And now we're leaving to join Beth and the Lambs. How do you feel about that?"

"Well . . . fine! I've been anxious to see you safely away from Washington." She wished she could pour out her true feelings, but this was no time to heap more cares on her mother's frail shoulders.

"Courtney, my darling, I don't have the strength to

252

work up to this tactfully, but there are things I want to say to you."

Courtney sensed that somehow Amity already knew. "All right."

"During the past weeks I've come to understand some things I could never face before. The difference between propriety and self-esteem . . . issues of that sort." She paused to sip the water. "I don't think you should marry Timothy Lamb."

"Wh-what?"

"Don't pretend I'm saying something that has never occurred to you, daughter." Amity smiled slightly, wisely, and the gray daylight emphasized her pallor. "I know you love Damon Sheffield, and I don't think you should let your father talk you out of it."

"But how? When?" Courtney could not believe she was having this conversation with her mother, who had always been so bland, so ready to obey her husband and the rules of etiquette.

"I've suspected for some time, but I've only felt certain this past month. Look in the bottom drawer of my bureau, under my winter bed gowns."

Bemused, Courtney did Amity's bidding and then let out a gasp. Folded neatly beneath the bed gowns was Sheffield's heavy wool cape, the one he had given her to wear home from the Union Tavern a month ago.

"Mrs. Belcher found it while cleaning the gardener's cottage and called me out to have a look. I didn't bring it inside until recently. I was afraid that if your father came home, she might show it to him, and I didn't want that to happen."

"What makes you so certain it belongs to Mr. Sheffield?" Courtney asked defensively.

Amity smiled. "Because it smells like him. I can't imagine any woman forgetting that scent once she's been near him."

Courtney's heart turned over, and she gulped back tears. "Oh, Mama . . . you understand!"

"Yes, but I had to be certain it wasn't simply a physical infatuation for you. Men like Mr. Sheffield can be absolutely irresistible, especially to susceptible females like you, my dear. Often there is little more to the relationship than that!"

"What makes you think our case is different?" Courtney could feel her heartbeat in her fingertips, temples, breast.

"Last night convinced me."

"Last night?"

"I may be older and sicker than you, my dear, but I'm not dead yet! Very little that happened in this house these past few hours escaped my notice."

"Do you mean you weren't really asleep when you let out that snore?" Courtney demanded incredulously.

Amity smiled her response, then added, "Listen to me now, for I am deadly serious. I heard what transpired beftween Gerald and Sheffield and you, and I know you buckled under your father's authority. Courtney, darling, you must not leave it this way. You will be miserable if you go north with us and marry Timothy, and so will he and Lisabeth and Damon . . . so, you see, the unhappiness goes round and round."

"It . . . it is very difficult for me to realize you're saying these things."

"I've you to thank for opening my eyes, my dear. Your father is in for a surprise, I fear."

"But, Mother, what can I do now? Damon has left, and I don't know where he's gone!"

"I have an idea. When Prudence Hatch was here yesterday, she said that although she couldn't wait for this certain person to return, it eased her mind to know he at least had a key and could find shelter if he needed it."

"And that person is Damon?"

Amity merely lifted her eyebrows.

Tears pooled in Courtney's amethyst eyes. "Mama . . . I can't leave you!"

"Your father is here, so I am certainly not alone, and besides, I *want* you to go. And if you want me to get well, you will go to Damon Sheffield. Please, darling . . . for my sake."

Gerald, bearing a tray laden with breakfast, brushed past his daughter in the hall. She ignored his icy stare and went into her bedchamber to pack. Before Amity had finished eating, Courtney's valise was stuffed with her most treasured possessions. She had managed to fit in half a dozen of her favorite gowns. Silently, she blessed the gauzy muslin of today's fashions.

After a final, bittersweet look around the bedchamber which had been hers since birth, Courtney opened the door and stepped into the hall.

"Daughter? Is that you?" boomed Gerald's deep voice, followed by the sound of his footsteps leaving Amity's sickbed. "It's time for us to have a serious discussion!"

Like a rabbit in a trap, Courtney froze a few feet away from the stairs. Would it be better to run or to face him with some semblance of courage?

"Just exactly what is the meaning of *that?*" Striding down the hall toward her, Gerald pointed at the valise. "I hope you're not entertaining thoughts of running away, back to your British lover!"

"I—"

"Courtney, my child, I thought you were far too bright to indulge in such fantasy," he chided. "Certainly you realize you could never find him. And even if you could, he's probably already soiling some other gullible young maiden."

When her father reached for the valise, she yanked it away and held fast. "I am not *soiled*. How dare you imply that I'm some empty-headed chit too starry-eyed to resist the flattery of a handsome man—"

"I'd advise you to curb that sharp tongue before it

gets you into trouble, my dear. I am still your father—"

"You don't know anything about me or Damon or even your own wife! I won't allow you to stand there, so smug and skeptical of honest emotions, and tell me I'm a fool! I know better! All my life you've tried to mold me, but, unlike Beth, I have a will of my own and ideas of my own about life and people. I don't need to adopt your secondhand philosophies in order to make intelligent conversation. I can develop my own. And—"

"I'm warning you, Courtney . . ." Gerald's eyes blazed at her as he spoke.

"Go ahead and warn me! I'm not afraid of you. I'm leaving this house, and when I'm gone, I want you to allow Mother's independent ideas to exist without your mean-spirited attempts to crush them. If you were as secure and confident as you pretend to be, you wouldn't be so threatened by—"

Suddenly his long, sinewy arms were hoisting her off the floor. "I'm locking you in your room, Courtney Amanda Ashton, until you're over this tantrum. When you are prepared to treat your father with the respect he deserves, I will consider letting you out, but there is one point I want to make clear. You are not going *anywhere*. As your parent, I have decided you will accompany your mother and me to Maryland and that you will then marry Representative Lamb—if he'll still have you! Is that clear?"

"No! Let go of me!" On the verge of tears, Courtney continued to cling to the overstuffed valise as he carried her toward the bedchamber.

"Gerald, set her free." Amity's voice was frail but firm. She stared calmly into two pairs of startled eyes while clasping her husband's pistol in thin, bony hands. "I said, set her free. I feel more strongly about this than you can imagine, and though you know I couldn't kill you, I would have no qualms about shooting you in the legs to ensure Courtney's escape from this house. We have both had enough of your tyranny, even though we love you." Her eyes brimmed with tears as she raised the pistol and took careful aim.

Chapter Twenty-three

Looking stunned and baffled, all at once Gerald Ashton did as his wife commanded.

"Courtney, darling, bring your valise over here." Amity waited until her duaghter was at hand, then continued softly. "Go and get Mr. Sheffield's cape. Put it on before you leave. You should have it, and already the rain has begun."

Courtney, feeling a trifle dazed herself, did as her mother bade and returned to her side. "Mama, how can I leave you here like this?" she whispered. "I'll be so worried! You shouldn't be out of bed, let alone aiming pistols."

"It's not loaded," Amity breathed into Courtney's ear, trying not to smile. "As for Gerald, I'm convinced he'll find me fascinating once this is over. Besides, it would have taken dozens of quarrels to convince him that I've changed and that his treatment of me must change. I've a feeling this dramatic scene has served to eliminate most of those."

"But, Mama, you look so pale!"

"Hush! I'll be fine once you are safely on your way."

"I love you," murmured Courtney, her throat aching. "You're magnificent!"

"No compliment could mean more, my dear. I love you, as well you know, and will keep you and Mr. Sheffield in my prayers."

After bestowing a heartfelt kiss on Amity's cheek, Courtney picked up her valise and took a few steps before turning back to add, "Tell Beth I love her, too. I know she'll be the ideal Mrs. Lamb, and I wish her and Timothy nothing but happiness."

Amity continued to direct the pistol toward her husband, but a tear stole down one ashen cheek. "God go with you, daughter."

When Courtney drew near Gerald, she tried not to look at him, but couldn't keep her emotion-filled gaze from his face. "Father, I'm so happy you're home and safe—for now, at least. If my joy had been less, I would have gone with Damon when he left here. Please wish me well. No matter where I am, my love will be with you and Mother."

Tears stung Gerald's blue eyes as he fought back an impulse to embrace his daughter. "You're a traitor! Go on. Leave my house!"

Somehow Courtney descended the stairs, pulled open the heavy front door and stepped out. A blast of wind forced her to struggle to close the door. The same wind buffeted her as she wrapped the cape tightly around her and started down the steps. The rain was sparse, but it pricked Courtney's face like little needles. Warily, she scanned the sky, which was nearly night-dark despite the advancement of morning. What if Damon weren't at Prudence Hatch's house and she couldn't get in? Crossing Duck Lane, Courtney looked back at the handsome brick home that had been hers for eighteen years. Would she ever enter it again?

Courtney progressed slowly to Cherry Alley and

turned the corner. Halfway along the row of narrow
houses, she recognized the home of Widow Hatch.
Courtney's heart sank when she saw that the windows
were dark and the curtains drawn, but she hurried to
the door nonetheless. After one long, urgent knock
went unanswered, she leaned forward to peer through
the sidelights bordering the door.

"Oh, thank you, God!" she whispered. There,
helter-skelter across the stair hall, were Damon's sad-
dlebags, telescope and wooden water keg, and the
black leather haversack and rum-filled horn which
British officers commonly wore slung around their
shoulders. Peeking from the haversack was a shirt
sleeve. For a moment Courtney forgot the wind and the
stinging raindrops in her delight at seeing the scattered
belongings of the man she loved. However, a second
round of knocking brought no response, the door was
locked and there was no sign of the gray stallion. It
would seem that Sheffield had hastily divested himself
of annoying excess weight before going off—where?
For how long?

The rain had grown more copious, and Courtney's
stomach rumbled loudly. Frowning, she pulled the wet
cloak closer and sat down on the stoop to wait.

"What in hades is that?" May Willing leaned over
from her seat on the chaise she was steering precari-
ously down Cherry Alley and loudly repeated her
question to the man who cantered nearby on a gray
stallion.

Damon Sheffield stared at the figure huddled against
Prudence's front door. *Was* it a person? No head was
visible. Instead, dark fabric was covering the bundle
from the elements. Suddenly a pair of eyes, a tiny nose
and a pretty mouth appeared, still surrounded by
midnight-blue wool.

"Courtney! *Courtney!* What the hell?" Sheffield
swung down from the stallion and vaulted up the steps,

leaving May to tie up not only her horse and chaise but his mount, too.

"I thought you'd never come!" Emotion welled up in Courtney, and she began to sob and hiccup at the same time.

"How long have you been here?" He pulled back the cape from her head, recognizing it, and winced to find the wool almost soaking wet.

"I came not long after you left our house."

"Oh, my God, Courtney! It's past two o'clock! Has it been more than five hours? No wonder you're wet through!" He was pulling a key from a pocket inside the red coat. "What's wrong? Is it your mother? Do you need help?" Opening the door, he drew Courtney inside, then remembered May and waited for her to enter.

The sight of May Willing had initially cheered Courtney's dreary mood, but when May removed her pelisse to reveal a fancy gown from Paris, with perfume and paint to match, Courtney blushed to the roots of her honey hair. She was certain the presence of Washington's most skilled courtesan could mean only one thing. Courtney's humiliation was increased by the realization of her own bedraggled appearance and of how, just hours before, she had succumbed to Damon's expert persuasions, caresses, kisses . . . lovemaking.

"Christ!" Sheffield exclaimed as he removed the sodden cape. "You look like a drowned rat, Courtney!"

She felt ill, particularly when she glanced down and discovered that her muslin gown was plastered against the bare skin beneath it. Hastily, she crossed her arms over chilled, taut breasts and puckered nipples, blushing anew at the sight of the flickering corners of Damon's mouth.

"So," he was saying, "tell us what's wrong."

"It's . . . not Mother. I hope. She says she'll be fine . . ."

May, recognizing Courtney's discomfort, spoke up

quickly. "You know, honey, I was afraid I'd never see you again! Major, I feel certain about what little Courtney needs, and if you'll excuse me, I'll fix it." Passing Damon, she whispered, "Where's the spirits?"

With difficulty, he repressed a grin and pointed her into the parlor. Then he turned to Courtney. "Look, why don't you put on some dry clothes? You'll feel better. Let me take you upstairs and find something of Prudence's—"

This newest indignation, heaped on top of the others, made too heavy a load for Courtney to bear. "Oh, that would be lovely! And what about underthings? I'll bet you know precisely where to find the Widow Hatch's chemises and pantalets and—"

"That's right." Sheffield grabbed her forearm and hauled her up the stairs. "I'm sure we can turn up something sleek and silky for you to enjoy!"

"How dare you?" she cried, digging in her heels on every step. "If you think I came here so you could flaunt your excessive sexual appetites in my face, you are sadly mistaken!"

Dragging her into the upstairs hallway, Sheffield was suddenly overcome with fatigue. "So help me, Courtney, I don't need this today. Either behave in a civilized fashion or get out of here." He threw open the door to Prudence's bedchamber. "If you'd like to put on something dry and clean, do come in. Otherwise I must ask that you take no more of my time."

Angrily, Courtney stared up at him, but her defiance melted at the sight of the network of tiny lines around his golden eyes and hard mouth. "I'm sorry. I don't want to leave. In fact, I can't. I know you must be exhausted . . . because I am, too."

He moved away so that she wouldn't be able to see the love in his eyes. Opening the cherry armoire, Sheffield rummaged through it, seemingly at random, until Courtney whispered over his shoulder, "If there's a bed gown in there, that'll be fine. I'd love to crawl into bed for a few hours."

He discovered one and turned to find her eyes burning into him like sapphire stars. "Do you . . . need assistance with your gown?"

Courtney was expert at reaching unreachable buttons, but this was too good to resist. Shyly, she turned her back to him and felt long, callused fingers brush the length of her spine as the dress fell open.

"You had better turn around," she said, feeling foolish in light of what they had so recently shared.

Smothering a smile, Damon complied. Off came Courtney's frock, then her chemise, and the bed gown slid over her head. "Thank you."

"Look . . ." He followed her to the bed. "I don't know what's bothering you—"

"You! I—"

"Hello!" yelled May Willing. "Don't mind me! I just wanted to bring this up to you, little girl." The older woman pushed through the door, holding a cup of warm whiskey in one hand, a glass of Jamaican rum in the other. "This whiskey is for Courtney, and I thought you might need the other, Major."

Courtney climbed into the snowy-lined bed and accepted the cup. "Perhaps a sip or two . . ."

May smiled in relief, then handed the glass to Sheffield. "I'll be downstairs, workin' on—well, you know."

When she had left the room, Courtney remarked, "Honestly, that perfume!"

"I thought you liked May!"

"Of course I do, but because of this situation, it's difficult to feel very friendly toward her."

"What situation?" Irritation edged his tone.

"Well . . . you and she—"

"For God's sake, Courtney, what do you take me for? May offered to come along and cook me a hot meal, and that is *all.* I encountered her today outside the *National Intelligencer* office. She seemed to be there for the sole purpose of making life difficult for Admiral Cockburn. He was in good spirits, so May escaped arrest, but I thought it would be wise to remove her from the scene before he lost his temper."

The corners of Courtney's mouth turned up. "She is rather incorrigible."

"That's putting it mildly! The sight and smell of her rather obviously gave Cockburn ideas, but when he wrapped an arm around her and announced that he wanted a kiss, May replied, 'Not today, sir!' and landed a left hook on the admiral's nose."

"Oh, no!" Courtney giggled. "In front of his troops?"

"Oh, God, yes. The crowd was gigantic. I was certain May was on her way back to the outhouse—probably forever—but Cockburn seemed to like her. He said she had more spirit than the entire American army." Sheffield arched an ironic eyebrow, remembering. "However, Mistress Willing took pleasure in pressing her luck, so I thought I'd better save her from herself."

"Damon, what about the *Intelligencer?* They didn't burn it, did they? Or harm Joe Gales?"

"Gales wasn't around, though I think the admiral had some evil plans for him. I convinced Cockburn not to destroy the entire building, but I couldn't save the presses or the books, which he had torched in the street. When I left with May, Cockburn was seeing to it that all the *C*'s in the type box were destroyed—therefore Gales would have no further means of abusing his name!"

Courtney felt like crying. "That animal! Hasn't he done enough damage? Why don't they go away and leave us alone?"

"Darling, I'm afraid we're in a war."

"How can you bear to be one of them? How can you condone the barbaric acts the British have committed?"

"Unfortunately, I am not the Prime Minister or the commander of the British army. All I can do is help my country win this damned war and try to lend some reason to the madness."

She pressed her fingertips to throbbing temples and groaned. "I'm so confused. Part of me feels that Father was right, that I'm a traitor to be here with you."

"I think some of those feelings will be resolved when you hear the full story."

Before Courtney could respond, May Willing appeared in the doorway. "I know you two'll be real sad to hear this, but I've got to be goin'," she said with a knowing grin. "You know what they say—three's a crowd! I made a nice soup. Just let it cook another hour or so."

"I don't know if it's safe out there." Damon stood up and crossed the room to look out the window.

"All the more reason why I should get home now, before the storm comes. It's goin' to be a bad one, and I don't think you'd want me hidin' under the covers with you."

"I'll escort you—"

"Nonsense! You stay right here and take care of this little girl." She hugged Courtney, who almost choked on the overpowering smell of perfume. "You know how I hate redcoats," she whispered, "but this one's all right."

"Thank you, May, for everything," Courtney murmured, kissing her cheek.

With a last wink, May Willing disappeared into the hallway. Damon followed her out to the chaise. Minutes later, he returned to find Courtney snuggled under the covers, eyes closed.

"Don't fall asleep yet," he whispered.

One blue eye opened slowly. "Hmm?"

"While I was outside, I saw your parents traveling down Duck Lane in a large, well-packed wagon."

"You did?" She opened both eyes, instantly alert. "Did you see Mother? How did she look?"

"As a matter of fact, she was sitting up in front beside your father, leaning against him."

"Really?" Courtney beamed with relief. "That's wonderful!"

"I thought perhaps he had changed his mind about leaving so soon for Maryland and that you might still be planning to accompany them, but I can see that's not the case."

A lump of panic formed in Courtney's throat. "Do you mind? You did say, before, that I could come with you—"

"You won't change *your* mind?"

"No," she assured him meekly.

Sheffield removed his jacket, then sat down on the edge of the bed to pull off the black knee boots. "How did you know where to find me?"

"Prudence Hatch came to see Mother last night and offered us transportation out of Georgetown. She mentioned she'd been waiting for you and that if you needed shelter, you had a key for it. You see . . ." Courtney stared at the far wall, feeling penetrating amber eyes on her face. "Mother encouraged me to come here. She knows I . . . uh . . . care for you."

"You *do?*" Damon pressed a hand to his waistcoat, feigning joyful surprise. "Lucky me."

"I don't appreciate being laughed at!" Her heart beat crazily as she watched him strip off the waistcoat and untie his stock.

Sheffield merely smiled wickedly in response while draping his shirt over a nearby chair.

"You certainly are at home here," Courtney accused, searching for a way to reverse the defensive position he had forced her into. "I may have been rather hasty and unfair about May Willing, but that doesn't mean I've forgiven you for what you did with Prudence Hatch . . . on the same night you came to me! If you think I'll lie with you in *her* bed—"

"What? When did I come to you?"

He was looking at her as though she had gone mad. Courtney squirmed. "I had a personal conversation with the Widow Hatch, so you needn't pretend. She told me herself that you were in her bed after our garden party."

"I came to you that night?" Damon persisted, mischief in his eyes.

Courtney wondered why the sight of him unbuttoning his snug white breeches made her feel like a virgin on her wedding night. "You know what I mean! Stop trying to change the subject! Will you deny that you left her in this very bed the same night I gave you my maidenhood?"

"Egad, how dramatic!" Unperturbed, Damon climbed into bed. "Courtney, my sweet, just because I was here that night, you needn't assume I made love to Prudence."

"What's that supposed to mean? Why else would you be in her bed? She didn't mention any illness, and I know *you* weren't sick!"

"You and I have shared physical encounters which have gone unconsummated, so I find it amazing that you should be baffled by such a development."

"Well . . . that was different!" Courtney flinched as his hand slid over her hip. "Are you going to deny you have made love to Prudence Hatch?"

"Why do I feel as if I'm on trial?" laughed Damon. "No, I won't deny that, but I will deny I made love to her that night, and I swear my feelings for you were the cause of that . . . ah . . . omission."

Feeling his hand wander up to tease a breast through her bed gown, Courtney shivered. "This story of yours is farfetched, and I don't know why I should believe it!"

"Frankly, I don't care if you do, unless you love me. In which case, I care very much. And if you do love me, I have no doubt you'll believe whatever I tell you."

She closed her eyes, thinking she would be a fool to trust him in light of all that had occurred. "Damon . . . do you love *me?*" she faltered.

"Yes."

Courtney looked at him and finally believed it. Under the covers, strong hands lifted the cotton gown and touched her bare legs. Courtney slid into the safety of Damon's embrace, melting against his steely warmth, dimly aware that torrents of rain pelted the window while the wind howled ominously.

"I love you, too, but I've already told you. Too often."

As she spoke, Damon lifted her hand and began to kiss the palm with leisurely heat. Something made her move back slightly and look at him. For the first time, she was able to see Damon clearly, without clothing, in full daylight. Audaciously, she drew back the sheet and stared at all of him, drinking in each magnificent line.

"You *hussy,*" he laughed.

She loved the way he didn't flinch under her gaze, but reclined proudly, like a panther, until she hitched up her garment and straddled his hips. Casually, Damon reached out to lift the gown over her head. Courtney blushed.

"Silly chit!" he admonished. "I suppose, however, I should be glad you're so modest. Too many of the women I've known—"

One of Courtney's hands smothered the rest of Damon's sentence. "I *don't* want to hear it!" she laughed, sliding down until his hardness pressed her belly, and her breasts, grazing the hair on his chest, became even more taut.

Damon endured the hand over his mouth, but the trail of kisses Courtney was nibbling across his collarbone was another matter. Suddenly, steely hands clasped her waist and pulled her forward until she let her hand slip away so that he might kiss her. Then, taking advantage of her weakened state, Damon brushed warm lips over one ear, across her elegant throat and down to the valley where Courtney's heartbeat answered his sensuous kiss.

"Oh . . . oh, my . . ." she gasped, bracing herself as Damon's tongue circled a taut nipple until it ached. Finally, when she could bear no more, he slowly embraced it with his mouth, kissing and caressing with the tip of his tongue. Farther down, a hot, tingling need was building in Courtney's loins. Damon's fingers sought it out, skillfully touching just enough to make her feverish.

"This isn't fair . . ." she moaned. "I wanted to kiss *you,* to look at you and show you how much—"

Damon smiled against her other breast and lifted her away. One quick push of his hands against the feather tick and he was half sitting, knees bent, pillows cushioning his wide, brown back. Courtney found herself sitting squarely on Damon's urgent hardness. She blushed again, feeling his eyes on all of her, but she let him lift her hips and show her how to guide his manhood into her eager body.

"Courtney, my love," Damon murmured, holding her hands and touching them to his chest, "don't worry. You and I have all the time in the world. . . ."

Epilogue

February 14, 1815

Seated before a roaring fire in his library, Gerald Ashton was sipping brandy and discussing the news of the Treaty of Ghent with his son-in-law Timothy Lamb. Just that afternoon, Henry Carroll had arrived from New York with President Madison's copy of the newly ratified treaty. The document had been signed almost two months earlier, but America's victory had been underscored at New Orleans on January 8. England had learned the hard way that her former colonies would not be bullied. Now, with the treaty in the President's hands, the end of the arduous war was definite. The District of Columbia was exploding with celebration.

Upstairs in the Ashton house, Amity and Lisabeth were dressing for the party to be held that evening at Octagon House. Since the dark day when the British had burned the President's Mansion nearly six months ago, the Madisons had been living in the former residence of the French minister. In fact, more than a half-dozen government offices had been resettled; the Congress was currently located at Blodgett's Hotel.

The British had not been the only destructive force in Washington that week in August. The gray sky and eerie winds that had followed Gerald and Amity's wagon out of Georgetown had barely hinted at the ensuing storm. A tornado had ripped through the streets, pulling trees from the ground and roofs off houses. After the frightened British had retreated and the Ashton and Lamb families had been able to return home, they had found, luckily, the house on Duck Lane still intact. Amity, who had almost completely recovered by then, had discovered an envelope in a certain drawer in the gardener's cottage. The enclosed letter had been written by Courtney before she and Damon Sheffield had left Georgetown. In it, she'd assured her family that they were safe, having waited out the storm at the Widow Hatch's house. In addition, she had become Mrs. Sheffield. Once her parents knew the complete tale of Damon's life, she'd felt confident they would understand and empathize with him as she did . . . and perhaps, eventually, learn to love him. However, Courtney had scrawled, that story would have to wait for a later letter. She and her husband were leaving for England within the hour. Wellington had called Damon home. She didn't know what awaited her, but she did know that as long as she was with the man she loved, happiness was inevitable.

Five and a half months had passed since then.

"Are you men prepared to be dazzled?" Amity called from the hallway in her gaiest voice.

Gerald, in midst of refilling his brandy snifter, paused to smile knowingly at Timothy.

"I think we're ready!" replied the younger man.

As the wives paraded through the door, Gerald gazed at Amity and wondered if it were possible for part of Courtney's spirit to have entered her mother's body. He missed Courtney terribly, yet these new sparks radiating from Amity were so familiar, enchanting and maddening.

"Ah, Beth!" Timothy crowed. "You're radiant!"

"Oh, thank you, darling!" Lisabeth bent to tickle his chin with the ostrich plume that sprang from her fillet-bound hair. "And how handsome *you* look! Don't forget to talk to Mr. Carroll tonight about your views concerning the—"

"Excuse me." Mrs. Belcher burst into the room. "A letter's just arrived. I thought ye might be interested. Says it's from a duchess!" She handed the crested envelope to Gerald, but bent to whisper to Amity, "Didn't know ye had any duchesses for friends!"

After the housekeeper had left the library, the family clustered on love seats near the fire while Gerald opened the letter, muttering, "Curious, curious." He squinted at the parchment sheets inside and emitted one last "What's this? Hmm, curious!" before his wife snatched the letter from him.

"Honestly, Gerald, when will you admit that you need to wear your spectacles?"

Beth glanced at Timothy, still astonished at her mother's newfound audacity. Meanwhile, Gerald bit back a smile and replied gruffly, "I'll admit it when it's true! But if it pleases you to be a shrew, then go on and read the thing. I'll just close my eyes."

Amity fondly shook her head at her husband, then returned to the mysterious letter. "It says it's from the Duchess of Wyndham. Perhaps she is someone who has news of Courtney."

Suddenly all eyes were on the sheets of parchment.

December 10, 1814

My dearest family:

I know you must be concerned for my welfare, so first I want to assure all of you that I am not only fine but happier and more fulfilled than I have ever been. Of course I miss Mother, Father, Beth, Timothy, the Madisons and even Mrs. Belcher, but somehow, even after so short a time, I feel at home here in England. I hope that when the war is officially ended, you will be able to visit me here.

I would put you to sleep if I explained in detail what has happened to me since Damon and I married and left Georgetown, so I shall strive for brevity. Do you know, all the way to England, and even for a fortnight after our arrival, I didn't have any idea that my new husband was a duke! Honestly, I seethe whenever I remember the air of mystery Damon affected. We spent nearly two weeks in London while he conferred with the Prime Minister and a lot of military men whose names I've forgotten. All along I assumed we'd be taking a small house there, but Damon said that first we must travel north to visit his mother. I knew his father had died when he was young, as well as an older brother, and that his mother had been trying to control Damon's life ever since. What I didn't know, until the night of the tornado in Georgetown, was that his father had been killed at Yorktown, which led to an abnormal resentment of America in the Sheffield household. That was the reason why, when the Duke of Wellington asked Damon to go on from France and scout the situation in Washington, he was happy to strike a retaliating blow on his father's behalf. However, Damon's feelings about America mellowed considerably afterward, and though you may not believe it, he ended up by trying to stave off most of the merciless maneuvers by the British. He told me he felt he could do more good that way. . . .

I sense myself growing long-winded! Suffice it to say, Damon is the man of character and fairness I always felt him to be. He has proved his mettle to me over and over again. I love him very much!

Back to my first view of Wyndham House. If you could have seen my face! I had thought myself married to a poor, professional soldier. I never dreamed! It was the responsibility of being the Duke of Wyndham that his mother, the Dowager Duchess, was driving him to distraction over. Damon used the war with France to escape her. Can you imagine, she even had a wife chosen for him! The girl lived on the neighboring estate, and their marriage would have doubled the Wyndham holdings. Needless to say, the Dowager Duchess was a tiny bit surprised to meet me! I was in a state of shock, staring at the cupolas and spires, the magnificent paintings and gigantic rooms, the lake with its swans and arched stone bridge . . . It is all inexpressibly lovely! I do think, however, that Damon's mother would have been pleased if I had fallen headfirst into that lake when no one was looking!

Eventually, she came to realize it was no use fighting with Damon, since he was perfectly prepared to leave again and possibly never come back. He and I discussed the situation and decided to make our home here. Damon said he could enjoy the estate and the challenges of rebuilding it if I were with him. There is so much to straighten out— problems with the tenants, upkeep of the grounds, restoration of the mansion, ad infinitum. The Dowager Duchess went off to London in a tiff, to stay at the family house there and forget her hurt in society. As you might guess, we don't miss her a bit! I adore our new home, and we get along very well with the staff. Damon and I are like little children at times, playing in a castle. Our bedchamber is enormous, with two huge fireplaces that one can walk into, and a bed that looks as if it were built for William the

Conquerer! Fortunately, there are heavy velvet curtains to keep out the drafts at night.

While waiting for the appearance of real children, which we're both eager for, we spend part of our time in London. Last month I acquired a stunning new wardrobe on Bond Street, against my own protestations, and we attended several fetes at Carlton House at the invitation of the Prince Regent. The Prince is lacking the type of image he covets most, so he finds friends who have it. Namely, Damon! My husband, however, has a low tolerance for society, so the Prince never spends as much time with him as he would like. These experiences are interesting for me. You can't imagine the way women look at Damon. They're positively predatory, and when they discover my existence, their eyes narrow as though they wish me dead! Fortunately for my self-esteem, I have admirers of my own, which may be the reason Damon wants to take me home so early! All this talk of socializing with English aristocracy must make me sound fickle, but I assure you that I continue to love America with all my heart, as our friends here fully realize.

I wish you could see me as I write this! I have a little hideaway room in the tallest tower. As a surprise for me, Damon had it outfitted with a French escritoire, a revolving, well-stocked bookcase and a plush chaise covered with peach velvet. I am looking out over a snowy countryside that sparkles in the sunlight like a carpet of diamonds. There are marvelous woods to the east which I like to imagine King Arthur had explored as a child, perhaps in the company of Merlin the Magician and a dragon or two.

I must end this, regretfully, since I hear Damon climbing the curving stone staircase and I know it's time for our morning ride. Perhaps I can persuade him to change our route in favor of the village, where we could post this letter immediately.

My thoughts and love are ever with you, particularly as I approach my first Christmas away from Duck Lane. I have no doubt that all of you—Mother and Father, Beth and Timothy—are basking in the exquisite happiness that results from relationships grounded in love and mutual respect.

Damon is kissing my neck and sends his warm regards to my family also. He says, "All's well that ends well," but after all, this is just the beginning—for all of us!

I remain

ever your Courtney

Postscript—If any of you should happen to meet either Prudence Hatch or a lady named May Willing, who lives on Pennsylvania Avenue, do pass along a grateful hug from the Duke and Duchess of Wyndham.